Praise for Karen Bergreen's Debut Novel, *Following Polly*

"*Following Polly* sparkles. It's got wit and energy, along with fabulous characters to love (and loathe)."

— Susan Isaacs, author of *Close Relations*

"It's like Comedy Central picked up *Law & Order* for an episode. . . . Combines edgy thrills with a wicked sense of humor and an endearing heart of gold."   — *Publishers Weekly*

"Stalking, dysfunctional family, murder, and unrequited love— what could be more delightful? It's a great read!"
— Joan Rivers, author of *Men Are Stupid. . . . and They Like Big Boobs*

"*Following Polly* is a delicious debut novel. Murder most foul is most fun, and Alice Teakle is so clever and quirky a protagonist— or is she a perp?—that you won't be able to stop reading. Bergreen is a wonderful new voice."

— Linda Fairstein, author of *Hell Gate*

"A laugh-out-loud page-turner."   — *The Huffington Post*

"Karen Bergreen has created a lovable heroine who is a bundle of totally unique neuroses. I couldn't put it down!"
— Susie Essman, author of *What Would Susie Say?*

PERFECT IS OVERRATED

ALSO BY KAREN BERGREEN

Following Polly

PERFECT IS OVERRATED

· · · · · · · · · · ·

KAREN BERGREEN

ST. MARTIN'S GRIFFIN 🏔 NEW YORK

This is a work of fiction. All of the characters, organizations, and events portrayed in this novel are either products of the author's imagination or are used fictitiously.

www.stmartins.com

Library of Congress Cataloging-in-Publication Data

Bergreen, Karen.
    Perfect is overrated / Karen Bergreen. — 1st ed.
        p. cm.
    ISBN 978-1-250-00176-4 (trade pbk.)
    ISBN 978-1-4668-0191-2 (e-book)
  1. Childbirth—Fiction. 2. Postpartum depression—Fiction. 3. Separation
(Law)—Fiction. 4. Murder—Investigation—Fiction. I. Title.
    PS3602.E756P47 2012
    813'.6—dc23

                                                          2012007567

First Edition: July 2012

10 9 8 7 6 5 4 3 2 1

To my husband, Dan,
who is just the right amount of perfect

ACKNOWLEDGMENTS

I'm a needy person. I can't even change a battery without a team of cheerleading friends to advise and coach me along the way. Here is my abridged statement of gratitude:

Thank you to my agent, Victoria Skurnick, for everything (I can't list it all because St. Martin's would charge me for the paper). And a big thanks to Levine Greenberg Literary Agency for navigating the literary waters for me.

Thank you to Kara Unterberg, Christina Malle, Cari Shane, Sarina Ogden, Nona Collin, Jeannie Gaffigan, Susan Kozacik Rodgers, Andy Engel, Amy Plum, Stacey Shepherd, Kelly and Harlan Levy, Julianne Yazbek, Beth Lobel, Marlane Melican, Nancy Tainiter, Bonnie Hurry, Brad Zimmerman, Debby Solomon, Lexi Diamond, Lita Alonso, Maria Verde, Christine Frissore, Amanda Vance Moran, my brothers, Tim and Tom, and my fantastic parents, Barbara and Bernard Bergreen.

Also a big thank-you to my GNO ladies who have turned complaining into its rightful place as a high art form.

To the best kids ever, Danny and Teddy, thank you for making me laugh all the time.

Dan, I already dedicated the book to you, but thank you for setting me right on some of the information in here that I didn't completely make up.

Thank you oh so much to my peeps at St. Martin's Press: to

my editor, the glammy, brilliant (has no obvious flaws) Elizabeth Beier, to Michelle Richter, who seems to double as my therapist, to the Art Department (I adore this cover so), and to Rachel Ekstrom, for getting the word out.

I love, love, love my new friends at February Partners, DeeDee DeBartlo, Gretchen Crary, and Kimberly Cowser and their friends Jennifer Katz and Corinne Ray, who are behind my crazy videos.

Also, a big thank-you to all of my Facebook friends for making me feel incredibly popular.

(And finally, a big thank you to the parenthesis.)

PERFECT IS OVERRATED

I emerge from my depression the moment I learn of Beverly Hastings's death. She's not just dead. She's been murdered. Someone, apparently, liked her even less than I did.

I get out of bed, where I have been spending way too much time. And alone, at that. I turn the volume up on the television. A reporter is standing outside Beverly's East Side town house, and cops are everywhere.

"Very little is known about the murder of Beverly Hastings. Police are withholding what appear to be gruesome details."

Gruesome details. I perk up even more.

"I just feel sorry for the child." An older woman identified as Sarah, Beverly's neighbor, is speaking.

I, too, feel sorry for the child, but on the bright side, Bitsy will never again have to wear bloomers.

I unravel my Disney princess comforter—Molly's actually, as mine has been in the laundry for two months—and start looking for the telephone. I haven't used it in days, a lingering by-product of my acute, protracted depression. It's not in the cradle. My apartment, once a masterwork of cleanliness and organization, is now a prime example of college-dorm-style disarray. I straighten Paul's old NYPD sweatshirt and pick up the jeans that I left on the floor after returning to bed this morning. Then I shuffle from my lightless bedroom into the kitchen, which owes its brightness to the building's architect rather than to any feat of mine. I realize I'm wearing one sneaker.

After I had returned home from dropping my daughter at school, I'd cleared off the counters, pleased that I had chosen a dark marble to hide the stains and grime. The dishes, Molly's octopus bowl and cup, to be specific, are still in the sink, and so, apparently, is the phone. *Please, battery, don't be out. I promise to recharge you every day from now on.* It works. I dial a number that is more familiar than my home phone.

Voice mail. I could have predicted that. "You've reached Detective Paul Alger. Leave a message."

"Paul, it's me." I do my best to sound conversational. Although frankly, mere murder is nothing next to the rage I feel every time I hear the dulcet tones of my ex-husband. "Could you call me when you have a sec? Thanks."

I put the phone back in its cradle as promised, and it starts to ring.

"Katie, is everything okay?"

"Oh, yeah. Molly's fine, *I'm* fine. I should have said it wasn't an emergency, but do you know anything about this Beverly Hastings murder?"

"Nothing."

"I don't believe you."

"Then why did you ask?"

"I did it for Molly."

Slightly energized, I scrub my daughter's octopus bowl as I talk.

"Molly doesn't even know Beverly."

"Not true, they have met a few times. And she does know Bitsy."

"But they're not friends."

"They're four. At this age, they're all friends."

"You know I can't say anything, Katie."

"I know."

"You're sure you're okay?" He's convinced that I'll never be okay.

"Truly, I am." Truly I am. In fact, I'm sweeping. "I'll drop Molly off later."

" 'Kay."

He's trying to be familiar, but I hang up in lieu of partaking in our old routine.

I will never forgive him. He makes my skin crawl. But we share a daughter.

And, he's gotta know something.

I met Paul Alger in the Eleventh Precinct when I was an assistant district attorney and he was a homicide detective, first grade. It was Christmastime. I was picking up a file from a junior officer, and I grabbed a chocolate Santa from a bowl on his desk.

"Committing petit larceny in a police station?"

I heard a rich, low voice behind me and turned around. Standing there was the most handsome man I had ever seen—excluding television and movies. He had dark, wavy hair, olive skin, light brown eyes, and a large but lean build. Like in a scene in a Greek tragedy, I heard what sounded like a Delphic voice say, *You are going to marry this man.*

"Excuse me?" I said to both the man and the crazy voice in my head.

"You are stealing items from that individual's desk. Technically, that's a petit larceny."

"Technically, it's the holiday season and a dish of candy is everyone's property." It didn't sound convincing, so I added, "There's legal precedent."

"Legal precedent, huh?" He winked at me. "I'm giving you a verbal warning now, but if I catch you stealing any more sweets, I'm not going to let you off so easily."

I smiled. I also perused the room for another bowl of candy before leaving the building.

A few days later, I attended the precinct Christmas party, the kind of social event I typically dreaded. Everybody was either on call and downing Diet Coke, or overdoing it on soured beer and ecru cheese cubes. Inevitably, the holiday colloquy transformed into tales of career conquests. I often ate these up, but that night I found myself looking for something else—namely, the handsome, aggressive cop. Strictly a pantsuit lawyer, I had dusted off a dress that morning, a formfitting, black Tahari number that, along with an impressively high-heeled pair of jet suede sling-backs, gave me the slice of femininity called for under the circumstances.

I had gotten to the party early, careful to stake out a piece of cheddar, a place to stand, and a glass of wine. Detective Ken Sawicki, a stocky, balding cop with big blue eyes and pale, pale skin, offered to get me another drink, but then held it hostage in his drying, fleshy hands until he finished this year's telling of arresting the mayor's kid for shoplifting a pack of watermelon Bubblicious. Don't get me wrong. I love hearing a good war story, especially from a cop, but he could do better than gum.

I nodded politely to Sawicki, attempting telepathically to make him hand over the Sauvignon Blanc.

And then *he* walked in.

"Alger," Sawicki screamed to him, lifting his glass as if to toast while mine lay limply in his other hand, "merry, merry. What can I get you?"

"I'll have what she's having," Paul said, taking my glass out of Sawicki's fingers and handing it to me.

"Minus the story," I whispered under my breath.

"Paul Alger." He stuck out his hand.

He was even more alluring than I had remembered, and he clearly hadn't dolled himself up for the occasion. In a fraying white oxford shirt and khaki pants, he was the best-looking man in the room. I studied him more carefully. Chocolate hair and striking, if asymmetric, cheekbones offset his amber eyes. He wore an expression that suggested an imminent wealth of emotion, which upgraded him from merely attractive to mesmerizing.

"Kate Hagen."

"Kate? As in *Kiss Me, Kate*?" He paused for a second. "I bet you never heard that before."

"It's a first from a cop."

"He's no ordinary cop," Sawicki said. "He's a crime fighter."

"Do you wear a leotard?" I couldn't resist.

"Only when I'm working undercover." Paul Alger was still holding my hand.

"Gotta love Paul," Sawicki declared.

I already did.

"It would be fun to work together." I sounded, I'm not proud to admit, like a fourth-grader looking for a school-project buddy.

"My thoughts exactly," Paul agreed. "Let's get out of here."

I'm switching the channels desperate for some Hastings coverage. News trucks with satellite dishes are parked outside the East Sixty-fourth Street town house. Cops are weaving in and around the slew of reporters. I look for a familiar face.

Neighbors are weighing in on the murder.

"We're just baffled," remarks a bespectacled man in a bow tie.

"It just goes to show you," another explains.

I notice that the news crew haven't produced anybody to publicly mourn Beverly.

I first met Beverly Hastings about two years ago, when we were trying to get Molly into the Hawthorne Preschool. I had long since heard the lore about applying early. Some Manhattan parents believed that the firm deadline for applications to New York's top three preschools, Hawthorne being number one, was the second trimester of pregnancy. Others emphasized the dual imperative of a huge cash donation and a recommendation from a Nobel laureate. Rejection meant a life of homeschooling and a college degree from the Internet.

"Ignore the nonsense and apply," Peg, my former boss, mentor, and best friend, chided. "How many people know a Nobel laureate? Not only do I not know a Nobel laureate, but I don't think I know anybody who knows one."

Peg, in her mid-fifties, looks forty-two. To be fair, she looked forty-two when she was twenty-seven, and she'll look forty-two at ninety-five. She has long, undyed brown hair, which she habitually wears in a low ponytail folded into a bun, and she almost always wears a clingy wrap dress that emphasizes her thinness rather than stirring up prurient desires.

"I actually do know one," I confessed. "Albert Brettschneider, my college chemistry professor, won it three years ago."

"Okay, Ms. Smarty-Pants. Get the chemistry teacher to call the preschool."

It did sound ridiculous. Peg had a way of putting things in perspective for me. She was sitting, as she always did during these biweekly visits, in the kitchen nook, making full use of our banquette. In return for her company, I'm expected to whip out the cappuccino maker she got me for my wedding and give her as many cups of foamy coffee as she desires. Just as former heroin addicts become doughnut devotees when they go cold turkey, Peg developed her caffeine dependence in 1991, when she finally stopped smoking two packs a day.

"And if Molly doesn't get in, what's the worst that could happen?"

Peg and I had had this discussion before. Paul and I wanted Molly to go to Hawthorne so that she could get into one of the top private schools in New York. Peg thought it was all nonsense.

"My kids went to public school their whole lives and it didn't hurt them at all." Peg, the daughter of two relentless union organizers, had shown remarkable restraint in this discussion.

Boy, was she right. Her older son, David, was enjoying his Fulbright in Ghana, and her younger son, Matthew, was about to enter Yale Law School. Both of them were products of New York City public schools.

Secretly I agreed with Peg, but Paul's parents are consumed with Molly's getting the best education possible and are willing to pay for it. Not what people would expect from a cop's parents, but Paul's life hasn't followed a predictable path.

"Peg, you are aware, are you not, that your kids have inherited your superhero genes?"

"True, but your gene pool isn't so bad either. Apply. Ignore the talk. Molly will be fine. She has you as a mother."

"That's what I'm worried about."

On Peg's urgings, I sent Molly's applications to three of New York's top-rated preschools.

"And the Emily Dickinson look may not work with these people, so before you go for your school interview, you might want to take a walk or a run or something. Gray may be in this year, but not in skin tone. Buy a dress or some shoes."

"I get it, Peg."

"Some of these schools are in a church. You don't want them redirecting you to the food bank."

"I get it."

Peg was the only person who understood my mental state. Despite her anti-elitist leanings, she knew that my applying for schools was a sign that I had graduated from the ocean-floor depths of my noxious depression to my current state of somewhat functional dysthymia.

But I had lost a husband in the process.

Beverly Hastings had been sitting across from me on a wooden bench in the austere waiting area outside Hawthorne's office of admissions. The walls, which needed another coat of wintergreen paint, were bare, except for a portrait of Ledyard Webster Wheeling Hawthorne. He could have been the twin of Rutherford B. Hayes, Molly's current commander in chief of choice from her Meet-the-Presidents place mat. The portrait of Hawthorne had been painted in 1879, the year he commissioned the preschool. It was well-known that Ledyard himself had nothing to do with the school. His wife, Katherine, was concerned that her five children, living in an urban and privileged environment, would grow lazy by age four. She developed a detailed curriculum integrating the social urban experience of young people with physical activity. Within ten years, she had hired several tutors to teach her progeny, extended family members, and acquaintances with similar social credentials.

Considered by many to be the supreme preschool in all of New York, the school boasts the highest percentage of admissions to New York City's most prestigious private schools. They also claim to have the most impressive college admissions in the country. One would be hard-pressed to find many institutions with the financial resources to embark on a research project tracking the long-term education of their five-year-olds.

"Here, Bitsy."

I thought Beverly Hastings, as I later learned her name to be, had brought the family dog on an interview. Then she pulled out an iPod and headphones and planted them on the little girl's head.

"Bitsy loves Rachmaninoff," Beverly informed me as she tucked a handful of her freshly cut-and-colored vanilla bob behind her ear only to reveal a gold shell earring.

She probably likes wearing the headphones so she doesn't have to listen to Mommy, I could almost hear Paul quipping. Thankfully, though, he had called me just as I was entering the building to say that an emergency had arisen and he wouldn't make the interview, yet another thing he had failed to make. His presence would have been nerve-racking, since we had just separated. I didn't know if I could hide my post-betrayal indignation and Paul's permanent state of stunned despair from Miss Margaret Talbott, Hawthorne's director of admissions and fund-raising. Admissions people can sense strife.

"You must be so proud," I said as I straightened my dress.

I had pulled out the old Tahari winner for the occasion. Upon Peg's urging, I had applied a coat of berry lipstick she pretended to accidentally leave on my kitchen table. I even found a five-year-old working mascara, which I'm sure was breeding high amounts of contagious bacteria, in the old black leather purse I brought with me to the interview. Beverly wasn't listening to me.

"Bitsy, Bitsy, Bitsy," she trilled, "do you want some hummus?"

Bitsy shook her large head no.

Molly, who had been intrigued by the both of them from the moment we had arrived, was inspired by the sight of food. She ambled right over to Bitsy's mother, hopeful that she might be offered a little taste.

"She's not sick, is she?" Bitsy's mother accused. "Bitsy doesn't like germs."

Before I could answer, Beverly addressed Molly. "The hummus is for Bitsy, dear." She straightened out her plaid Burberry tunic, which matched the one worn by her little girl.

I distracted my daughter with some old saltines that had been sitting in my purse since her days as an embryo.

Bitsy's mother stared at me. "Ooh, you do *salt*?" Then she turned to her charge. "Bitsy, sweetie. Mommy is going to help Bitsy out of her stroller. And then Bitsy can give Mommy a kiss. Mommy loves Bitsy."

Bitsy threw up all over her mother.

Molly took the second saltine out of its plastic wrap and handed it to the little girl.

Once Paul and I were out of the precinct, he put his arm around me and drew me in. Neither of us said anything.

As we walked up Sixty-seventh Street toward Park Avenue, I was determined to speak. "It got even colder outsi—"

Before I could finish my sentence, Paul was pulling me even

closer. I wanted to tell him that maybe we should take a walk or share a conversation before we exchanged saliva, but I was the person doing most of the kissing. There we were, yards away from our colleagues, making out like teenagers. A voice in my head was demanding that I stop. I was about to assert myself when Paul started kissing my neck.

"Maybe we should have a conversation first." For the record, Paul made the suggestion.

"Do you have a preferred topic?"

"I'm fairly certain we will be getting married."

I was relieved that he'd had that eerie feeling as well and replied, "To each other? Otherwise you are just relying on statistical probabilities."

"I'm not relying on statistical probabilities."

We were still planted outside the Park Avenue Armory, an ambitious nineteenth-century urban fortress. Paul waved down a cab. "Any objections to going downtown?"

"That's what you cops say when you are arresting someone."

"My precinct is here."

"Downtown it is."

Once in the cab, Paul and I continued not to talk, but we didn't make out either. We just sat there, his large, warm hands holding mine, both of us feeling that something important was happening. The cabdriver stayed on Park Avenue. On one side, the islands of Christmas trees sparkled in the cold, still night. On the other, an endless row of office buildings remained partially lit to support the smattering of after-hours workers.

Paul kissed me as we rolled through the MetLife Building underpass in the mid-Forties. Right after we emerged, he pulled away and squeezed my hand more tightly. Park Avenue was uncharacteristically empty: a response to the arctic chill that was hampering everyone's holiday plans. But after we passed Union Square and started heading east, the streets were filled with intrepid revelers.

At the corner of Second Avenue and Ninth Street, Paul instructed the driver to stop. He jumped out and handed him some cash. He led me into a compact Italian restaurant, the kind with red-checkered tablecloths and single carnations in the water glasses in the middle of each table. *The New York Times* would never deign to review this kind of restaurant, but it would always be filled with customers keen for a hearty Bolognese or anything Parmesan.

They seemed to know Paul. A few of them were hugging and kissing him, while others shifted the wobbly wooden tables around so that we could sit in the corner and eat our dinner.

Despite the comforting smell and bubbling tomatoes, we didn't do much eating. My stomach had climbed into my throat, making it impossible for me to ingest any food. Also, Paul wouldn't let go of my hands. Or was it I who wouldn't let go of his? We pretended to eat minestrone and then pretended to eat fettuccine and then pretended to eat monkfish with capers. We skipped pretending to eat the *tartufo*.

We didn't exchange our life stories right away. Paul preferred to ask specific questions rather than general ones, as did I. Too much time in interrogation training.

"What was your favorite day as a kid?"

"That one is easy. September thirteenth, 1987, my tenth birthday. My mom took me to Bryce Canyon as a present. My mom is a nature lady."

"You don't seem that crunchy granola to me." He was gazing at my formfitting dress.

"No, I'm not. I mean, I'm not anti-nature, but I take in

energy from the city. My mother would be happy to sit in a wheat field. But, anyway . . ."

I had lost my train of thought. I was focused on his lips, remembering our kiss from minutes before and longing to continue right then, regardless of the venue.

Paul read my mind, gently kissed me on the lips as if promising more, and coaxed me to talk more about my favorite day.

"Even though I'm not Miss Nature, I am a little obsessed with astronomy. When I was three, I learned the names of all the planets in our galaxy. By five, I had memorized a random array of facts about them. A year later, I knew all eighty-eight constellations. And then I discovered Greek mythology. I loved the stories behind the stars. They made sense to me."

"Were you some kind of child prodigy?" He sounded more interested than intimidated.

"No, Mom read me all the Greek myths when I was little. The ancients devised these legends as a way to make sense of star formations. I was a kid. I liked the stories, and the stars were pretty."

He didn't say anything, so I kept talking.

"When I was ten, she took me on this trip to Bryce Canyon. She wanted to spend all day looking at rock formations, and I wanted to spend all night looking at star formations. It was about fifty degrees, but I stayed outside the whole night, wearing long johns and my mom's treasured Big Sur sweatshirt over my *Moonlighting* sweatshirt and under my orange L.L. Bean Windbreaker. Around eleven, with only a crappy pair of binoculars, I saw the Andromeda Galaxy. I have chills thinking about it."

Paul was smiling.

"What, you think I'm a dork?"

"No, I am focused on you and your long johns."

"I was ten, Officer."

"That's *Detective*. And no, I don't think you're a dork. I like it when kids have passions like that. Keeps them out of trouble."

"Now you."

"Now me, what?"

"Tell me your happiest day as a kid."

"Oh, it will pale."

"I'm sure it won't."

I meant it. He could have told me he loved burning bugs with a magnifying glass on the sidewalk and it would have endeared him to me, so intense was my attraction.

"By far the best day of my youth happened the summer my brother made me vice president of his club."

"Good for you," I said at my most maternal. "What was the club?"

"The Invention Club."

"See, I wasn't the only geeky kid. What did you invent?"

"Glop."

"What's glop?"

"It was a combination of mayonnaise, dirt, and broken crayons."

"What did you do with glop?"

"Oh, nothing. We just invented it."

"That's it? You just invented it? It had no purpose?"

"Excuse me, Copernicus, I was five and my brother was seven. The bringing together of mayonnaise, dirt, and color was inspired. Besides, being elected by my brother to be VP was like getting made in the mob. It was an honor."

"You're right. That is an honor."

I'm an only child, but I had witnessed similar ceremonies

among my friends and their siblings throughout my youth. "How many people were in the club?"

"Two."

"You and your brother, and only two other people?"

"No, just me and my brother."

I paused to envision my beautiful date as a lovely boy with a domineering older brother, playing in the mud and breaking crayons.

"Hold on to that memory," I said.

"I do every day," he replied solemnly.

The rest of our dinner conversation had more to do with the present than the past. Neither of us was in a relationship. We were both overly connected to our jobs: he captured criminals; I did my best to punish them. We agreed that these were the perfect careers for us as we shared a fondness for rules and structure.

Paul believed that people were either good or evil. Being the daughter of a therapist, I was much more inclined to use terms such as *destructive* or *productive*.

We agreed most strongly on our good fortune at having met. Paul professed his profound attraction over coffee. Once it became clear that our philosophies and interests were congruous, we both used words such as *fate* and *soul mate* on our way back to his apartment.

Needless to say, the lovemaking was spectacular.

Beverly has been dead for two days, and scant information has come out about her murder. She lived in a town house on Sixty-fourth Street off Lexington Avenue, and as of yet, no one has claimed to have seen any odd individuals entering or leaving her front door. A garden was out back, but it was pouring rain the night she was killed, so there was no evidence of any footprints or human traffic.

Little has been said on the news about the state of her house. Aside from the dead body and the blood spray, the place looks fairly clean. And why not? Beverly had a lot of household help. Rumor had it that she hired illegal immigrants fresh to the United States, offering them steady work, one meal a day, six dollars an hour, and a day off on Christmas. She had a staff of four, one to cook, two to tidy, and one to watch over Bitsy. As soon as one of her laborers politely brought to her attention that their counterparts made about three times that amount, plus days off and vacation time, Beverly would remind them that she was chummy with Immigration Services. Which, by the way, she was not. Bitsy has had six caretakers since I met her two years ago.

Articles and stories in the news all proclaim that Bitsy's mother was bludgeoned to death by a yet-to-be-identified dense object. At first, police suspected a baseball bat, but recent reports suggest that a wider object, like an iron, was used. Dumpster searches throughout the area have produced nothing.

I've learned nothing from Paul. He never called me back. Not such a shock. But in the old days, this would have been foreplay. Was she struck from behind? Were there multiple hits? Was the rest of her body intact? I once assisted in the prosecution of a perp who beat up his victim endlessly, even after it was certain the guy was dead. Was there a lot of blood on the scene? Did the killer take anything? This is the kind of information I crave. I am tempted to call Peg and ask her.

All the crime pundits are talking about the murder, putting out thirty-minute and sixty-minute specials promising new details on the atrocity. But they have only about two and a half minutes of real information. They know little about Beverly other than her obvious affluence and her devotion to her child.

"Beverly was determined when it came to her daughter," Helen Yeong, the family music teacher, is saying. "She was planning on surprising Bitsy with a harp for Christmas."

Other professionals speak in similar terms. According to her art teacher, Lenore Voulet, Bitsy shows zeal for gouache. Rob, her craft teacher, says that the Hastings family just purchased a loom so that Bitsy could follow through on her enthusiasm for weaving.

I try a Google search for recent criminal activity in our neighborhood. We live seven blocks from the Hastings family, and the only crimes I was hearing about were car theft, pickpocketing, and a string of high-end jewelry-store robberies. My search uncovers only thirteen assaults, all of them domestic disputes.

The police have not pointed to Beverly's husband as a suspect or as a person of interest. Little has been said about him aside from the acknowledgment of his seemingly authentic grief.

"They should look at the husband on this thing," a female passerby on the TV screen disagrees with me. "It's always the husband."

"Or somebody else," I say to my screen.

I grew up in Boulder, Colorado, the daughter of the coolest woman in the state. My father, Gary Hagen, disappeared when I was three. It was one of those cliché stories: he left to get a cup of coffee, never to return.

My mother didn't miss a beat. I never heard her say a bitter word about him. He wasn't ready for parental responsibility, and it was in all of our interests that he have nothing to do with me from that point forward. She made his departure and her solo raising of me seem as if that had been her intention from the beginning.

I don't remember my father at all, what he looked like, what he smelled like, or what he sounded like. Occasionally, I have the fantasy that I will see him in the street or at an airport or on a movie line and I will instinctively know who he is. Sometimes I envision giving him a piece of my mind, reciting a killer closing statement outlining the breadth of his irresponsibility. My vision of his reaction to me is less particularized. When I'm square with myself, I think I want him to feel bad. Not so much about forsaking me; he barely even knew me. But who in his right mind would walk away from my mother?

Mom has said over the years that he wasn't in his right mind. She suspects that he was bipolar—or is, if he is still alive. After he left, she got her Ph.D. in psychology and is now a successful therapist. Her take on my father is that she married a man with a colorful personality and was, along with her child, abandoned by a troubled and immature individual. She has been through years of therapy herself and generally confronts conflict in a way that is most healthy. She is also magnetic and charming.

My childhood friends loved coming to my house. They were frequently disappointed if my mother wasn't around. In tenth grade, when Sandy Weisler was preparing for the imminent loss of her virginity, my mother talked her out of it. My friend Miriam Nooge—Paul calls her Nudge—left her toothbrush and spare pair of pajamas in my room. Her mother, Mary Beth, a onetime beauty queen, relinquished a potentially boring and predictable suburban existence for an addiction to pills, booze, and high-fructose corn syrup. She was both out of it and enormous. Had there been a celebrity rehab show at that time and had she been a celebrity, she would most certainly have been a contestant. Miriam's father, Todd, proprietor of Boulder County's most successful car dealership, ignored his wife even before she took up her vices—and perhaps brought them about—in favor of a salesgirl or two in his workplace.

Miriam's response to the neglect was to become a permanent fixture at our kitchen table and on my bedroom floor. Other friends also telephoned my house a lot just to speak with my mother. I didn't resent it at all. I appreciated how cool my mother was as much as they did. She loved and loves being my mother. We even have a nice grown-up compatibility. We still go on trips together that offer beautiful natural scenery for her and breathtaking stargazing for me. We went to India together, she was the maid of honor in my wedding, and she sends me a friendship cake every Valentine's Day.

When I am visiting home in Colorado, my friends always ask me to bring Virginia—aka Mom—along.

She was a great mother. She is a great mother. It is unclear to me how on earth we could possibly be related.

Where she's impromptu, I'm rigid. She's the most flexible and accommodating person on earth. I am in desperate need of structure and rules. My mother was probably the only woman west of the Mississippi who harbored dreams of her daughter's teaching circus arts or opening an organic bakery. What did I become? An Ivy-educated lawyer.

"That's who you are, Katie," she said, beaming at my Columbia Law School graduation. "Love every day of it."

And she meant it. Because she really is the world's most perfect person.

"You are far and away the best thing that ever happened to me, Katie. I loved having you in my belly, I enjoyed you thoroughly as a child, and I am drawn to you as an adult."

All of this made my postpartum depression all the more depressing.

On our first official date, Paul asked me about the worst day in my life. Recalling my interest in the night sky, he had gotten us tickets to the Hayden Planetarium.

"How thoughtful—" I had started to say.

"Before you go on and on," Paul interrupted me, "I didn't do this for you. You've probably been here a jillion times. You could probably give lectures here."

He was right. I could. I had at one time considered taking a leave of absence from my job and writing a book about the stars and their stories.

"I did this for me," he continued. "If we're going to be together, I need to know about this stuff. I don't want my eyes glazing over every time you get excited about seeing O'Brien."

"Orion," I corrected him.

"Right. O'Brien was my first partner on the force. See, I need to know that stuff." His eyes were twinkling. He knew it wasn't called O'Brien. "So I thought you could explain some of this stuff to me."

Before seeing a great space show, I whisked Paul through the Hall of Galaxies and led him to each of the planets and some of my favorite constellations.

I told him about the lore in many ancient cultures surrounding the planets. I showed him the Andromeda constellation, an outline of a woman with her arms extended and chained at the wrists.

"I could make a tasteless joke here," Paul said.

"Please don't. Andromeda was the daughter of Cassiopeia and Cepheus, the king and queen of Ethiopia. Cassiopeia had a vanity problem. She bragged to anyone who would listen that she was more beautiful than the Nereids."

"And the Nereids were . . . ?"

"Part of Poseidon's entourage. They were sea nymphs, beautiful and typically nice. But Cassiopeia's boasting enraged them and they complained to Poseidon, who you might remember is the god of the sea. Poseidon, protecting his retinue, sent a horrible sea monster to the coast of Ethiopia to destroy Cassiopeia and Cepheus's kingdom. Cepheus consulted with an infallible prophet on how to save his kingdom. The only thing he could do was to chain his daughter to a rock and leave her to the mercy of the sea monster."

"Just because the mother said she was prettier than the goddesses? That seems a little drastic."

"Vanity and boastfulness come with a high price," I said.

"So, that's it. The daughter who was completely innocent loses her life because of her mother?"

"There is more to the story."

"Phew."

"Do you remember Perseus?"

"Sort of. He chopped off the head that turned people to stone?"

"Very good." I was impressed. "The Medusa."

"Oh, yeah, fourth grade is coming back to me. He had a flying horse?"

"We prefer to call it winged. He rescued Andromeda and married her."

"At least something went right for her."

"But it was his decision, not hers. Perseus just happened to be passing through Ethiopia on his flying horse and he saw Andromeda bound to the rock and told her parents he would rescue her if he could marry her. But by all accounts, she liked him. Although there was one messy incident at the wedding when Andromeda's former fiancé, Phineas, showed up and threatened to ruin the whole thing. Perseus saved the day again when he turned him into stone with—"

"The Medusa," Paul interrupted. "This would have been a lot less complicated if Cepheus had chained Cassiopeia to the rock instead of the daughter."

"Good point. But Cassiopeia is being eternally punished. When she died, she got to be in heaven, but if you look at her constellation, here"—I pointed to the diagram of the Cassiopeia constellation—"she is sitting on her throne with her head toward the North Star, Polaris, and so she spends half of every night upside down. Rather undignified."

"Well, that ended right."

I agreed. "Many of them end right. Sometimes the gods overreact. Don't even get me started on what they did to Odysseus. But ultimately they need to proscribe our behavior."

I was inclined to think that Paul would like the space show better than my tour, but we spent the entire program making out.

"I thought you said you wanted to learn," I teased him on our way out.

"Your lecture in the beginning was so thorough that I was comfortable with missing out on the virtual field trip to the moon."

He told me I had to pick our dinner spot because he was the one who selected the planetarium. I whisked him down to Hell's Kitchen on a crowded C train and led him to my favorite diner there, the Artemis.

"Is this part of the Greek-god thing?" Paul inquired.

A huge mural of Apollo and his chariot was on the wall facing the front door. The ceiling was painted light blue, with a circle of green laurels in the center. Sketches of columns and nymphs offset the fluorescent sconces.

"No." I laughed. "They just renamed and redecorated this place about eight months ago. It used to be called New York's Best Diner, and then I guess someone wanted to go for a theme. I'm a big fan of breakfast foods after nine p.m. This place has the best hash browns in the city, and my friends all like their pancakes."

We sat at a booth for four hours, long after they took our plates away, continuing our deep conversation from the Christmas-party evening three nights before.

"You've told me the best day when you were a kid," Paul challenged me. "What was the worst?"

"The day my father left. My memory is so fuzzy. I don't remember crying. I don't even remember what the man looked like. My most vivid recollection was my mother spending hours and hours on the phone. I knew something important had happened, and it wasn't good. And then I realized something was missing. It wasn't obvious that it was my father. But my mother was acting sad—no, not sad. Odd. It was as if we had moved to a different house. Except we hadn't."

I heard myself sigh. "It was my worst day not because my life went downhill afterwards or that I missed my father terribly. I just remember that I had a general but strong sense of loss. I don't know if this affected me in any obvious way; my mom was so fantastic and strong and empathetic."

"You seem pretty well-adjusted," Paul remarked.

"I know. I keep waiting for all of the abandonment fallout to manifest itself, but I'm pretty happy."

I was being honest. I had never been an especially depressed person. I liked my life. I loved my mother, my friends, and my career. Life did not seem as hard for me as it did for some of my pals who struggled with eating disorders, drug and alcohol problems, or weird-boyfriend stuff.

"You're an anomaly," Trisha, one of my college roommates, a psych major and now a research psychologist, had said to me. "You should have a whole range of problems."

"Maybe I'm lucky," I'd said to her. "If my father didn't want to be around, better for him to leave than to torture me every day with his malaise."

"Yeah, but you should hate yourself for the abandonment part."

"I'll try harder."

"No, I don't mean that you deserved it. It's just that people do horrible things to each other and there are always consequences. It's like Newton's laws of motion as applied to the human psyche."

This was Trish's summa cum laude thesis topic.

"Except it's not." I was confident. "I'm a lucky person." That was the way I felt, and I was grateful. I credited my mother with her parenting, plus some sturdy emotional genes, which I had most certainly not inherited from my father.

"I think that's why I'm so attracted to rules and order," I confided to Paul. "There's something very comforting about consistency and structure."

"So, that's why you like astronomy?" he said over our shared rice pudding.

"What do you mean?"

"At first glance, the sky looks arbitrary, but once you learn where everything is, there is predictability to it. It must be nice for you to know that on a given day, you will see a given star.

And then to see the pictures in the stars—which make sense out of their placement and which dictate a moral code—must be extremely satisfying."

"Are you sure you're a cop?" I asked.

"I am certain I'm a cop."

"I just rambled on about my worst day, what about yours?"

"I had a brother."

"Oh, yeah, the president of the club," I said. Too flippant, I quickly realized. Paul had used the past tense.

"That one. My only brother. He was the best."

"What was his name?" My heart was in my throat.

"Mark. Mark was it for me. My father was old-school. He didn't really have much to do with the day-to-day of child rearing. So my brother was my role model. He was only two years older, but he seemed to know everything. He taught me how to read. He taught me about superheroes. Everyone loved him, and I was happy to bask in some of his leftover glory."

"He sounds great," I said, realizing I was using the present tense.

"He was. But—" Paul's eyes filled with tears and he grabbed my hands.

"You don't have to tell me if you're not ready."

"I don't know if I'm ever ready. This is a horrible story and it will never be okay."

I didn't say anything. I just held tightly to his hands.

"One night, my parents took us to a movie. I was six. Mark was eight. It was some arty movie at a film festival. The name of it was *A Whale of a Tail*. My mother thought it would be educational for us, and we walked out after it became clear that the movie was a documentary about a couple's shared sexual fetish with whales and other large sea mammals."

I couldn't picture it, but I knew this wasn't the point of Paul's story.

"We left the movie, and on our way home, Mark, always the prankster, ran away from us while we weren't looking. We were all used to these spontaneous games of hide–and–seek, so my parents were more irritated than alarmed . . . at least for the first few minutes. Then something like ten minutes went by, and there was no sign of him. Then fifteen, then twenty. After a half hour, my parents called the police. We were thinking he might have gotten kidnapped.

"Pretty soon a young cop came over to my father and whispered something in his ear. He kind of held my father up and led him away. When my father came back, he was screaming in a way I had never heard before and only occasionally hear in other men now. Mark had been stabbed. They speculated that he had gone into an alley to hide from us and had accidentally walked in on a knife fight between two gangs. One gang member had attempted to murder another. Maybe he was afraid that Mark would rat him out. Whatever it was, he stabbed him and ran away, leaving both of them. The other guy ended up recovering and Mark died within minutes."

I couldn't speak. Paul's story made my little account of my father's abandonment look like a quaint tale.

"I don't know what to say," I finally said.

"There is nothing to say. Nothing. My whole family has been angry ever since, and we will be angry until we die."

"Is that why you became a cop?"

"That's exactly why. My parents are medical educators. My father is the dean of Cornell Medical School and my mother is a professor of infectious diseases there. It was understood when we were little boys that we would both go into medicine, and then, after . . . it was assumed that I would go into medicine. I'm the first in my family never to have gone to graduate school. It's the opposite of the American dream."

"Do your parents still want you to go into medicine?"

"Of course. My father tells me I can save more lives that way. He might be right, but, like your Greek gods, I have a vengeful heart."

I'm dating Batman, I thought. "I hope you don't take this the wrong way, but you don't seem vengeful. You seem gentle."

"I channel it." His face was starting to soften again. "My wrath really is limited to the bad guys."

Boy, was he not kidding. Paul was obsessed. We talked about work all the time, and it didn't bother me at all. He was passionate. After we had been dating for two months, I offered to replace his bulky 1990s Sony television with a sleek flat-screen model from the ultracool, trendy Xtech store in Times Square. On the way to the grand opening, he couldn't contain his excitement, but once in the store, he couldn't even focus on his gift or appreciate the cool gadgets. He merely shook his head.

"Whoever planned the layout of this store should be fired."

I looked around. The store was stunning. "I'm not a techno geek, but the sleek, organized displays make me want to grab a few TVs and laptops right now."

"And you could, without even paying for them. The merchandise is way too close to the door. The security guard is acting as a greeter. The cameras should be panning the aisles, not the registers."

Paul was right. The shoplifting incidents at the store made the front page of *New York, New York* magazine. He loved preventing crime. A girlfriend in the DA's office completed the picture. I was a dream come true.

"I can't wait to introduce you to my parents. They are going to love the fact that you have a law degree."

He was right. They did. Paul's parents, Franklin and Mary, are quiet academic types. They appreciate their son's passion, but they revere degrees.

"I have a Ph.D. and an M.D.," Franklin told me within five minutes of meeting him, "and Mary has a Ph.D., an M.D., and a master's. We had always assumed that Paul would go to professional school."

"Like Eliot Ness," Mary concluded.

"Or Melvin Purvis," I offered.

"You know Melvin Purvis?"

"Not personally. Do I look that old?"

Paul laughed. "Whenever I mention Melvin Purvis, I get blank looks from people."

"How often do you mention Melvin Purvis?"

"He's a staple in family discussions," said Franklin. "We," he said emphatically, "all collect Melvin Purvis memorabilia."

"I have his toothbrush," Mary said.

I want to be in this family, I thought. Franklin and Mary, despite their disappointment with Paul's BA, were obviously proud of the work he had done.

"Never shot anyone," Mary said. "And he could have." I had heard this about Paul. He had trained in jujitsu for years and was routinely able to physically restrain a fleeing or aggressive suspect without pulling his gun.

"The key is focus," he would tell me. "You can't worry about your safety. The focus has to be on the perp."

"So, Kate," Franklin said, "I have a feeling you are going

to be talking about Melvin Purvis a lot more than you ever dreamed."

"Nah. She'll be talking about Anthony Trentano more."

"Who?" I asked.

"Anthony Trentano. He was around the same time as Ness and Purvis, but no one has ever heard of him."

"That's because he didn't have a law degree," Mary said.

"No. It's because he weeded corruption out of the police department and cops don't want to perpetuate a history of corruption."

"I must say I have never heard of him," I told Paul.

"That'll change," Franklin said. "When we went on a family trip to Italy a few years ago, we had to go to Adeppa, a small town outside of Rome, to visit the birthplace of his father."

"Giuseppe," Paul added. "Anthony's Italian heritage was a significant factor in shaping his commitment to fight corruption. Everyone assumed that because he was of Italian descent, he was connected to the mob. He was able to infiltrate a huge cluster of dirty cops in New York City simply by telling people his name. He was responsible for the arrests of seventy-three corrupt officers."

"I have never heard of him," I repeated.

"You'll hear of him soon enough," Franklin said, and winked. "Welcome to the family."

The next day, Paul delivered a wrapped gift to my office.

"A book?" Peg asked when she saw it on my desk. "No flowers? I love this guy."

I felt the package. "It's actually two books." I opened it up.

Not just books. Homemade books. On top, one with a yellow-and-black cover entitled *Crime Lore for Dummies* in Paul's handwriting. Paul had stuck a Post-it inside the front cover.

If we're going to be together, you have to know this stuff. Your homework for tomorrow: read the first chapter on Anthony Trentano, and then read the stuff on the Yankee Stadium Syndicate.

I looked at the other book with the same cover design. Although it was empty inside, Paul had designed a similar cover and entitled the book *Constellations for Even Bigger Dummies*.

"That one has a Post-it too," Peg said. "It's inside."

You fill this one in for me. So we can be even.

Paul and I always knew we would become parents. We even had a plan B in case one of us had malfunctioning equipment. On our third date, he took me ice-skating at Rockefeller Center. He fell, I picked him up, and he told me he wanted to make babies with me.

Babies?

Babies!

Babies.

It was a given. We would be married. We would have children. We just had to work out the details. We were both obsessive workaholics, spending twelve-hour days on the job, talking about our careers the rest of the time. He was passionate about catching criminals, and I was hooked on putting them in jail. I liked the idea of having a baby. I loved the reality of my job.

We dated for two years through promotions, food poisoning, a broken wrist, and the life and death of our pet fish, Sal. We were both big talkers and spent a good deal of our time together negotiating which one of us could offer up his or her story first. We kept nothing from each other. I learned that Paul was heartbroken when his ex-girlfriend Elaine got married fourteen weeks after she dumped him for a Wall Street guy; Paul knew that I'd had an on-again, off-again romance with my next-door neighbor Russ, an out-of-work screenwriter, whose movies' central theme was the hopelessness of love. Paul knew all the gossip in my office: the affairs, the dissatisfactions, the occasional transgender surgery. He even confided to me the long-standing tradition in his office that if a spouse called looking for an officer—an officer who was most likely engaging in an extramarital relationship—whoever answered the phone was required to tell the spouse that the missing officer was at a seminar.

"Why a seminar?" I asked.

"Ten years ago, Sawicki answered the phone when LouEllen Dempsey called hysterically looking for her husband, Mike. Sawicki knew that Dempsey was with someone else. He didn't want to say that Dempsey was out on a job because the wife could have worried herself to death. On the spot, he said Mike was at a seminar. That way, they could fudge on the time and the wife wouldn't be freaking."

"And he could aid and abet his infidelity."

"That's between them."

I didn't like the "seminar" code. It sounded conspiratorial. Although I enjoyed being in on the conspiracy.

We got married at City Hall. My mother and Peg were there, as well as Paul's parents. For our reception, we invited 119 guests for a twilight cruise around Manhattan. We had a crescent moon, a symbol in Greek mythology of fertility. Babies would be coming.

We honeymooned in Crete and returned seventeen days later, energized to start our life together.

I had worked on a high-profile case, prosecuting a brother/sister team who befriended newlyweds, lured them into bogus business deals, then tortured and killed them. Quite by accident, I was honored with trying the case. Not honored quite so much as being in the right place at the right time. I had been assisting a senior prosecutor in our office, and he'd had to take an emergency leave of absence to care for his ailing wife. I had never worked as hard. We went to trial, and the jury returned a guilty verdict in less than four hours on three counts of murder and eleven counts of fraud. I was high on myself. I was cocky.

I was selecting my wardrobe for a nicely timed news conference when the court of its own volition dismissed the case. Apparently, juror number five had gone against the judge's instructions to refrain from reading about the case. He had researched it thoroughly on the Internet and shared everything he learned during jury deliberations.

My mother was soothing. "Sometimes these horrible letdowns can be opportunities."

"Don't tell me things happen for a reason."

"I'm not saying that, Katie. But maybe you can *make* reason of it. Maybe this is the perfect time for you to start a family. It will pull your focus away from your job temporarily, so you can heal, and then you'll end up with a wonderful little baby."

I was a bit nervous about having a baby. My mother was so perfect because she was patient and flexible. I told her my fears.

"In my opinion, Katie, the most important aspect of parenting is empathy, and you are the most empathetic person I know."

I was terrified by my ignorance of the administrative aspects of child rearing: how to fold a stroller, how to change a diaper, how to keep the little things from setting themselves on fire.

"You know a lot more than you think," Peg prompted me. "You've spent time with my kids for the past six years. You've taken them camping all by yourself."

"Your kids are teenagers. I didn't have to dress them."

Peg reminded me that I had spent a week in Chicago helping my friend Susan when her twins were born. I remembered more vividly avoiding the babies and taking the older kids to the Science Museum, sneaking them ice cream and video games.

"Very few women know this stuff until they have to do it." Peg laughed. "Bear in mind, stupid people have kids, too."

"In that case, I'm on board." I wasn't kidding.

True to my then superorganized, type A form, I resolved to learn everything about babies and parenting. I learned early on that honey could kill a child if he eats it before his first birthday. Honey! Who knew?

Paul didn't.

"And to think you could have given our baby honey," I jokingly scolded him.

"Kate, you're not even pregnant yet. You have plenty of time to learn all of that stuff."

I scoured the Internet for every spot of information. I bought every book on parenting trends, then took old parenting tomes out of the library to see if any out-of-fashion baby-raising advice made any sense to me. I read *The New England Journal of Medicine,* making frequent calls to Frank and Mary about medical terms. I learned that parenting meant a year at least of breast-feeding, intense sleep training to be instituted at four months, and an organic diet. I took copious notes on all of it. I developed a bizarre addiction to cable TV shows that

highlighted baby and pregnancy themes. Most of them involved individuals who were unaware of their pregnancy until
they gave birth. I wrote this stuff down as well.

"You could do a pregnancy PowerPoint," Paul teased. "I'll
get you an overhead projector."

"Paul, I like lists. I like cards. I like color codes. This is how
I learn. This was how I studied in law school, it was how I
passed the bar, and it was how I successfully prosecuted some
serious evildoers."

"Serious evildoers." Paul laughed. "You sound like a comic
book."

"Yes, and that's why I need to write stuff down. Extempo-
raneous speaking was never my forte. If I'm going to parent, I
need to play to my strengths."

"You're right. Here, let me add to your list." Paul grabbed
my index card and wrote, *Let's go at it like bunnies until you
got a baby in there.*

And we did.

I got pregnant right away.

Mom and Paul were thrilled. As was I. Mom was right. I
later apologized for my earlier ambivalence, but she told me it
was understandable given my huge work disappointment. My
failed trial faded away. It was as if it never happened. I didn't
want any of the negative criminal energy touching us—me
and my little baby.

That's how I thought of myself: us. "Bye, Paul, we're going
to work." Or, "Yes, Your Honor, we can meet you in chambers
at four."

The only parts about "us" I didn't like were the nausea and
fatigue, but my books, *Pregnancy Fitness* magazine, and the
Learning Channel assured me it would go away.

"One day, you'll wake up, and you'll feel like you did before," Peg promised.

I did. It was just as they said. I woke up one day and felt fantastic. Alive and libidinous. In fact, I made Paul late for work. I made "us" late for work, too.

The next day, at my eleven-week checkup, my doctor was her usual chatty self until she got to the ultrasound.

"Hmmm," she said, as she rubbed the wand over my belly.

"Everything okay in there?" I asked.

"I'm sorry, Kate." Her tone had turned somber.

Despite the fact that I could visualize the words "thirty percent chance of miscarriage in the first trimester" smack on top of the pile of index cards on my desk, I didn't understand.

"What? Everything's okay, right?"

"No, Kate. It's not. I'm sorry to have to tell you this, but there's no heartbeat."

"Can you check again?"

"Yes." I watched her as she moved the wand all over my slightly puffed belly. She gave me a consoling look.

"Nothing?"

"I'm afraid so."

"But I'm fine. I've never felt better."

"I know, Kate." Dr. Wanzell took my hand. "Unfortunately, you probably feel better because the baby isn't taking nutrients from your system anymore."

No more. "So, that's it? I'm not pregnant now? No baby?"

"I'll schedule a D and C for you, and then you guys can start again. The good news is that you can get pregnant."

"And the bad news is that I'm not."

I had the procedure that afternoon. Paul wanted to come with me. I didn't let him.

I threw myself back into my work. Paul threw himself back into his work. It seemed to me he didn't miss a beat.

"We got the ball rolling, babe," he said. He thought he sounded like an optimist. I thought he sounded like a jerk.

Franklin and Mary called that night. "We just want you to know how much we love you," they trilled into the voice mail.

I know they were hoping for a grandson—another way to bring back Mark.

I felt as if we had moved backward. I didn't approach my job with the same kind of vigor I'd had before the pregnancy. As soon as I had committed myself to having a baby, I wanted a baby. Everyone had one. Pregnant tummies and strollers were everywhere. Where had they come from?

"Enjoy the peace and quiet," Peg said. "You'll get your baby."

Easy for you to say, I wanted to tell her. She had two.

My mother called every day. "Your feelings are totally normal," she said.

All the same, I felt disconnected from everything in my life.

Work was busy for Paul and me. For three months we put one foot in front of the other. Or, I guess, two feet in front of the others. Then one day I felt the nausea again. Watching a cartoon tuna-fish commercial made me gag. I went to the drugstore, bought the sticks, and voilà: I was pregnant again.

I called Paul. He was on a stakeout. "We're back in business," I said on his voice mail.

My husband knew better than to talk about the baby with me this time around. Instead, he exerted all of his attention on *my* well-being, lavishing me with back rubs, coconut ice cream, and "Are you okay?"

I kept my condition a secret, superstitious that my telling

people had caused my previous miscarriage, and not the diagnosed trisomy 13.

It was easy for me to focus on my job. The brother/sister trial that had been dismissed before I'd gotten pregnant the first time was fortuitously scheduled for retrial during this pregnancy. My hormone-induced fatigue was counteracted by my endless excitement about my case. I was adamant that the defense attorneys not attempt any delays to keep me from trying it on the date that was originally scheduled by the judge. At five months, I was forced to inform everyone of my condition. My normal size-six frame was looking like a mutant balloon.

"What exactly do the rolls of fat on my legs do for the baby's development?" I asked Paul.

He ran over to me, kissed my stomach, and squeezed a huge portion of my fleshy thigh. "Just accept that you are going to be a big girl for a while."

I took to calling the baby "my tenant." When I was hungry, I would remark that "my tenant" was hungry; when I was sleepy, I'd attribute it to "my tenant."

By distancing myself from my baby, I knew I could concentrate on my work and could stave off the potential disappointment of another miscarriage. The stack of pregnancy index cards that had been relegated to the back corner of my bottom desk drawer after my miscarriage remained there. For the first time in my life, I didn't prepare.

And I didn't let myself get excited.

The trial was set to begin when I was thirty-two weeks along, and would end at thirty-four weeks. Two weeks was a good estimate of how long it might last. After it was over, I would have a few weeks to reassign my cases and tie up the loose ends for my maternity leave.

I went for my ultrasound the day before trial. The technician, Daphnia, was an overly chatty woman from Central Asia, although her accent was so thick I couldn't understand whether she said Uzbekistan or Turkmenistan. She just kept saying, "How cute, how cute," as she rubbed the wand over my belly.

Then: "Excuse me. I have to go for a second."

"Oh, God," I said, having an immediate flashback to my miscarriage.

Something wasn't right, I just knew it. I tried to tell myself it was going to be okay. After all, she kept saying, "How cute." Who says "How cute" under dire circumstances?

She was gone maybe five minutes, but it seemed like an eternity. I closed my eyes and thought about the sky. I wasn't going for any astrological predictions. My fascination with the stars and the planets is astronomical, not psychic. But thinking about the bigness of the universe was soothing. I envisioned the blank sky and then stuffed it with new planets and stars. I played connect-the-dots to form my own stories.

Three weeks earlier, I'd seen a grouping of stars around the North Star, including the ones that make up Ursa Minor and the Little Dipper. Why had no one seen this before? There it was. If you rethought Cygnus, the Little Dipper, and Ursa Minor, it looked exactly like a woman giving birth. It was so obvious to me, more defined than its previous grouping. I didn't tell anyone—not even Paul. My constellation seemed more real to me in some ways than the baby growing in my belly. Better to think about a newly identified constellation than to run down the hall demanding to know what the hell was going on.

Daphnia returned with an elderly man, wearing what appeared to be magnifying glasses on his eyes. He came over to me, held out his hand, and said, "I'm Dr. Schloss, chairman of Prenatal Radiology."

I gulped in lieu of introducing myself.

"You have a condition called vasa previa. This is very rare. If we don't take your baby out, there could be very tragic consequences. I've called Dr. Wanzell, but she is on vacation through tomorrow. Dr. Lamb will be performing your surgery. If we take the baby out now, everyone will be fine."

"But can't we wait until Dr. Wanzell gets back?"

"I would normally say yes, but I'm noticing a tiny dilation in your cervix. We want to avoid labor at all costs."

"What about my husband?"

"Our office called him. He's on his way."

They wheeled me into surgery, praising me for skipping breakfast.

The eponymous Dr. Lamb walked in, small, young, and wobbly.

"You okay?" she asked in a high-pitched voice.

"I'd like to wait for my husband." *More important,* I thought, *I'd like to wait for you to go through puberty.*

"We can do that."

As she was leaving, an enormous, hirsute, scrubs-clad bear entered the room. He introduced himself as the anesthesiologist and instructed me to sign the release.

Always the conscientious legal scholar, I signed it without even glancing at the words. What was I going to do? Go to another hospital?

They wheeled me into the operating room.

"Please, can we wait for my husband to get here?" I was terrified.

"No, we really can't," Dr. Lamb squawked.

The burly anesthesiologist jabbed me with my pre-epidural and then injected me with the real thing.

Within minutes, Dr. Lamb was carving my abdomen and pressing down on my chest. I smelled something burning, but decided against asking about it. Moments later she said, "Congratulations, Kate, you have a baby girl."

And I passed out.

Miriam is at my door. In my situation I don't really want to see her. Miriam is my one old friend from Boulder who lives in New York. She's an actress. Her claim to fame was an infomercial for the Abbisaucer, a sit-up enabler that has been a top seller for the past six years, largely due to Miriam's spectacular abdomen. She only uses the Abbisaucer when shooting the commercial, but she keeps herself fit and trim by maintaining a firm sit-up regimen and anorectic diet habits. Her other screen credits include three lines in *Slaughter at Snowcap*, a straight-to-DVD movie about a serial killer who lives in the mountains, juror number seven in *Presumed Guilty*, a failed social science-fiction television series about the legal system of our future, and a national commercial for Carly Button's floor wax.

Miriam sees herself as a star, and to some extent she is. Although no one appears to know who she is at first, there is always a glimmer of recognition when she displays her midsection. To be fair, the rest of Miriam is pretty fabulous looking: a heart-shaped face with wavy, inky-black hair and bright blue eyes. She had a pimple one time but fought it mercilessly until it informed all other blemishes to stay away. Her figure, not just the stomach, is enviable.

Miriam looks great in clothes. "I have a gift," she told me once. "I know how to throw things on."

Miriam and I have different interpretations of *throw*. I see her more as dressing in slow motion, trying items on for twenty or thirty minutes before she decides upon an outfit. Makeup and hair usually take her another forty minutes.

"If I were at a shoot," Miriam explained, "this would take me two hours."

"True, but we are going to the dry cleaner," I told her. I didn't think a ten-minute debate on whether the bangles were flattering with her wrap dress was warranted.

"We have different priorities," she told me.

Last year, Miriam lost her job at Abbisaucer, not through any fault of her own. The company went out of business after the CEO was convicted of statutory rape.

"So the girl was fifteen. She told him she was eighteen. How was he to know?" This was Miriam's reaction. "She saw him and she saw big bucks. She knew what she was getting into."

"They call it rape because the law doesn't believe that a fifteen-year-old can make those decisions." My friend had forgotten that I used to prosecute sex crimes.

"Yeah, well, whatever," Miriam said. "Now I have to get work."

She has been job-hunting for three months and has found nothing. She never seems to run out of cash. Every time she comes here, which is often, she shows up with a box of Leonidas truffles or a Gratelli orchid. She isn't in the business for money: she wants to be a star.

"It's all about who you know," she instructs me as she buzzes around all of New York's networking events.

She knows a lot of people. She was in acting school with Rebecca Gillers, star of *URGENT!*—television's longest-running medical drama. Rebecca has introduced Miriam to all of her contacts: her manager, her agent, her producers. But it has yet to get Miriam anywhere.

"You know . . ." Miriam starts 56 percent of her sentences with "You know."

"Yes?" I have to prod her because one of the side effects of her hunger is that it makes her slow to finish a sentence.

"It's just so the right place at the right time," Miriam says, reciting her mantra.

"With the right talent and the right personality," Paul had once whispered in my ear.

But I've got to hand it to her; she doesn't give up, and there's usually a payoff.

"It's all about perseverance," she's telling me now.

Miriam is lounging on the banquette while I spray my counters. My house is reverting to its clean self. I dust the metal bulletin board, the only spot in the house that has weathered my mood dip. It's Molly's board really: her class list, complete with phone numbers and addresses, her potty-training certificate, her police badge, and her first ultrasound. That's only because she insists that I show it to her so often, I might as well keep it out.

"And the right place at the right time," I remind her. I'm de-germing the trash.

"That is so true."

"Tell me why you are friends with her," Paul had said on the way to meeting her for the first time. He and I had been dating for a while. When it was clear that I had no choice other than to introduce them, I dragged him to meet her at a champagne tasting in SoHo.

"It's great because you can limit your calorie intake and get drunk at the very same time," I had said, imitating her voice on the subway ride on the way down. "She's family. She's the sister I love and hate."

Something about the two of us being from the same small city and ending up in New York was reassuring. When I first moved here for law school, I had hoped to have a decent social life. But I learned quickly that my classmates for the most part didn't have such aspirations. They were focused on school alone and felt that a night out here and there could hamper their chances for law review and a high-paying position as a summer associate. I was bored and lonely and needed a night out to be more focused when it was necessary.

Miriam was always game. She showed up at my door the first week of school with a plate of homemade cookies (they were from a Pillsbury log, but that's homemade for Miriam, and, for that matter, for me). Then she took me out to dinner, which for her was a bowl of broth. In all fairness, she paid for my chicken. Miriam is incredibly generous that way. She would invite me to lavish meals, expensive shows, and galas, and if I was low on cash, she never grumbled about picking up the check. And she was willing. Every time I needed a break from legal scholarship, I would call Miriam. A scholar she wasn't.

But she was fun and she was a lifeline to my past. Besides, she had been a fixture in my house all throughout my childhood, so she was easy to be around. My mother and I knew why she was practically living under our roof.

"Mom's on Percocet and Dad is with his perky set" was Miriam's standard joking way to ask for an invitation.

"She's self-medicating," my mom would console her.

"She used to be so beautiful." Miriam carried a picture of her mother in her purse when she was in high school. "I just don't get how she would let herself get like this."

Todd Nooge felt the same way. When it was clear that Mary Beth's baby weight wouldn't melt away as it had for Lucille Ball, he spent less and less time with his wife and daughter, and more and more time with his salesgirl Carolee and her sister, Kelly.

"If she just lost the weight, he would come back to us," Miriam would cry.

"I don't think it's that simple," my mother would tell her.

But Miriam did think it was that simple. "There's no way I'm letting myself go like that when I'm older," she announced.

"It's not just that," Mom explained.

"You are so right, Dr. Hagen. My mother is a serious drag. Of course he doesn't want to spend time with her. She never wants to do anything fun."

"That could be the drugs," I suggested.

"No. She's not fun. I am fun, and I'm going to stay that way."

So while Miriam may be a lightweight in the depth department, she can be counted on for a good time.

"I had an epiphany today," she said to me when we went out after my first-year exams. "I can give myself a manicure if I don't need the pedi."

While these conversations tire me now to some extent as a nonworking mother, they were the perfect antidote to single-minded law geeks. Miriam was good for a movie, a free seat at the theater, and a single gal's nighttime adventure—she had an endless supply of unserious men looking for a fun night in the city. While I was in law school, unlike most of my fellow classmates, I ate at the trendiest restaurants in the city, attended private openings for up-and-coming artists, saw the *Ring Cycle* at the Metropolitan Opera, and was a staple at private Central Park Zoo parties. I was on a first-name basis with Gus the polar bear. I learned I preferred Mozart to Wagner, hated sea urchin but liked black-pepper ice cream, and thought all abstract paintings would benefit from the color red.

I have Miriam to thank for all these experiences. She got me out of the law school trap. The men who invited us on these excursions were not ungentlemanly; they just weren't boyfriend material. It was obvious to me, but Miriam never seemed to pick that up.

"But he said I had a body that makes men weep," she said when one hadn't called after a week.

Her gentlemen callers were a blur to me—as I am sure we were to them.

"I don't get it," Miriam said, but she was always hopeful. Like a goldfish, she kept swimming around the bowl looking for the treasure.

"Kate, your life is different now. You have deeper friend-ships. Lots of people come from troubled homes and lots of people are fun." Paul repeated this frequently. "Don't you think you would benefit from hanging around with somebody more mature? You don't need to be her friend for the rest of her life."

"I know. I can't explain it."

And I can't. It's as if she's family. She will always have a place at my kitchen table, even if she always hogs the banquette.

"You know, I'm so over the business." Miriam is talking about show business. "I go in for meetings and auditions, and they're all loving me, and then it's like I don't hear from them."

Let me clarify: she doesn't hear from them.

I pretend for the sake of our well-worn dynamic that we have never had this discussion before.

"And you know, if they don't know I'm great, it's their loss. I'm better than that. Do you want to see my new headshots?"

Before I can answer, she whips out a contact sheet. She

really is quite pretty. Cherub-faced with crystal blue eyes, black, curly hair, and unblemished skin. Not to mention the perfect stomach.

"Now, which do you like the best?"

Before I can answer, she tells me that numbers seventeen and thirty-two are her favorites because, you know, they make her look sexy and mysterious, yet warm and approachable.

"Sure." There's no point in not agreeing.

"But don't you think so?" Miriam pulls a Rene des Toiles Lavender Vanilla Body Cream out of her bag and massages it into her limbs.

"Sure." I agree again.

"Great. Great. Enough about me. Do you have any diet soda?"

She puts the cream back. The house smells like a cupcake. While she is sipping her soda, I ask her if she has heard about Beverly Hastings.

"No, what?" Her expression suggests dismay that the conversation has moved away from her.

"She was murdered."

"Murdered? No. Murdered?"

"Murdered." I head to the sink, and surprisingly enthusiastic, I scrub a pot.

"Do they know who did it?"

"Not a clue. But I must say, it has piqued my interest."

"Wow. Who did you say was murdered?"

"Beverly Hastings."

"Who is Beverly Hastings?"

"She's a mom from Molly's school—her class actually."

"A mom, really? What did you say her name was?"

"Beverly Hastings."

"What's the kid's name?"

"Bitsy," I say as I mount my campaign against a three-year-old cluster of crud at the bottom of my pot.

"Where did she live? I mean, you know, it could have been a robbery."

"Could be. Sixty-fourth between Lexington and Third. Seven blocks from here. I've been trying to get information from Paul." The pot is coming along nicely.

"Would he even tell you? Do you think thirteen is okay?"

"What?"

"Thirteen. Picture thirteen. If I'm going to commit to a headshot, it has to be flawless." Miriam was finished with our murder investigation.

"Thirteen is great."

"But don't you think it is?"

This is how our conversations go. I agree with her on a topic, and she answers me as if I don't.

"You know, I'm going to do something crazy and pick thirteen."

All the mothers in Molly's class have agreed that we have to attend Beverly's funeral.

"It seems like the right thing to do," Liane Tulsch says.

I sense that Liane liked Beverly as much as I did, namely, not at all. Although my frail emotional health has caused me to feel remote from the other nursery-school moms, it's hard to escape the "What about Bitsy?" buzz. The girl hasn't been in school for the last few days, and Bitsy's father has been in seclusion.

"Maybe he did it," one of the mothers whispers, echoing the sentiments of New Yorkers everywhere.

I try to picture Bitsy's father in a homicidal rage. He appears pleasant in an I-just-had-a-lobotomy sort of way. Every time I run into him, he asks, "So good to see you?"—unsure if it is our first meeting. To his credit, he dresses well.

Three looks at the funeral the way he always does. Yes, Beverly married a man named Three.

"He is a Third, you know," she had informed me last year during the girls' second week of school.

I wondered what name could be so bad that you trade it in for a number.

"George," she volunteered. "You know George the Third has bad connotations, losing the colonies and all."

"So true," I responded.

"So we call him Three."

Problem solved.

St. Christopher's Chapel is lit only by its extensive stained-glass paneling. A scene depicting Abraham, Sarah, and Hagar illuminates Three holding little Bitsy's hand. She is in a crimson-and-forest-green plaid cashmere coat with a forest-green velvet collar. She has on forest-green tights and black patent-leather Mary Janes.

It is the first time that I feel genuine sadness for Beverly—she can't see her daughter like this. She looks adorable. Flanked by grandparents, household help, and a beautiful woman of unknown origin, Bitsy seems emotionally okay, or at least she is distracted by the ninety-five-year-old organist playing Pachelbel's Canon. They are standing at the front of the stone chapel, an intimate place of worship for New York's rich and connected. I, being neither rich nor connected, know nobody here except for the Hawthorne parents who have overtaken the rear seating of the elegant and bleak room.

Molly's class has sixteen mothers. I count only fourteen in attendance. Beverly, number fifteen, is lying dead in the closed coffin. I notice that Johanna Crump, Caleb's mother, isn't present. Hmm. Interesting. Maybe she's trying to make a statement. Maybe Caleb is ill. Maybe she killed Beverly. I look at Paul. He should be told that Johanna isn't here. After all that has gone on, a piece of me longs to team up with him on this as we occasionally did in the past. Another piece of me would like to see him locked in a storage closet for the next twenty-five or thirty years.

I locate him occupying a spot under the David-and-Goliath window. I didn't detect him at first as he is so good at blending in. But there he is in his navy-blue suit holding a little notebook. Paul can't go anywhere without the notebook, a Mead Composition in black and white. Sticking to my better intention, I reluctantly try to catch his eye. He sees me. His eyes rest on mine for a second and then move away.

The service goes by at top speed. Am I just a bitch, or did Beverly's early demise fail to reach the height of tragedy that one might have expected?

I glance over at Paul's face once again to search for information. Nothing. The man is unreadable on duty.

I go home, considering whether Three could have been responsible for Beverly's death. I decide he lacks the requisite verve.

As I walk into the apartment building, Alfred, our creepy doorman who resembles Peter Lorre in stature and voice quality, asks me if I heard that there's been another murder.

Another murder?

"Another Hawthorne mother," he whispers. As he opens

the door for one of my neighbors, I could swear that I still hear the church organ.

I press the elevator button over and over, a habit I had acquired long ago when I was chronically rushing. Alfred is staring at me with his bug eyes, his lips a straight line, his face offering no vestige of an inner life. He rarely sees me this jittery. In fact, he frequently calls me Mrs. Calm, misreading my emotional coma as composure.

Another murder.

I get to the eighth floor, run down the long, beige, permanently meat-loaf-scented hallway, let myself into my apartment, and turn on the little television set in the kitchen. I'm shaking. New York One, the all-news channel, is wrapping up the weather for the week, and, yes, Breaking News.

"It seems another Upper East Side mother has been killed," the unfazed reporter tells the camera. "Johanna Crump was found dead in her bathtub. The cause of death: electrocution."

Johanna Crump is dead. Dead. My heart starts beating fast. Johanna? Who would want her dead?

This is business, I tell myself, and I call Paul. I don't even wrestle over the choice of whether to call him. I get his voice mail. This time, I don't leave a message.

The phone rings.

"Hey," I say without looking at the caller ID. It's most likely Paul.

"Sweetheart? You sound good." It's my mother.

"Mom, I can't talk. There's been another murder."

"Do you need me to come take care of you, sweetheart?"

I can picture her, barefoot, clad in white yoga pants and a fading sea-foam SAVE THE BURROWED OWL T-shirt, seated on her yellow physioball drinking a watermelon-wheatgrass shake, and playing with her long, brown braid. Mom fully misunderstands the situation. She thinks the murders will send me back to bed.

"Thanks but, no, really. We can look after ourselves." I dig into my desk drawer and find a weathered but unused pack of index cards. I rip them open and scribble Beverly on the top one, then Johanna on the next. I forget that they are murder victims here.

"You're sure."

"Of course."

"You sound okay," she concedes.

"Let's talk later, Mom."

She's been pestering me to become a social creature once again. Just last night, I was instructed to go out more. This is code for *go on a date*. Mom is a big believer in physical contact. Not that she wants me to be a slut, but she says touch has a therapeutic aspect.

She has been hinting about this for months. "Get out of bed, sweetheart. You're over the worst of it. Molly's in school. Before you know it, she'll have friends."

Until today, I have been ignoring her. I *was* lonely, but I wanted to be alone. Now I'm not so sure. I put down the cards and look in the mirror. I am temporarily sporting a waifish physique, a by-product of my depression. Objectively speaking, I am attractive enough, but I am certainly not making the best of myself. My brown hair hits my shoulders, but the split ends start at my ears. I haven't worn makeup or applied moisturizer since my first trimester—Molly is now four—and my wardrobe needs sprucing.

The doorbell rings, and I go to answer it.

"The trick is to hook someone before you get jowly," Miriam says when I convey to her the essence of my mother's advice.

Miriam reads a lot of magazines and is on top of the talk shows. Frequently, she joins pyramid schemes that hawk vitamins and creams. "Meet someone when you look your best," she trills. "Obviously you won't find someone as cute as Paul, but let's face it; you're a little less cute than you were back then."

Miriam herself is luckless with men. She has no trouble meeting them, but she can't upgrade from initial attraction to deep connection. Paul's theory on this is that they skip right from attraction to boredom and flight. Her relationships typically involve a lot of champagne and a pricey dinner, which she happily pushes around her plate. She learned this trick from a diet specialist who assured her that no one would notice. The meal is then followed by a night of passionate lovemaking, which Miriam tends to describe in profligate detail.

"I mean the guy is a specialist with his tongue."

I routinely change the subject at the onset of these discussions on the theory that she will curtail the description, but she enjoys herself too much to hear me.

"Men never call her back for the same reason that producers and casting directors never call her back. They don't want to see her anymore," Paul had said to me when I was pregnant.

"So we can be best girlfriends and go out and meet the guys." Miriam was genuinely thrilled. "I know the best bra store in NYC."

Miriam, unfortunately, has seen many a bar-cruising girlfriend get married and leave her behind.

However, she was also an incredibly loyal friend to me during my divorce. Minutes after Paul moved out of here for good, in a lapse of judgment I answered her call.

"Oh, good," she said when she realized it wasn't the machine.

"I think I'm in love." She had begun explicit carnal play-by-play when I cut her off.

"Paul left."

"Is there any hope for us?" she said, thrusting me further into my black hole of despair.

But she came right over—that is, just after she ironed her hair and dressed in a somber black cloak—with three pints of ice cream and a shopping bag filled with old vitamins and makeup. She had her hair done for the occasion.

"This always helps me during a breakup," she advised.

I didn't have the heart to suggest that her relationships didn't quite hit the intensity of my marriage, because perhaps losing a potential relationship can be more devastating than losing an actual one.

Today, Miriam is hopeful. "I've got it. We can go get mani-pedis and then hit the bars. I'm wearing my favorite dress. I never knew green could be so divine, but it is quietly sophisticated, you know, especially if you wear fabulous earrings."

"I have to watch Molly."

"Can't Paul watch Molly?" Miriam is wearing an Yves Saint Laurent, neon-green halter dress and a pair of white hoop earrings. "I mean, I even left my panties at home." She giggles.

"He's working." Molly can be exhausting and mind-numbing, but with all that's going on, I don't want to spend time apart from her unless I have to.

"Wow. He works a lot."

"Yup. He's looking into the Beverly Hastings murder. I just heard another Hawthorne mother has been murdered."

"Do you think they're related?"

Do I think they're related? Was the second plane that flew into the World Trade Center related to the first?

"Two moms. Upper East Side. Knew each other. They must be."

"Maybe it's a crafty mom-hater."

For once, Miriam and I are sharing the same thought.

Johanna Crump was not as grating as Beverly. Whereas it is easy to imagine Beverly's repetitive braggadocio and inherent meanness sending someone into a homicidal rage, I would not say that about Johanna. She was good-natured and gentle. I wish I could say the same thing about her son, Caleb. I cannot. By the end of the first week of school, Caleb had bitten every kid in the class. He is said to be "wild." That is a jauntier description than I would have chosen.

Constantly in the administrative office, Caleb was warned—via his mother—that if this behavior didn't stop, he would be asked to leave the Hawthorne Preschool.

"Caleb is a spirited child. He doesn't respond well to discipline. It makes him cry." Johanna would whisper this to each mother as she apologized for the biting. "We feel that Caleb will learn this organically. Unnaturally interfering with the learning process will turn him into someone he isn't."

"He's a monster," Liane had whispered to me.

Had Beverly Hastings not been found dead in her kitchen the week before, I would have assumed that spirited little Caleb slaughtered his own mother.

I go upstairs to the apartment above mine, Paul's, to pick up Molly. Every time I'm there, I am stunned by its sparseness. It's just not Paul, or should I say, the Paul he used to be? I spent the night of our first date in his apartment and was shocked by the amount of stuff he had. The place looked like a museum. He loved memorabilia and made sure to cover every surface with it.

He was a superheroes fan: action figures, comic books, graphic novels, and odd accessories took over one wall. He was also an unlikely collector of maps.

"The world keeps reorganizing itself," Paul had explained as I lay on top of him. "I've got to keep up."

There were also magazine collections, notably every issue of *Running* since 1992.

"That was the year I took up the sport. I needed to commemorate it."

That was Paul, *il formaggio grande* of Commemoration.

When we moved in together, I told him that the magazines had to be switched over to microfiche. All the same, I found his nostalgia endearing. In fact, I contributed to the clutter, finding obscure superhero paraphernalia at flea markets and in online auctions. I got him a gold-plated Batman utility belt as an engagement present.

As our marriage started to fall apart, Paul's stuff began to irritate me. "Your trinkets are taking up way too much space. Where do you expect Molly to put her things?"

"Molly's three months old. She can't put her things anywhere," Paul had said in a lighthearted tone.

"So, *I* have to put everything away?" With huge gestures, I started rearranging items that needed rearranging.

Paul tried to calm me down. "When Molly gets bigger, I'll try to shave some of it off."

But he didn't. The stuff just kept proliferating. When Molly was eight months old, we received a new shipment of maps, and Paul was furiously increasing his superhero collection. "I hope to give these to Molly someday," Paul had said.

"Molly's a girl."

"Katie, girls like superheroes. I don't know how you can be so sexist."

"You have got to be kidding me. You leave your crap all over the place and *I'm* the sexist." I was lying in an unmade bed, wearing only a single gym sock and an oversize shirt, a souvenir from a Greek-myths show at the Met, which read in fading letters GODDESS.

"Huh?"

"You're the one who wanted a baby, but you don't want to change your lifestyle one iota. And you make me pick up your junk." I didn't budge from the bed.

"I have never asked you to pick it up."

"Not with words. But you leave it in silly piles all over the place and then run away to do your important work."

And so it went.

Paul has de-accumulated. His bedroom is adorned only with blinds, a twin bed, and a chest of drawers. His living room consists of a drab green corduroy couch and two matching drab green corduroy chairs. His coffee table betrays something of his former decorating style, piled high with maps, magazines, figurines, and old postcards.

But Molly's room is filled. Her ceiling is painted dark blue. She has adopted my interest in constellations, and Paul has inaccurately, but with my approval, placed all of the fun ones up there: Pegasus, Hercules, and Cassiopeia. He also threw a moon in the corner for good measure. Her walls are covered in rainbows and depictions of traffic lights, her relentless obsession.

The hallway smells like chocolate chip cookies. I ring the doorbell, although Paul has given me a key for an emergency.

Molly answers the door. "Hi, Mommy." She greets me as if she's hosting a dinner party. "Me and Willa are making chocolate chip cookies."

"Who's Wi—"

Before I can finish, a beautiful, glowing twentysomething girl emerges from the kitchen.

"Hi. I'm Willa. Your daughter is delightful."

Who are you? I want to say.

"Me and Willa stayed up all night last night. She likes red, too."

This cannot be a babysitter. It must be Paul being Paul. His bedroom door is shut, a sign that he is most likely napping or showering. I'm tempted to march in there and demand a background check on this Willa. Sure, she looks sweet and innocent, but that means nothing. She could be out killing all the moms. Not to mention shtupping the ex.

Paul, fully dressed, ambles in from his room. "I see you've met Willa," he says, checking his BlackBerry. He doesn't look up. His nonchalance further inflames my lack of nonchalance.

"Yes."

"Willa makes a mean cookie." He proudly pats her shoulder.

"I'm sure she does."

"No, she doesn't," Molly's little voice pipes in. "Willa's cookies are nice like Willa is."

"That's just something that grown-ups say," I reassure her, a reprimand to my ex-husband about his inappropriate use of the English language in front of our young daughter. "Come on, pumpkin. Give Daddy a kiss good-bye. We have to go."

"But I want to stay here with Willa and Daddy."

"I know you do, sweet pumpkin." I try not to sound wounded. "We have all sorts of fun things at home."

"Can Willa come?"

Why, little buttercup, you would have to ask your father about that one, I chuckle bitterly to myself.

"No, baby," Willa says. "Why don't you bring some of the cookies with you." And then, with extreme reverence: "If your mommy says it's okay."

"Mommy, Willa said I could bring cookies."

"Of course you can, Molly." I am feeling unpleasantly competitive. "Say good-bye to Willa." Whoever that is. "And to your daddy."

" 'Kay." Molly runs over to Paul. "Bye, Daddy."

"I love you, Mol," Paul says.

She runs over to Willa. "Bye, Willa."

"Bye, baby." And they hug. Willa hands me the bowl of cookies.

"I love you so much, Willa," Molly concludes.

When we get into the ninth-floor hallway, I have to keep myself from heading into interrogation mode.

"Did you have fun with Daddy?"

"Uh-huh," Molly says, her mouth filled with cookies.

"And with Willa?"

"Uh-huh." She keeps chewing.

"Have you met Willa a lot?" I trace the edge of the cookie bowl, suggesting a bribe is in the works.

"Lots and lots and lots and lots." She is singing.

"Is Daddy there when you play with her?" I say as I open the fire door onto the eighth floor.

"Sometimes."

This kid is impossible to break.

"For how long? Like just a couple of minutes, or do the three of you do big things together?" Why am I asking her this?

"Willa makes cookies."

I already got that. *Spit it out, sister, or I'm going to have to take you down to the station.* "With Daddy?"

Molly doesn't answer.

This is my first cross-examination in four and a half years and I'm terrible.

"Molly, sweetheart, does Daddy give Willa money to spend time with you?"

I half wait for Molly to say, *What do you think? Willa is some kind of whore?*

Instead, she says nothing.

"This is a great sign," my mother says as I relay the whole story on the phone.

"What's a great sign? That Paul has a hot girlfriend or a sizzling babysitter?"

"No, that you're jealous."

"I'm not jealous."

"You interrogated your daughter." Mom's tone suggests I had water-boarded Molly.

"I need to know the kinds of people Molly hangs out with. This Willa could be a child predator or a—"

"Or a love interest?" Mom interrupts me.

"I was going to say 'or a very bad person.'"

"Paul's a cop."

Paul's a cop who has been in a seminar, I remind myself. "True, but he may not be wearing his shield when there's a pretty woman around." I sound as if I pen soft porn.

"The point is, Willa is under your skin. You're having flutterings. The fact that you're having flutterings is another sign that you're coming out of this dark depression. After the flutterings, you'll have attractions. And then, after the attractions, you'll be having dates involving good conversation and sexual fulfillment. You're on your way."

Leave it to my mother to put a positive spin on the nymphet

cookie maker who's hugging my kid and doing goodness knows what with my ex-husband.

I realize that my sudden preoccupation with Willa distracted me from asking Paul about Johanna Crump's murder. I don't want to give him the satisfaction of thinking that my nosiness about the recent murder is a pretext for my nosiness about Willa.

I google Johanna Crump. There is no real update.

"As to whether Mrs. Crump's death is related to that of Beverly Hastings, anything is possible," Officer Robbins told reporters, but another police officer who prefers to remain anonymous sums it up with "What do you think? If I were a betting man, I'd say it was the same doer."

The article continues with the more personal information about the Crumps. Choosing not to identity Caleb by name, the article merely says that their four-year-old son will continue to live in New York City with his father. I learn that Johanna, like me, was not an Easterner. She was raised in Montana. Before moving to New York City, she led extreme hiking tours in Glacier National Park. During that time, she attended the University of Montana, where she got her Ph.D. in biology. Upon graduation, she moved to New York City and worked at the Museum of Natural History. There, she curated their highly touted bear exhibit in the year 2000. During that time, Johanna Turner, as her name was then, met and fell in love with noted ad exec and museum board member Robert Crump. Crump encouraged her to continue at the museum as special events curator. The couple married in 2002 and Johanna quit her job in 2006 when Caleb was born.

I google *Johanna Turner* and find dozens of articles written by her: "Bear Community Arrangement," "Repercussions of the Increasing Greenhouse Gases on the Bear Diet," and "Bear Coupling in Captivity." The woman certainly knew her bears.

I remember Johanna only as Caleb's mother, picking him up and dropping him off at school, putting in her time at class cocktail parties and holiday recitals. The subject of bears never came up. Not that it would have done so naturally.

Hi, I'm Molly's mom, former assistant district attorney and now a divorced depressive.

Nice to meet you. I'm Caleb's mother and a world authority on all things bear.

I had regarded her only as a mother who failed to discipline her kid. Maybe she was raised without boundaries. Perhaps this is what gave her the confidence to live among the beasts. Maybe Caleb is, or at least *was,* destined to do something great.

I feel emptier now that I did not know Johanna the bear expert. Depression is fertile ground for dismissiveness. Still, I wonder why she never mentioned it. Did she not think it was relevant anymore, that her career chapter was closed? Maybe she was burned-out and didn't feel like sharing. Did she have her bear friends and her mom friends? Did she just abandon her bear people when she became Mrs. Robert Crump?

I call Peg. I'm lucky to find her at her desk. At precisely this moment I conclude it is in my best interest to resume my daily bed-making habit.

"Katie, so good to hear from you." I hear her gnawing at her Venus No. 2 pencil.

I ignore the salutations and cut to the chase as I swipe off the top and bottom sheets almost simultaneously.

"When David and Matthew were in nursery school, were you involved in all the school stuff?"

"When it was remotely possible, yes." Peg's voice has a 1930s movie-star twang.

I head into my linen closet and pull out a crisp set of autumn-hued sheets. They smell like Ivory Snow.

"Did people know who you were? I mean, what you did?"

When David was Molly's age, Peg achieved some fame for her prosecution of a group of high school seniors. They were all rich kids from the elite, private Lincoln School who had raped a poor freshman girl from a public school. It was in the papers every day for months.

"I didn't advertise at the time. For safety reasons. I didn't want anyone to know I had children. I had a lot of enemies who had no qualms about breaking the law."

"But you didn't hide your job from the other parents?"

"It really didn't come up." I put the phone down for a second to tuck the bottom sheet onto the mattress, but I can still hear Peg saying, "When the boys were in school, there were many mothers who worked and some who didn't. No one seemed to care what I did beyond the 'Are you going to help at the bake sale or will you be stuck at work?'"

"Did that bother you? Here you were a star in one arena, at the top of your career, and worthwhile in another only to the extent that you provided baked goods?" Without thinking, I execute the hospital corners.

"First, I resent your saying I was at the top of my game. I'm hopeful that the top of my game hasn't happened yet. And second, no, it didn't bother me. In the context of school, I was David and Matthew's mommy. I didn't want to bring all of that nonsense into their Play-Doh."

I think about Johanna. Was she like Peg? Hawthorne, after all, was about Caleb—not Johanna's expertise on the bear population.

"Are you working on the mommy murders?" I ask Peg breezily.

"Not yet. But I'll be sure to fill you in on all of the confidential information as soon as it comes my way."

The thought that Peg, a stickler for ethics, would divulge any private information with a former ADA is ridiculous. The first summer I met Peg, she took me out to Gristle's, a DA hangout, to meet for drinks. Her husband showed up after she had downed two Bloody Marys and casually asked her what she was working on. She held up her hands and said, "No way," in a manner suggesting that bin Laden's whereabouts would more easily be discovered than the details of his wife's job.

"She only tells me after the fact," he said to me. "Like that's going to be interesting. What's the point of marrying a hotshot if you can't get the inside scoop?"

"Oh, be quiet," Peg fake-scolded. "Most men are dying for a woman who can keep her mouth shut."

Despite this I argue, "I don't want the confidential stuff. I just want to—"

"To live vicariously?" she challenged. "Why don't you come back to work here? You'll be up-to-date on everything, and you'll make a little cash."

"And I'll never see my daughter."

"You'll see her in a more structured way, like the millions of other working mothers around the globe."

"I can't do it. I tried and it didn't work."

"You came back to work too early, Katie. The baby was too small. That was before. She's in school now. Pretty soon, she'll be in college. Your connections to this office will be gone, you'll have lapsed on your bar requirements, and you'll have to work as a barista."

"It's not going to happen, Peg. I can't come back just so I can be in on office gossip."

I hear a little voice next to me. "Mommmeee, I wanna play."

"Good-bye, kiddo."

"Bye, Peg."

She has already hung up.

Tonight is the parent/teacher cocktail party. Typically, a couple host it at their house. Tonight, we are at the home of Phillippa and Edwin von Eck. The couple, along with their issue and their servants, reside at a spacious duplex apartment on Park Avenue and Seventy-first Street.

Phillippa, I have concluded from my three interactions with her, is awful. She is often absent from school functions because of her frequent volunteer work, i.e., luncheons and cocktail parties for various New York charities. Other times, she has made a vocation of self-beautifying treatments. With those, Phillippa has been able to transform her natural equine look into an artificial equine look. She has God-given large teeth, ample lips, an isosceles nose, full brows, and thick hair that was sprayed into position in 1989 and hasn't moved since. Phillippa always wears a suit, alternating between Chanel and St. John. Every part of her body is aggressively thin except for a pair of turgid ankles, which are not necessarily shown in their best light by her dedication to ballet flats. She carries an old Louis Vuitton tote.

Her better half, and I assume he's better because no one could be worse, is far more comely than she. Edwin von Eck is positively handsome. Like Phillippa, he is perfectly coiffed, and he dresses impeccably in custom-made suits and Hermès ties. He has the look of a retired model.

I put out my hand to Phillippa. "Kate Alger. Molly's mom."

"Nice to see you," Edwin says to me with surprising affability.

Not a sparkle of recognition comes from Phillippa. As she says hello, she grazes my hand for so short a time, I do not feel her touch.

The first time Phillippa and I had any interaction was about a year and a half ago, during Molly's first week in school. I was picking her up as I do every day. There was the usual mix of moms and nannies, plus one stay-at-home dad. Phillippa would pick Woodrow up only if she had to meet our school director, Irene Druvier, about fund-raising. Even then she brought the nanny.

Woodrow was the most overdressed person in the school. Had he been invited, he would have been the most overdressed person at my wedding. The kid wore a bow tie every day. I was tempted to call my friends at Family Services and tell them to come and collect him. The other children spanned a huge range in attire. Bitsy generally wore an eerily short skirt, the child-molester special. Caleb was usually dressed in a cool pair of jeans and a shirt that augured well for his chain-gang years to come. The others wore casual little dresses or pants.

Molly was going through a pants phase. "Dresses are much more beautiful," she told me earnestly, "but pants are easier. You can put me in a dress for when we make a party."

So she went to school every day in what I had believed were cute little pants outfits.

On this one afternoon, my daughter was wearing a pair of berry-colored velour trousers and a white turtleneck with berry-colored elephants. I noticed that Phillippa and Manuela, one of her help, were both present for pickup. The grown-ups were watching the children in their last minutes of free play before they would be scooped up and taken home. A group of kids had spontaneously kicked off an intense game of ring-around-the-rosy, welcoming anyone who wanted to join the circle. They would burst into hysterical laughter as they all fell down. The parents and caregivers were sharing in the children's delight. It was a memorable and perfect moment.

Phillippa, impermeable to joy, was staring at the group. She was fixated on Molly. I entertained the thought that Phillippa admired my little angel and was contemplating a playdate for Molly and Woodrow. When the game was over, the kids ran up to their babysitters and mothers. Molly, flushed and nearly breathless, was still singing, "Ashes, ashes," as she ran up to me. Simultaneously, Phillippa summoned me with her index finger.

How would I explain to her that I was weary of playdates? I considered being honest and telling her that I went into a deep depression soon after Molly's birth and now I was happy just to hang on. Then I considered lying, telling her that I worked from home and that I put Molly in afternoon classes under the care of a babysitter. Instead, I decided I would wing it. I went over to her, smiling, primed to come clean with a reason why I carried no day planner.

"You really should tell the mother not to dress the girl like that for school, for God's sake. This is a place of learning, not a sandbox."

I nodded and left. I did not mention that the Hawthorne

Preschool boasted the biggest preschool sandbox in all of Manhattan. Donated by the von Ecks.

I spot Liane Tulsch. I can imagine being friends with her at the peak of mental well-being, although I know nothing about her other than she has a bright boy named Max and a newish baby girl at home.

I wave and go over to her.

"Hey," I say.

"Oh, good, a familiar face." She is downing wine with impressive speed.

I smile. "I know. There's a huge contingent here that I have never seen before."

"They're called dads." We chuckle because it is true. "You must at least recognize the von Eck staff."

Unlike the Hastingses' revolving door of household workers, the von Eck workforce were born into their positions. Not only do they have an actual butler in their employ, he is also the son of the butler who served the von Ecks in the previous generation.

"I feel weird being at a party under these circumstances," I tell Liane, hoping that she might have a little more information than is in my possession.

"I've known Phillippa since the first grade, and she wouldn't cancel a party if she herself had been murdered."

Liane, I sense, is searching for a waiter who will drop another glass of wine in her hand.

"First grade, huh?"

"She looked exactly the same then as she does now."

I can't think of two more opposite people than Liane and

Phillippa. Liane is not a Chanel person, and doesn't appear to be an enthusiast of designer attire. She has long black hair, flecked with gray, freckled skin, slightly wrinkled, a small mouth, and perfect teeth. She always wears a white silk blouse, delicate jade earrings, and black trousers. I've never seen her husband.

"Did she wear Chanel back then?"

A waiter appears and hands us each a glass of wine. Unlike Liane, I imbibe with caution. I haven't had more than a few sips since Molly's birth.

"No, St. John."

"And the swords? Did she have those as well?"

I have had this question in my head since last year's parent/teacher cocktail party. The von Ecks have a prolific collection of Japanese samurai swords about which they show no modesty. Word in the school is that Phillippa will not attend any Hawthorne events unless they are at her home. She prefers her interior, she told Ms. Druvier's ineffectual assistant, Bree, to any others. When Bree asked her if she had seen everybody else's home, Phillippa laughed ("'Ha, ha, ha'—high-pitched and sharp, just like the Wicked Witch of the West," according to Bree) and said, "I don't need to." While Bree hadn't initially intended to report this conversation to anybody and had promised Phillippa that everything that was said in Ms. Druvier's office was confidential, Bree ultimately, thirty minutes later, felt compelled to repeat it. Just to Howard Montgomery's mom.

"She was in a bad mood. I thought it would cheer her up," Bree candidly defended herself to her boss, Ms. Druvier, who heard the story only two and a half hours after Mrs. Montgomery had. Irene, afraid of Phillippa's wrath, threatened to fire her sweet-but-less-than-bright hand. In the end, the story never got back to Phillippa. Everyone knows that she is a kill-the-messenger type.

"Oh, the swords are all Edwin's," Liane tells me. "If those had been in Phillippa's family, she wouldn't have gotten through her adolescence without slicing someone's head off."

I giggle. "Is it safe for her to be in the house with them now?"

"No one is safe. She would think nothing of ending someone's life, and the staff must have murderous fantasies about her. But her husband is obsessed with these things. His father started collecting the swords in World War Two. He bought his first in Guadalcanal. And then after the war, he traveled throughout Japan buying them from antique dealers and pawnshops."

It's hard to believe that Phillippa owns anything from a pawnshop.

"The oldest one is from the eleventh century. They are extremely valuable."

"How did you learn this?" I have been somewhat curious about the swords since I saw them last year. I could have predicted the George II mahogany armchair and the delft thirteen-nozzle flower holder, but it would never have occurred to me that Phillippa would share a home with sixty-four Japanese weapons.

"Maybe she's into geishas," Miriam, who loves to know everything about rich and famous people, had responded when I gave her every detail about the party last year. It had been a mistake to tell her. "You know, because geishas are Japanese, too."

This was the kind of conversation I once upon a time enjoyed with Paul. A bit of an aggregator himself, he can sympathize with that obsession. He probably knows a bit about swords because, well, he seems to know a bit about everything. He also liked to poke fun at the upper crust.

"It's a world I know well," he had confided to me when I was relaxing on his couch one Sunday morning, enjoying the Style section of *The New York Times*. "Both my parents are well-known doctors. They have all sorts of well-heeled friends. I have been to their opera box seats, their basketball floor seats, their six-course, six-hour, six-figure banquets, and I tell you I would prefer to party with a room of street-smart cops than a bunch of uptight rich people."

"What about freethinking rich people? Would you party with them?"

"Always the lawyer." Paul climbed on top of me and tossed the paper to the floor.

The conversation ended.

"Honey, I don't know, but I know everything," Liane interrupts my memory. Her manner is warm and chummy. *See, Paul,* I think to myself, *an example of the unpretentious privileged.*

And I happen to like her son.

Like Molly, Max is four, but he already knows how to read. Yesterday, he used the word *verbose* in a sentence.

"Max is a great kid," I offer.

"Thanks, Molly is a lot of fun, too. We should do a playdate." She grabs another wine.

"Sure," I falter, wondering if I can really go through with another designated social event. I think of my mother, telling me to push through the discomfort. "Yes, that would be wonderful. I'm free pretty much all the time." There. I sound pathetic, but open.

"Lucky you. I work, but at least it's freelance, so it can be flexible."

"Great."

Her answer makes me uneasy. Is it that I'm disinclined to ask Liane what she does for work? She says she's flexible. *Freelance* sounds like a writer, although some of my law school classmates are now freelance attorneys. Maybe she's a dog walker, or a personal trainer. Or not. She's a Hawthorne mother after all. She could be an art consultant or an editor. Why don't I just ask? Ironically, I know that her husband, Arthur, is a top executive at Login.com. In fact, I know what everyone's husband does, but little about what the moms may do. It doesn't come up.

Paul enters. You would think he would be a fish out of water here in a room filled with uptight business folks. Not Paul. I think that's why he is such a successful detective. He is chameleonlike. And it doesn't hurt that he grew up on the Upper East Side.

Paul nods to the men in the room. He's less social than usual. Neither of us is at our best when the other is around. Or perhaps he and Willa got into a disagreement. Most likely, he's just in work mode. After all, two of tonight's prospective guests have met their unnatural demise in his precinct. He's studying Phillippa. I know that look. He's sizing her up. Is she the one behind these murders? Is she next in line? Or is he simply taking in her awfulness?

For her part, Phillippa is talking to an extremely attractive young man. He can't be more than thirty. He is positively chiseled, with thick, wavy black hair neatly combed (but not too neatly), a perfectly carved nose and slightly asymmetrical lips, and dark brown eyes with lashes that even Ferdinand the Bull would envy. Although neat and crisp in appearance, the man exudes heterosexual.

I take a small sip of wine. "Who is that?" I whisper to Wendy Walker, our class parent.

"Oh, that's Mr. Mykonos, the new science teacher."

"Science teacher. These kids are four."

"Their minds are like sponges." Wendy takes on a professorial tone. "This is the perfect time to learn science."

Great. I have to go home and bone up on my molecular biology.

Funny, Molly hasn't mentioned Mr. Mykonos. She has, however, absconded with my flashlight. The other night I caught her in the bathroom with the lights out, flashlight in her mouth.

"I'm looking at my blood," she announced. "It's in my face. Look, it's on my arms, too."

Before I knew it, Wendy was waving to Mr. Adonis. "Steve, come over here."

Mr. Mykonos walks over to me. He puts out his delicate albeit masculine hand.

"Hi, I'm Molly's mother."

"Wow. What a privilege that must be. I thoroughly enjoy your daughter, and," he whispers, "I can't say that about everyone."

I know he must be thinking about Caleb. I take another sip. "Thank you."

Let me state for the record that Steve Mykonos is not my type. He is way too neat in appearance. I like a guy who emanates scruff. When I was in law school, I was obsessed with my classmate Nat Golden, a stubby little guy whose hair, what little was left, flew every which way. When I showed his picture to Peg, she thought I was joking.

"That guy," she roared. "He looks like Danny DeVito in *Taxi*."

"What's wrong with Danny DeVito?" I had asked her defensively.

"Nothing. He's brilliant and at times charming, but in spite of his appearance not because of it.

"I can't explain it. I think he's hot." And indeed I did. I was like Jell-O around little Nat.

Peg urged me to ask Louie out. That's what she called him, Louie. He wasn't just Danny DeVito. He was Louie De Palma, the sour, bullying dispatcher.

It turns out Louie's looks were his most appealing quality. He was on law review, and he brought an article that needed proofreading along on our date. He asked me if I wouldn't mind doing it.

"You mean now?"

"If you don't mind."

"I was thinking we could go to a movie."

Louie looked confused. "I find that a movie interferes with my process."

Not wanting to be rude, I read Louie's article, entitled "Producing Reductionist Complexity: The Evolution of the Internal Revenue Code 402(d)(6)." Louie's article needed a lot of proofreading. There were typos everywhere. We stayed at a coffeehouse for two hours while I marked it up with a red pen. Afterward, exhausted and miserable, I gave it back to him.

He grabbed me, thrust his head forward, and started sucking my lips into his mouth.

"Is it wrong to say that this turns me on?" he asked.

"Yes."

Okay, so he really was Louie De Palma.

"Good luck with the article."

Just to clarify. Paul is, by all objective standards, a handsome man. He just happens to have the scruffiness I am drawn to.

Steve Mykonos is staring at me with intensity. I look to the back of the room, and I notice Paul notice us. I have a flashback to being at his apartment with Willa. In a move not characteristic of my recent state, I make my facial expression match Steve's fervor.

"So, how long have you been teaching science to the toddler set?"

"Only a couple of weeks. I've been getting my Ph.D. at Columbia, and my grant money has shrunk in the financial crisis. So I'm making a little where I can."

"Good for you." Oops, I sound so condescending. But Steve doesn't look as if he minds. "How did you end up at Hawthorne?"

"I met Phillippa, I mean"—Steve clutches his throat—"Mrs. von Eck, at an aeronautics shindig her husband had funded. She suggested that I teach here at Hawthorne."

Steve sees Phillippa concentrating on us. He salutes his glass to her.

"Mrs. von Eck"—he is back to me immediately—"is very concerned with the intellectual development of all the little minds here at Hawthorne," I say, trying not to sound sarcastic.

"I'm grateful for the opportunity. I am surprisingly impressed with the kids, and it has been a pleasure, so far, to interact with the parents. And it just keeps getting better." Steve is quiet for a moment. Is he gazing at me? "Excuse me." His hand grazes my arm.

And off he goes to chat up Howard Montgomery's mother.

"Whoa," Liane says, her words a touch slurred, "if I didn't know better, I would say that you and Dr. Science had a moment."

"I don't know. I don't really have moments."

Liane is tactful, not asking what happened between Paul and me.

Finally, the ex makes his way over. I can tell he hasn't shaved today. About a quarter of a centimeter of hair is on his face. The familiarity of it unnerves me. We immediately engage in the more-polite-than-thou patter that has decorated our public relationship for the past three years.

"I see you've met Molly's chemistry teacher."

"She's four. At four, it's science. Also, he's a physicist."

"I could have sworn it was chemistry," Paul says as he pulls his BlackBerry out of his pocket.

"Are you here strictly as a parent?" I change the subject. "Or are you here on business?"

"Strictly as a parent," he lies, not removing his eyes from his little screen, "though it's hard not to associate this group with the murders."

It is difficult to let go of my hostility, but I know I have to if I'm going to get the information I want. "Thoughts?"

"Just one."

"Yes?"

He finally looks at me. "Mr. Physics isn't your type."

As if it matters to him. "On the murders, Paul."

"Nothing yet."

I can't tell if he is being honest. He has mastered the art of withholding information.

I maintain my artificial sweetness. "You must find it interesting that two women were murdered on the Upper East Side within a week."

"I do."

"And you must find it interesting that they both have four-year-olds?"

"I do."

"And you must find it interesting that they both go to Hawthorne?"

Paul doesn't say anything.

"Well?"

Still nothing.

"Well?"

"You know what I find more interesting?" Paul says.

"What?"

"That you find it interesting. It's been a long time, Kate."

"Well, well." Aimi Wentz is standing next to us. "I love seeing a divorced couple that can stand each other."

"Thank you," Paul says, and walks away.

Aimi disregards this and directs her conversation to me. "I was at my Reiki consult, and I couldn't switch. Ashanti Sanna was in from LA, and I want to show him how serious I am about Reiki, so he selects me to go on the retreat next month."

"Retreat?"

Aimi was hoping I would ask. "To India. He's leading a spiritual tour. Everyone wants to go so badly. It's incredibly competitive."

"Really?" People are now competing over who is more spiritual?

"Oh, yes," Aimi says, not smiling. "It's harder than getting into law school."

This was completely expected of Aimi. When I met her a year and a half ago, she was a cabalist, then she started with an obscure form of Hinduism. Now she is practicing Reiki. I suppose she is trying to find happiness. *Me, too,* I think. And she's done a great job with her daughter, Tess, especially with no partner in the picture.

"Tess is my greatest joy," Aimi had once told me. "She landed on my lap as a gift from heaven."

As far as I know, no one has ever asked Aimi about Tess's

origins. It isn't clear whether she adopted her or gave birth to her. They don't look particularly similar. Tess is a dark-haired Shirley Temple, fair skin, blue eyes, and dark brown ringlets. Aimi has long, straight, dirty-blond hair and hazel eyes. So Aimi could have adopted Tess or she could have given birth to a girl who inherited every single one of her physical traits from her biological father.

Aimi has always spoken of Tess's arrival in vague spiritual terms. We've never discussed pregnancy or delivery. That said, I know plenty of Upper East Side women who are loath to hash out the gory details of natural birth, let alone semen selection or turkey basters. Aimi may be keeping the details of her daughter's birth private in fear that the Phillippa von Ecks of the world would judge her.

Indeed, Phillippa has often remarked on the unfortunate trend of admitting broken families into Hawthorne. She is referring to the divorced: Paul and me. I wonder if she knows he's a cop. She might lobby for him to work as a school security guard rather than a parent.

As far as I know, however, Phillippa doesn't know about Paul's vocation. She just knows that we are not together anymore. On the one hand, this fuels her concern about the future of the Hawthorne community, and on the other, it reinforces her feeling of superiority.

A man comes by with the smallest piece of white bread I have ever seen, topped with a microscopic piece of tuna.

"Canapé?" he inquires, assessing my outfit.

"Sure," I say, thinking I had better grab four. It's clear that food is not a priority in this household.

"No, thank you," Aimi says. "I happen to be allergic to both wheat and tuna."

"Oh, do you carry the pen?"

Molly wants an EpiPen. She says that Howard Montgomery always has it with him because he's allergic to peanuts.

"Oh, no, it's nothing like that. I just notice that when I eat certain foods, I gain weight."

I'm not sure this is an allergy, but I am fascinated.

"Wheat, dairy, sugar, of course nightshades, all animal products, legumes, citrus, and green, leafy vegetables."

"Oh my. There's nothing left. What do you eat?"

"Clementines and chicken broth."

"Isn't chicken broth an animal product?"

"It would seem that way, but I don't have an allergic reaction to chicken broth."

I decide not to ask about the clementines.

"I'll send you to my guy."

"Oh. So far, I only have a slight reaction to bee stings."

"You don't know. You could be allergic to a whole bunch of stuff and not even know it."

"I guess what I don't know won't hurt me."

"A lot of people make that mistake."

I plunk a canapé in my mouth.

"And by then it's too late."

Is Aimi implying that I'm fat? I check myself out in the von Ecks' mirrored hall. I'm wearing a Diane von Furstenberg sleeveless fuchsia dress, a gift from Peg. I'm still benefiting from the depression weight loss. My shrink, worried about my loss of appetite, sent me to my internist, who told me I was anemic, which impressed Miriam.

"That's confirmation of your thinness," she said.

"I am sure there are three-hundred-pound individuals who eat iron-free foods and are anemic."

"Name one."

Here, I decide not to challenge Aimi on her diet advice. She is committed to it. I don't share her enthusiasm enough to defend my own food preferences; besides, I do enjoy just about everything she's allergic to. This brings our conversation to a brief halt. Then Aimi notices handsome Steve, who appears in her line of vision.

"Ooh," she squeals, "I *have* to talk to him."

I stand alone for a second and relish the break. Attendance at social events remains too ambitious for me. I find them exhausting and sometimes depressing. Parents, even the ones who are squabbling, are usually coupled off arm in arm, and my erstwhile husband and I stay at a geographical distance from one another. When we both used to work and attended law enforcement gatherings, the parties were fine, but the after-party was the most gratifying. Usually a brisk walk to the Artemis, where we would compare notes on our cases, dissect office rumors, then go home and make love. Sometimes we just skipped the diner and went straight home.

I think about my mother's telling me that I am ready to meet somebody. Maybe she's right.

I will start dating again. I take a hearty gulp of wine. I look up. Steve Mykonos is smiling at me.

When I get home, I call Peg. "I think I'm ready to date," I blurt into the phone.

Peg is thrilled. Some excitement in my social calendar will make her life fun, she has assured me. "Where do we start? Soulmates.com, parenting groups, tennis clubs, spiritual workshops, citizenship classes?"

"Citizenship classes?" I ask.

"Oh, yeah. That's just if you want to get married. Let's focus on some romance first. I hear hiking trips are good."

"I thought it would happen more organically." Although I do find myself jotting the word *Date!* on an index card.

"Organic is for the twenty-seven-year-olds. You don't have that kind of time. You have to approach this like a job. You're not in law school anymore. You don't just get to meet a guy whenever and make out with him whenever. There's a framework already in place."

"I don't know." I am trying to picture myself hanging out at a citizenship class.

"Unless there's already someone you have in mind and you aren't telling me."

I don't say anything.

"It's Paul. You're going back to Paul. Or he's going back to you. I knew it. I knew—"

"It's not Paul. Why would I ever do that again? I want someone new."

"You have someone in mind. Spill it, Kate. Who is it? Some hot divorced dad? Did you have a moment?"

"Oh, no, nothing like that. There was no real moment. I was just at a parents' night at Molly's school and I met a cute someone."

"'A cute someone.' Molly is a cute someone. I need a name. I need a marital status. I need a profession. Throw in a few physical attributes while you're at it."

"Why, Peg, I do believe you are incredibly superficial." Without thinking, I pen the letters *S.T.E.V.E.* on the card.

"I'll be interested in his moral code after you have gone out with him."

She does have a point as I have no idea what Steve's moral code is.

"For now, I want something I can chew on. What does he look like? Don't tell me he's objectively repulsive."

"A Greek god in a suit. With combed hair." I trace over the letters.

"Oh, no. That's never going to work."

"I thought you'd be proud of me for lusting after a cute one. Are you saying he's too cute for me?"

"No. I'm saying he's too neat for you. You won't be attracted enough to see it through. On the other hand, he sounds perfect for me. I mean, if I ever needed to stray. But he's definitely a Felix."

Felix was Peg's code for crisp, neat-looking men. A lifelong fan of *The Odd Couple,* she has divided the male population into Felixes and Oscars. Martin, her husband, is more of a Felix than Tony Randall himself. That I'm partial to Oscars was her conclusion after seeing me swoon over a series of slovenly guys.

"He is a Felix, I agree, but he's breathtaking."

"No. You won't like him. Flirt away. It's a step in the right direction, but I'm not going to be planning my next boyfriend visit anytime soon."

"You sure know how to take the wind out of a girl's sails," I say, thinking that Paul also remarked that Steve Mykonos was not my type.

"Oh, no." Peg doesn't want to discourage me. "Pursue it. I don't want to ruin this for you. I am so proud of you for moving forward. I just think ultimately you won't want to take his clothes off."

"And yet the thought has entered my mind."

"Does Molly know him?"

"Yes." I pause before I say it, knowing that Peg is trying yet another tack to uncover his identity. Even though I am not ready to tell her that I am lusting after a young lad, I do want her to know I have Molly's best interests at heart.

"What does she think of him?"

"She hasn't invoked him, which is good. She's usually fairly critical. She's not a Miriam fan."

"Tell her to join the club. Why didn't I know this?"

"I know. It must have slipped my mind."

"You know I love the Miriam stories."

It wasn't much of a story. I had an important court date involving my divorce, and it went much longer than I'd anticipated. I couldn't get to Hawthorne fast enough to pick Molly up. I tried all my sitters. I tried Peg. Everyone was busy. Out of desperation, I called Miriam, who, I knew, would be sitting by the phone waiting for Hollywood to ring.

Miriam reminded me how busy she was, but agreed to help me out in light of the despair she heard in my voice. "This is why I don't have kids," she told me.

But Miriam, to my surprise, went to pick Molly up. In fact, she dolled herself up, assuming someone with a show-business connection would be there, or at least some hunky guy on the street would be taken with her acting maternal.

"Men love that," she said, suggesting that she had firsthand experience and I didn't.

When I finally reunited with Molly, Miriam was vague about the encounter. Her usual habit is to recount every molecule of oxygen she takes in and every bit of carbon dioxide she breathes out.

"It was great, just great," she kept repeating.

"Did you see the other moms?" I expected a long-winded fashion analysis.

"No, I was focused on Molly."

Huh?

When Molly and I were alone, she asked me why I wasn't there to pick her up.

"Oh, pumpkin, I am so sorry. Mommy made a big mistake. I thought it would be fun for you to go with Miriam."

"Mommy, you come the next time, okay?"

"Okay."

I was worried. "Was Miriam mean to you?"

"No, but I like Mommy better."

You and the rest of mankind, I could hear Peg saying.

"She liked Tess's shoes."

Tess's shoes? I tried to conjure up a picture in my head of her shoes. I had never noticed anything remarkable about that kid's footwear. By contrast, I could have sworn that Savannah Foie wore a little heel to the Christmas celebration.

"What kind of shoes?"

I had assumed that my daughter and Miriam had discussed it. Miriam told me that she could be Molly's fashion guru since I didn't put any effort into it. She always brings Molly lipstick and nail polish and keeps promising her a pedicure party. Last year, Miriam gave her a Prada bag for Christmas.

"A lady isn't a lady unless she carries a handbag," Molly chirped for three weeks.

But Miriam forwent the tutorial that day. And Molly felt rejected by Miriam's perceived preference for Tess.

I also decided against confiding all of this to Paul. While it was nothing, we were smack in the middle of divorce negotiations. Leaving her under the care of superficial Miriam may have given him ammunition. It was bad enough that I had become reclusive. But my darkness following Molly's birth didn't make me inattentive as a mother—only as a wife. And while I know that Miriam was not the greatest proxy pick,

I didn't think she was capable of outright neglect. When I questioned Miriam again on the details of the pickup, she reiterated that it was great and seemed anxious to change the subject.

"So Molly likes him?" Peg probes yet again.

"She has never mentioned him."

"That's approval?"

"For Molly it is. She doesn't like to gush."

"If he's good enough for Molly, then he's good enough for me," Peg pronounces.

"If that were my standard, I'd be rolling on the floor and doing it with Big Bird."

"At least he's scruffy," Peg reminds me.

I don't go to Johanna's funeral. The newspaper noted that it would be a private family event. Her death notice did state that friends could contribute to the International Bear Society in her name. I am going to the website to see if I can pay online when Molly comes into my room.

"Hi, Mommy. Why is there a Kodiak bear on your computer?"

Kodiak. I look on the screen. The bear is in fact a Kodiak.

"How did you know that, sweetheart? Did Caleb tell you?"

"Oh, no, Mama, I learned that in my school." She does a series of imperfect leaps.

"Who taught it to you?"

"Mr. Steve." Now she is in midplié.

Mr. Steve. Soon to be Dr. Mykonos, physicist to the tots.

What an interesting coincidence that Johanna's specialty was being explored in his class. A specialty it appears no one knew about. Maybe the school was aware of Johanna's former career. They could be developing a curriculum that reflects the occupations of the parents. Molly was looking for blood in her body with a flashlight, and Kevin Kim's father is one of New York City's top hematologists. She has been dumping paper towels in water, but she could have learned that from a cleaning person. I look around the apartment. For all of my anticlutter stance with Paul, it is an utter mess.

But the coincidence is striking.

Paul stops by the apartment. He always knocks the same way—two short knocks followed by two long ones. We started this ritual before we moved in together, and Paul still keeps it up. I don't have the strength to tell him that it's no longer appropriate. I don't want him to think I even notice it, especially since a part of me thinks he knows that his apparent ease or not-so-apparent presumptuousness is a stake to my heart. But for Molly's sake, we did have an agreement that we can stop by each other's apartment without phoning as long as we knock. It's strange that he would come by when he knows she's in school.

"I just wanted to see you," he says.

Oh, please. But I play nice. "Can I get you some coffee?"

"You know I love your coffee, Katie." He heads into the kitchen and gives the fridge a once-over, as if we're still married. I bite my tongue.

He's definitely up to something. Whenever he uses *Katie* in a sentence, he wants something. When we first started dating, it was, predictably, sex, and over the years it morphed into errands.

I pull out my coffee grinder and toss in a hefty portion of French roast. My chumminess is making me ill, but my customary hostility will do nothing for me.

"How's work?"

"Busy." He gives up nothing. I turn on the grinder.

"Anything new on those murders?"

"What?"

"Anything new on the murders?" I am screaming over the machine.

"What murders?" His condescension makes it hard to remain pleasant.

I turn the machine off. "Oh, you know. The ones that have dominated every headline of every newspaper in New York?"

"Oh, those women?"

I load up the filter. I envision grinding his head next.

"Those women who just happen to have been mothers from your daughter's school." I try a different strategy. "Should I be worried?" I fish around for two mugs that lack any sentimental value.

"No." He sounds defensive.

"No? That's it?" We are silent for what seems like an hour until I pour the first cup in a Ziggy mug and hand it to Paul.

"You're fine. You have a cop right above you."

"Separated by three inches of plaster. That's not going to help me when the killer is standing next to me with a large, blunt object."

"Katie, don't worry. You know I'm here for you. One thousand percent." He gives me a familiar look. Right in the eye. When we were courting, that gaze prefaced a declaration of love. But I know better than to misread it. Now, it is his display of concern. He wears it all the time. On nights when I have Molly and he isn't working, he shows up at our place for game night. "It gives her normalcy," he says.

Apparently, I'm not normal.

And when he's here, I catch him from the corner of my eye, looking at me. Waiting for the big breakdown.

And the murders aren't helping either. He's primed for my catatonia.

But I'm not even a little worried. I'm curious. What did somebody have against these women? On one level, I completely understand why someone would be tempted to kill Beverly. She was the most annoying person in the world. Killing her, however, seems drastic. And Johanna? She was perfectly nice. The woman loved bears. What's not to like? She was certainly far more appealing than her son.

"It seems extreme." I'm certain that batting my eyes will appeal to his inflated hero complex, but I can't stomach it.

He takes a sip of coffee.

"And it's so specific."

"Your new brand of coffee isn't working for me, Katie."

"I'll keep that in mind when I go grocery shopping."

"The sandwich fixings are looking thin, too."

"Duly noted. Are you done critiquing my food supply?"

"That depends. Are you done poking your nose in a murder investigation?"

"This is Hawthorne. The whole thing is really making me—"

Paul puts down his coffee cup and cuts me off. "Miss the DA's office perhaps?"

"I'm worried about Molly. Her friends are suddenly motherless, and she's going to be traumatized." I consider Johanna, a woman I might have befriended if I weren't so stuck. And I wonder if I am mourning the extinguished possibility of friendship. I forget for a moment that Paul is the enemy here.

"I worry about that, too. I'm talking to some law enforcement shrinks to see if there is anything we should be doing. Right now, they're dealing overtime with the Hastings and Crump kids. We should do whatever we can to make our little girl feel safe."

Yeah. Why weren't you thinking about that three years ago, Mr. Rogers? "Thanks, Paul," I say sweetly as I grit my teeth. Keep your friends close and keep your enemies closer.

"No problem." He heads back to the door. "I'll be upstairs when you need me."

I take a deep breath as I manufacture a bit o' sincerity. "And Paul?"

"Yes, Kate?"

"If you get any information, feel free to drop by."

"Got it," he says, and leaves the apartment.

I resist the urge to call out to him, *By the way, thanks for ruining the marriage.*

I don't really know when my marriage to Paul went downhill. I am inclined to say that it was right after Molly's birth, but I don't want to be misunderstood. Molly's birth was the best thing that has ever happened to me.

But it did change things.

As a three-and-a-half-pound preemie, her lungs weren't developed. The hospital admitted her to the NICU, which I found terrifying. Compared to the other babies, she was positively Olympian. But I would have been scared by any baby, even a full-term eight-pounder.

The first months of Molly's life were made more difficult by my lack of help. My mother had intended to take a leave of absence from her practice after the baby's birth and teach me the ins and outs of infant care for a couple of weeks. Days before my surgery she broke her hip in a biking accident and was bedridden for seven weeks with a prohibition against travel for at least six months.

The doctors, nurses, orderlies, and technicians were all telling me to rest while Molly was in the NICU. The nurses said my work would really begin once she got home. My doctor told me that my C-section would heal faster if I took care of myself.

How could I take care of myself when my little girl was hospitalized?

"The pediatrician says Molly will be home soon. Think of this around-the-clock nursing staff as an opportunity to rest," Paul urged me.

I ignored this. As far as I was concerned, my baby was fighting for her life. I spent every moment in the hospital, changing her diaper when the nurses would let me, holding my baby when I could. I used to sneak out of the apartment in the middle of the night to breast-feed her.

"This isn't necessary," Ella, our no-nonsense night nurse said. "Really. Your daughter will thrive with a healthy mother. The doctors are already supplementing with formula. She needs more than your body can give. Why don't you sleep during the night? If you feel you must expel milk, we can loan you a pump and you can do that in the middle of the night." Ella was trying to be kind, but I knew that wasn't enough.

"No. I have to be here," I insisted.

Paul was not as hospital-bound as I was. He was out buying baby things. Molly was so early, we didn't have anything except the box of secondhand baby clothes my friend Susan had sent from Chicago. But within a week we had all the paraphernalia.

"I built you a great-looking swing," Paul told our Lilliputian Molly through the glass of her incubator.

I ignored him.

"Aren't you glad I built our little girl a swing?"

I didn't care about any of it. I was gripped by anxiety. "How can you think of toys when Molly is in Intensive Care?"

"She's going to be out soon. And we need stuff. Not just stuff. We need a mom here. A fully functioning, nonhysterical mom."

"Are you calling me hysterical?" I asked, my voice high.

"Maybe not hysterical, but not rested."

"It may be easy for you to rest and hop from store to store when our little girl is barely breathing, but it's unthinkable for me."

Paul tried to hug me. I didn't reciprocate.

Molly was in the hospital for twenty-two days. I didn't sleep and I didn't eat. Paul slept, shopped, and even went to the precinct once or twice to see what was going on. I couldn't see how this was possible for him. It may have been the hormones or my lack of medical education, but I was convinced that Molly was on the brink of death. Regardless of the medical advice I received, I kept a vigil at her station and only paced the halls when the doctors kicked me out of the room.

When Molly weighed five pounds and was breathing on her own, she was released—without ceremony—from the hospital. We all went home together, Molly clad in her orange-pink-and-red-flowered leaving-the-hospital Onesies and matching hat, resting comfortably in her car seat—all thanks to Paul. I sat in the back with her, sick from my worry binge and sleeplessness.

Paul chirpily drove us home. This was the best day of his life, he told me, but he would have to go back to his post. He had already taken three weeks off, and his captain was joking that the Big Apple's crime rate had spiked.

While I was thrilled to have Molly at home with us and relieved by her good health, I was exhausted and alone.

"Maybe we should hire a nurse or a babysitter to help you," Paul said as he watched me change Molly's diaper twice within fifteen minutes. "You need sleep."

Despite Peg's mantra that even stupid people have babies, I managed to put Molly's diaper on backward twice within thirty minutes, and another time forgot to apply the diaper cream.

"No, I can do this," I told him, holding back the tears. "If I had no problem investigating a murderous gang and then prosecuting them for three months, I can lose a little sleep to feed a baby."

But it was hard.

Meanwhile, Paul was busy. He had just won an award from the mayor for his implementation of a street-crime-reduction program. I'd helped him to develop the plan several years before when we noticed that more and more evidence could be collected against street criminals who had been caught on private security video. A string of muggings in Tribeca had gone unsolved until a security video from the Better Bean caught a picture of the license plate the muggers had used in their getaway car. The video was set up only to take pictures of the interior and doorways of the café, but the revolving camera was focused on one of their signature oversize windows. If the crime had taken place during the day, the patrons would undoubtedly have seen the crime and stopped it, or been able to report it. But the mugging took place at night when the streets are sparsely populated and the cafés are closed. However, the Better Bean video surveillance was twenty-four hours and the entire getaway was caught on tape.

We had an idea. What if security videos were set up to film the exteriors of businesses, to the extent it was cinematically possible? Because this would be costly for business owners, Paul had the brilliant idea of offering a substantial tax advantage to business owners who supplemented their surveillance. He devised a plan and introduced it to the city council. It was named Mark's Break, after his brother.

Paul was hailed as a hero in the fight against street crime. There would be a ceremony for him at Gracie Mansion, the mayor's home. Paul was asked to prepare a speech. While he wasn't working at the office, he was at home writing and rehearsing his speech. He loved the idea of his wife taking care of his beautiful little girl while he fought crime in New York City. He didn't notice the reality: the wife was sinking into a deep depression.

I didn't notice either. I just thought I was tired. One evening Peg came over after work. Paul was, as usual, staying way past his shift. He was assisting in a rape trial. My friend Dawn was prosecuting, and she needed his help.

"Great about Paul's award, huh?" Peg said.

"Yup, it sure is." I did everything I could to look enthusiastic.

"You okay?"

"Sure. Maybe a little fatigued." I was slumped over a wooden chair.

"I've been there." It was hard to believe. There Peg was in a little pin-striped suit with a briefcase at her feet.

We sat in silence for a while. Peg offered to hold Molly when she started to cry. She suggested that I take a nap.

"No. I need to be on top of this."

"That's what I'm here for. We all need a break."

"Thanks. But Molly is really small, and I just need to monitor all this." It seemed to make so much sense at the time.

"Kate, you look exhausted. I have been through this. Twice. I also helped out my brother's wife and a couple of other friends. You need to sleep."

"Yes, but Molly is sick," I told Peg, not moving from the chair. "My circumstances are different."

"No, Kate, they are not. Molly isn't sick. She's great. She's strong. The doctors gave her a clean bill of health. I'm not so sure about you."

"I'm strong," I said weakly.

Peg didn't argue with me.

It didn't occur to me that I was depressed. I had heard of postpartum depression. I had even prosecuted a few domestic cases in which postpartum had been diagnosed in some abusive homes. The abuse always manifested in hostility toward the baby. I had no such thoughts. In my darkest moments, I only wanted to protect her. If I wanted to hurt anybody, it was me—or Paul.

"I would love to take my beautiful wife out for a date. How about we sneak out of the awards ceremony a little early and toast our family with a glass of champagne and some smooching?"

"You're kidding, right?" I asked him. Even I heard how bitter I sounded.

"No." Paul was confused.

"I can't very well drink champagne while I'm breast-feeding."

"Maybe not a bottle, but you can have a few sips."

"Not one sip, Paul. Molly is small. One sip could hurt her."

"Okay, we can drink seltzer. Better yet, we skip the drinking and go right to the smooching."

"I don't think so."

"Why?"

"I don't want to be away from her."

"You are going to have to be away from her at the awards ceremony. Peg said she would babysit, so what's another hour or two?"

"Paul, I don't think Molly's ready for a babysitter. Let me sit this one out."

Truth is, I didn't really want Paul to win the award. I was starting to harbor a grudge. He was home less and less. Some days he didn't even look at Molly. Occasionally, I would hear him on the phone saying "my daughter" this and "my daughter" that.

"You seem to spend a lot more time talking about your daughter than you spend being with her," I said to him one morning after he hung up from a twenty-five-minute call.

"She was asleep. Did you want me to wake her up?"

"When was the last time you saw your daughter awake?"

"I don't know. I'm always checking up on you guys."

"When was the last time you saw her awake, Paul?"

"Kate, you better get back to work soon because you look like someone who's craving a cross-examination."

"Don't put this on me." I started crying. "You may be a big crime fighter, but you have responsibilities, mister."

"I didn't know you felt like this."

"How could you not know?" I was screaming.

"You seem to want to do everything. You're breast-feeding, obviously. You told me you don't think I diaper correctly. You want to read to her because you say it's the closest thing to intellectual stimulation. These are all the jobs."

"The jobs," I said self-righteously with a hint of insanity, "are being a father." I couldn't respond to him logically. I just felt angry and alone.

"I am a father, and I'm taking care of us."

I left the room and closed the door. "Don't you worry, my baby," I said to my five-month-old. "Mama loves you."

Looking back on it, I see clearly I wasn't well, but at the time my rage had seemed so justified. Paul seemed to have lost faith in me. He had no idea what I was going through. He thought I hated him, and I was certain he considered me incapable of motherhood. I kept fantasizing about leaving him, serving him with divorce papers replete with details as to his shortcomings as a father and a husband. When he would try to touch me, I would flinch. When he would try to talk to me, I would avoid the conversation, fearing that my words of resentment would spew forth.

I called my mother daily complaining about him.

"Honey, you need to sleep. I wish I could be there. This should be the happiest time for you."

I kept thinking that myself. All my life my mother sang like a chorus about how perfect my infancy was. That she had felt blessed and happy every second. And I kept wondering why this wasn't true for me. I secretly believed I was a bad mother.

"You had a rough start," she said.

"No. But Molly's five months. I should be thrilled."

I wasn't thrilled. I was enraged. And I was fairly certain it was because of Paul.

That was almost four years ago. If I had known then what I know now, I would have realized that it was illogical of me to think that my experience would be identical to my mother's. It had never occurred to me that we wouldn't have this in common. I would probably have realized that my rage was born of exhaustion and some imperfections in my brain chemistry rather than Paul's misdoings. I would have realized that despite my love for Molly I was having postpartum blues. But I didn't know.

And it got worse.

The Manhattan DA's office offers three months of paid maternity leave and three months of unpaid maternity leave. During my pregnancy, I was leaning toward taking the paid leave only. When that time expired, I unwillingly went back.

"We did miss you," Peg had said, "but you don't have to come back if you don't feel ready."

When I got back to work, it didn't seem as if anyone had missed me. The wheels of justice hadn't skipped a beat. The expected genuinely excited patter about Molly and my return lasted for about forty-five seconds. People demanded pictures, questioned me about breast-feeding, and offered sympathy for my lack of sleep. But by eleven o'clock of my first morning back, my experiences of the past couple of months were no longer a concern.

I felt disconnected. In my stupor, the collegiality I had always adored in the office felt cliquish. I didn't know how to talk to my coworkers. My points of reference seemed exclusively Molly-related. I was an outcast.

More important, the work that had always fascinated me seemed not to matter much. So another criminal in New York City broke the law and had to be worked through the justice system. Who cared if I put this individual on trial or if some other prosecutor did?

Little Molly needed me.

"Are you sure?" Paul asked. "This isn't only about what Molly needs. It's also about what you need."

"Not all of us can afford to be selfish."

"Molly is entitled to have a happy and fulfilled mother, and you're entitled to be happy."

Not only did Paul want to be happy, he *was* happy. I remember hearing him humming in the morning. Humming everything: the Beatles, TV jingles, opera, Ricky Martin, everything. It was annoying for two reasons: he was a terrible hummer and he had no right.

"Would you just stop it?" I yelled.

By Molly's six-month birthday, Paul's patience had worn thin. He stopped complimenting me on my maternal talents. He stopped offering to help. He stopped trying to make plans with me. He started staying at work even longer.

As the months wore on, we ran out of things to talk about. Wanting to maintain my position as parent leader, I withheld information about Molly's progress. I didn't want to hear about work. It made me feel bad.

When Molly turned eight months old, Paul suggested that we go away for a weekend to try to reconnect.

I wasn't interested.

One afternoon when I was feeling particularly dreadful, Peg made a surprise uninvited appearance at my door. She pushed herself in, saying no when I offered to take her coat and ignoring me when I offered her coffee and snacks. She did deign to sit on the very edge of one of my kitchen chairs.

"Look, Kate. I don't have time, so here it is. You love Paul. Paul loves you. You had a baby. You have had some sort of psychotic break, and we have all been holding your hand as you flush your good fortune down the toilet."

"But I—"

"Don't interrupt. I don't have time. Really. This is what you're going to do. You're going to get yourself a therapist, which is easy, because I got one for you. She is the best. If you don't like her, I have a list of ten others who are all tied for second best. You will get well. While you are healing and figuring out what the hell is wrong with you, your husband, your biggest fan, will be at your side. Why? you ask. Because after I leave today, you will call him and tell him to come home early. You will dress up in some ridiculously sexy getup that I prefer not to envision in my head, for reasons I am sure you can understand. You will greet him in the sexy getup and seduce him. If you are not in the mood, close your eyes and think of England. It'll all come back. Then you will tell him that you love him, that you will do anything, I mean anything, to keep this family together. It sounds like a lot now, but you have no choice."

Peg handed me a piece of paper with eleven names on it. She had highlighted the top name, Judy Schmitt, with the notation *Friday, 11:00 a.m.*, next to it.

"Your appointment is for tomorrow morning."

Then she left.

I stared at the piece of paper and then at the telephone. Peg said I had no choice. She was right. I had no choice. I loved Paul, and if I could get over my resentment of him for . . . for . . . for . . . What did I resent him for anyway? I searched my brain for evidence that would justify my rage.

I found nothing.

I quickly logged on to the computer and purchased a gel curve bra at Principessa.com. The item promised "confidence in public, and pleasure in private." I certainly needed both.

I grabbed my phone and called Paul's number.

"You've reached Detective Paul Alger. Leave a message."

I hung up and called the main precinct number.

"Precinct," Helen Varvulis, who had been at the precinct since before we were born, answered.

I pictured Helen sitting at the main desk in her cobalt-blue, slightly sheer, polyester tie-blouse.

"Hey, Helen, it's Kate. Kate Hagen."

"Hi, Katie. How are you? How's that angel of yours?"

"She's getting big. She enjoys sweet potatoes and traffic lights."

Helen laughed. "What can I do for you?"

"Is Paul around?"

"Let me check." I heard her call, "Alger. Alger. Has anyone seen Alger?"

The other end of the line got quiet for a moment as I caught her putting her hand over the receiver.

After thirty seconds, Helen got back on the phone. "He's in a seminar, dear. Do you want me to leave a message?"

"No, um . . . Helen. No message. Don't even tell him I called. I don't want to bother him."

I never questioned Paul about his "seminar." He had obviously moved on.

I skipped the appointment with Dr. Schmitt. There seemed to be no point in repairing a marriage he had opted out of. I retreated further, never confronting him about his "seminar" and never giving him the speech Peg had urged me to give.

It was over for us. Paul's earnestness gave way to gloom, and I became silent.

All the untapped love we had was heaped on our baby. We couldn't get enough of Molly, and I came to recognize that

Paul was a decent father. When an apartment directly above ours went on the market, Paul put a bid on it and moved all of his things and half of Molly's upstairs.

But for the ceiling and a divorce decree, the family was intact.

Liane calls me out of the blue and asks if I want to go for coffee. Just the two of us. In the past four years, I've rarely gone out on a social occasion that didn't include Molly.

We meet at the Better Bean near Hawthorne. Liane is an easy coffee date. She is the kind of woman I befriended easily prior to having kids. She's smart, self-effacing, but not unconfident. I had prepared several conversation points just in case there was a lull.

But it wasn't necessary. Liane and I connect.

"What a good idea," I hear myself telling her, "to go out like this."

"I needed this. We've all got to bond now. These murders are freaking me out."

I'm relieved that Liane wants to discuss the murders. I was afraid that she wanted to compare notes on how to teach *please* and *thank you* to your kid.

"Yeah. It's all I can think about. I wonder what connects these two women. Other than Hawthorne."

"Maybe it is Hawthorne." I inhale my coffee's aroma. Boy, do I love the Better Bean.

"Maybe some deranged parent is desperate for his kid to get into kindergarten. And he saw Caleb and Bitsy as formidable competition."

"It does sound drastic," I say. "Not that the Hawthorne parents are immune to the drastic. Not to be ghoulish, but why not then kill the kids?"

"These surviving kids will be too traumatized to present an acceptable package as a prospective kindergartner. Easier to off the parents. The kids are young and oblivious." Liane notices the uneasy look on my face. "I know. It's sick. But this whole thing has me thinking. They actually did this plot on *Law and Order* about four years ago. These parents are that crazy. All over New York City. I do some real estate on the side. I hear these conversations."

Liane accidentally spills her coffee; I immediately wipe it with my napkin.

"I didn't know that about you," I say.

"I make it a point not to tell people because then they'll hound me for real-estate advice. I try to keep the two lives separate."

"Don't worry, I won't ask anything," I say, bursting to find out how much she thinks Paul's and my apartments are worth in today's market.

"Oh, you can do it. It's just that sometimes we're in a group and the discussion morphs into a free tutorial." In a lull in the conversation, she digs into her seemingly bottomless, disorganized purse and pulls out a box of Altoids.

"I get it." I hold off on my free appraisal until the next time. "Did you know that Johanna was a bear expert?"

"That's random."

"I think she gave up her bear stuff when she had Caleb. But she was probably the most notable bear person in the country."

"Maybe," Liane whispers, "she was killed by a bear."

This horrible, stupid, tasteless, ridiculous comment makes me laugh so hard I almost have coffee running out of my nose. "This is so wrong."

"I know." Liane is still chuckling. "We should be killed for laughing like this."

"Poor choice of words." I sober up.

Liane is fun and easy to talk to. I ask her where she bought her jade earrings. "I'm not much of a shopper," I confess, "but I've been admiring them for quite some time."

"Thank you. I actually made these in a jewelry-design class." She pulls one out of her ear. "They even showed us how to engrave our initials in it. This is a signed work."

"Very impressive. I would just engrave my initials on a pair I bought from Bloomingdale's."

"Don't think I haven't considered that. The real estate market is so slow. I refuse to be a mom who does nothing outside the home. I come from a long line of feministas. So I volunteer for anti-gun groups to fulfill my need to do something public-service-oriented. I always hated myself a little for selling real estate. For God's sake, I have a doctorate in women's history from Radcliffe. I feel as if my great-great-great-great-great-great-grandmother, who was at the first women's rights convention in Seneca Falls, is rolling in her grave every time I show a house." Liane smiles. "If I were superstitious, I would say she was the force behind the subprime-mortgage scandal." She takes a sip of her coffee. "She might have had higher hopes for me. So I meet her halfway. I do a little work here and there on the Women v. Guns Project. It makes me feel better about myself. Gun violence is a women's issue. Most victims of domestic violence are women."

I nod, as I know all of this from my own experience, but I'm not ready to share just yet.

"I hope I don't sound as if I'm recruiting you. I'm not. I promise." She takes a deep breath. "On the lighter side, I love the class. I can get you the information if you want. Oh, I'm recruiting again."

I shake my head. "Actually, that would be great."

Wow. A new friend. A potential new hobby. My mother will be proud. Liane opens the mints again.

We chat a little about her life. She knows all about Hawthorne. "I can't get away from the place. I graduated thirty-two years ago, and I get postcards and newsletters from the school on a weekly basis. Altoids?"

I grab the box. "Thanks. That's more than we get."

"Just wait until Molly leaves the place. She'll have to get her own mailbox. There are fund-raisers, a speaker series, and reunion parties."

"Reunions? For nursery school?"

"Anytime there's an opportunity to raise money, Hawthorne will do it. That's why they have such a large endowment."

I think of my nursery school in Colorado. The closest thing they had to an endowment was the jungle gym.

Liane reads my mind. "The amount of money at the school is a little repulsive. But it does keep the place in such nice shape and allows for an ample scholarship fund."

I wonder if Liane thinks that Molly is on scholarship. After all, the school's tuition would eat up most of Paul's after-tax salary. She must know that Paul is a cop. Does she know that his family is wealthy? All these hens at Hawthorne seem to know everything. And Liane is in real estate. They have cash sensors in that business. She probably knows the net worth of every parent at the school.

"Have you been to any of the reunions?" I ask. I'm dying for another cup of coffee, but I don't want to kill the flow of conversation.

"Just one. Phillippa von Ick had one at her house."

"And how was that?"

"It was exactly the same as the parent/teacher conference the other night. Same paltry hors d'oeuvres, same waiters, same samurai swords on display. She was probably wearing the same outfit to accompany the same sour face."

"I guess you don't like Phillippa." I take a phantom sip of coffee out of the empty cup.

"What is there to like? She's awful."

I couldn't agree more. "Her husband seems sort of nice and he's really handsome. Hard to know what he sees in her."

"He sees a big bank account."

"Really, that's it?" I sound so naïve for a woman who prosecuted many a greedy pants over the years.

"That's the word anyway. She's rich, and she has the added bonus of being frigid."

"Gosh." Again I sound like a second-grader, but I'm honestly fascinated. I should have gone out for coffee a long time ago.

"Truthfully, I have no idea if she's frigid. She acts like it. And he's supposedly gay and trying to hide it. He's probably the happiest husband in the class."

I don't say anything.

"Oh. Sorry. Are you sensitive when I say *husband*?"

I laugh. "Oh, no. Don't worry. These sorts of conversations don't bother me." They bother me a little.

"If you ever want to talk about it," Liane says kindly, "I'm happy to listen."

"That's so nice of you. I don't think there's anything to talk about. Paul and I grew apart, but we still respect each other. We do fine—sort of. You know, out of necessity. For Molly." I omit the part about Paul cheating on me and breaking my heart.

"Well, not everyone is as mature about this stuff as you are, especially when your ex looks like that. He's devastating. And sometimes, I see him look at you a certain way at the parent functions, and I feel as if I should give you some privacy."

"Don't be fooled. That's his default look."

"I like it. Are you blushing?"

"No." I hold my breath. "You are just looking for drama."

"Probably. And if you're ever in the mood to be set up, I'll keep my eyes open. I'm in real estate, so I know everybody!"

"I'll keep that in mind."

I'm not thinking of Liane's potential fix-up. I'm not even thinking about getting coffee. I'm not even thinking about Paul. I'm thinking of Steve Mykonos.

Some women feel reenergized after they divorce. Nothing about divorcing Paul was pleasant or uplifting. When I was still married, I had walked my good friend Pam through her divorce from her philandering husband, Dennis. The night the papers were signed, I offered to take her out. I was being a good friend.

Pam was fine. She felt liberated. While downing her third shot, she confided that Dennis was "cheap" in the sack. "I'll leave it at that," she said, then handed out her business card to several male admirers. "I'm sending out energy. They can tell I'm free and I'm game." She was right; she was radiant.

When Paul left, I didn't feel liberated. I felt abandoned and furious. I focused on Molly, tending to her every need, keeping her clean, feeding her, reading to her, but never quite enjoying her. I didn't enjoy anything. Laundry never quite made it out of the basket. Some laundry never made it into the basket. I took to wearing the same sweatpants every day. I cut off most of my friends. I stopped making lists, I stopped cooking, and I stopped eating.

"You need to see Schmitt," Peg nagged during one of our

many phone calls, referring to the shrink she'd recommended to me. "She could help you get over this. Abandonment is a theme with you. And besides, you're starting to smell."

Peg was referring to my father's leaving my mother and me. But my father was most likely mentally ill. Paul wasn't.

"It doesn't matter. It doesn't matter if it's Paul or your father, or some other schmuck you might love. The excuses are different, but the pain is the same. See the shrink. Take care of your kid. Take a shower. Get back to work. Meet someone new."

Peg spoke as if she were reading a grocery list. But I knew she cared. She wanted me to get better. "I miss my friend. You're the little sister I never had."

"I miss you too, Peg." Then I crawled back into bed.

Weeks after Paul and I split, I willed myself to leave the apartment and meet Miriam for lunch. "It's my treat," she said. "You need to get out, girlfriend." She said this as if she had been calling me girlfriend for years and I thought it was cute. "You need some sunshine. Put on a sundress. We'll go to La Lolalu and drink iced teas and meet guys."

La Lolalu.

I got it.

It had seemed uncharacteristic of Miriam to eat lunch. Lunch was something she had once, maybe twice a year, and it usually meant sucking on a lettuce leaf and admiring a crab salad being consumed at another table. But she gave herself away when she mentioned La Lolalu. She had mentioned meeting the owner of what was a trendy joint when she was at the opera last Saturday.

"See, I told you I liked Mozart," she said as she described

the guy's sexy premature-gray hair, his sexy blue eyes, and his sexy big hands.

She had asked me along so she'd have company while she scoped him out. I went along with it. I, who had always had an endless supply of friends, was suddenly alone. I was tired of the tired routine. Paul had Molly that whole week because he was about to go undercover. Sleeping had lost its luster. Miriam arrived just as I was putting on my sandals.

"Let me take a look at *you*," she said.

She might have been self-absorbed and self-deluded, but as has been the case for the last thirty years, she was also there when I needed her.

I looked good considering I hadn't seen the light of day in months. But I wore a red linen sundress, a bittersweet souvenir of my honeymoon.

I did a mock twirl and held out my arms.

"Oh my God," she screamed in terror.

Not the response I was expecting. "What?"

"Your arm! The back of your arm."

"Miriam, you know I'm devoted to our noncompete clause when it comes to our bodies. I haven't been to the gym in a thousand years. Take it as a sign of my love for you. My arm is a little flabby."

"No, that's not it." She looked more horrified than the time she caught herself taking a third french fry from my plate at Cafe Luxembourg three years before.

I realized she was serious and ran into the bathroom. I contorted my triceps so that it could be reflected in the mirror. Miriam was right. I had a big black spot. I had never seen it before. Except in pamphlets.

Cancer. Miriam and I were both thinking the same thing, but we didn't dare say the word.

"I have a terrific dermatologist," she said as she applied a fresh coat of lipstick. "He does a great microdermabrasion and laser hair removal. Once you get this gross mark taken care of, you should consider getting some of that pesky leg hair permanently removed."

To her credit, she called the doctor on her cell phone and secured me an appointment for that very afternoon. "We are superlucky. He had a cancellation. Otherwise you might have had to wait months. We'll go to lunch another time."

"I can't believe you are giving up lunch at La Lolalu," I told her. "Thank you. I owe you."

"My pleasure. That's what best girlfriends are for."

Miriam does have her moments.

It turned out that I did have cancer. Melanoma. The doctor was fairly certain when he looked at my arm. When he called me five days later with the biopsy results, he told me how lucky I was.

"In situ," I then told Peg on the phone. "That means that the cancer didn't go anywhere. Stage zero."

"Oh my! Oh my! Oh my!" she said. "We have to go celebrate."

"Celebrate? I have cancer." I collapsed on my hard wooden chair.

"Yes, sweetheart. You do, and I am so sorry, but you're fine. You are fine. You dodged a bullet. I always knew that Miriam would be good for something."

"No, you didn't. You said she was vapid and hard work to be around."

"You're right, but all that hard work paid off. She did in fact save your life. This is great."

It didn't feel great. I felt vulnerable to attack. "I don't know, Peg. I dodged a bullet with the melanoma. Molly and I dodged a bullet with the vasa previa. At some point the bullet is going to find me."

"You can't live that way. You are very lucky."

Which made me feel like a failure. Instead of feeling triumphant over the deadly growth, I felt further paralyzed. What would happen next?

"You need to see Schmitt," Peg admonished.

But she also invited me *and* Miriam out for a celebratory dinner. Okay, outside of a thank-you toast, Peg did not exactly spew loving fellowship toward Miriam, and Miriam did not exactly chow down on the steak she ordered—Peg later claimed that had we measured the distance Miriam had moved the meat around, it would have taken the slab of beef from Manhattan all the way to Newark—but that night was one of the happiest I had in the past four years. My closest friends were never going to be glued to each other, but they loved me enough to be civil. In retrospect, my excessive appreciation of that event should have signaled to me just how emotionally distraught I really was.

In keeping with my commitment to participate in the world, I check my e-mail. There's a note from Liane.

Hi Kate,

Just thought you'd be interested to know that the Hastings town house is for sale. Check Lysorp & Fowlkes Realty. Just in case you had a few extra million sitting around. I would love to go for another gossip session, formally known as coffee, soon.

Best,
Liane

I'm heartened on so many levels. I sense a burgeoning friendship. And I have a new way to get information on the murder.

I do as Liane says. I check out today's real-estate listings on the Lysorp & Fowlkes website. I find it within seconds.

Stunning Manhattan mansion. Victorian splendor offset by space-age amenities. 8 bedrooms, 3 public rooms including great room with Manhattan's highest ceiling, state-of-the-art kitchen, warming room, museum-ready staircase, breakfast garden.

What in God's name is a warming room? I e-mail back to Liane.

I call the Realtor's number on the listing and speak to Serena Fowlkes herself. She is showing the apartment tomorrow and is delighted to tell me that the tour has room for one more. I make up a history for myself. I am married with no children, and my husband and I have just moved here from London, where he worked with an investment bank. My husband can't make the meeting, I inform her, as he will be in Geneva. We are currently a little cramped in our quarters at the Carlyle, but we couldn't resist the opportunity to be yards from the Whitney Museum, where a brief but critically acclaimed exhibit is devoted to pi, called Mathematical Constant: Making Sense of the Irrational in a Rational World. Serena eats this up. As do I. I don't know that the lying is necessary, but it makes me more committed to the investigation.

A new e-mail from Liane:

Subject: Warming Room
Many town houses have kitchens and dining spaces on separate floors. It is illegal in New York City for a dwelling

*to have more than one kitchen, so property owners have re-
sorted to creating a faux kitchen next to dining areas to keep
the food fresh.*

L

I type back, *Good to know. I'll try to remember to bring a
quiche with me.*

I don't tell her about my appointment with Serena Fowlkes.
I'm not about to go all *Murder, She Wrote* on my new friend.
For now, I just pretend to be the mom who likes a little bit of
gossip.

As I contemplate the visit, I realize how little I know of Beverly Hastings. I exit my e-mail and Google her. The first thing
that comes up is the *New York Times* wedding announcement. I see that she and Three were married at St. Christopher's Chapel, same as her funeral. Nice, and not surprising.
The announcement has a lot about the groom's side. Not so
much about Three himself. More about his family. His great-
great-great-great-grandfather Chester Hastings founded the
Dairy Bank of New York City in the early nineteenth century.
It is now known as Dairy Bank Worldwide. Chester's innova-
tion in forming a bank around the dairy industry was initially
a New York venture, but his business model was adopted all
over the country, and he emerged as a global powerhouse. The
family had been extremely philanthropic for more than a hundred years, but their charitable enthusiasm had waned I guess
when Doris Hastings, Three's grandmother, created a false
charity for the purpose of providing her tennis instructor, Leo
Faneuil, a spacious apartment in Gramercy Park and a summer cottage in Sag Harbor. This was in the early 1960s. Three,
like his father and grandfather, is a graduate of Yale and the
Harvard Business School.

Mrs. Three was from Delville, Ohio. I have never heard of Delville. I guess Bitsy's mommy forgot to mention it when she spoke of the importance of raising a child in Manhattan proper. After graduating from James Garfield High School, Beverly got her degree in massage therapy from Rhinebeck University in New York.

I wish I had known this when she was alive. I can't have fun with it now. It would be improper. Seriously, I have never heard of Rhinebeck University. I type it into the computer. And, yes, Rhinebeck University is in Rhinebeck, New York. Who knew? Rhinebeck offers degrees in refrigeration, massage, executive assistance, and security.

I recall hearing Beverly on several occasions refer to people who didn't go to Ivy League schools as uneducated trash. Is this how she saw herself?

Was she hiding it? How humiliating for her and Bitsy if there was a chunk on Page Six devoted to her unremarkable beginnings. Maybe someone from her past was threatening to expose her. This seems unlikely, as I was able to acquire this information in a basic Google search. Maybe someone from her past was jealous of her.

But then, why is Johanna Crump dead?

I rush through drop-off at school, thankful I don't see Liane. First, she would question why I have cast my ratty jeans and sneakers aside in favor of a swanky suit, and then I, who never need to rush to anything, would be forced to fabricate a morning appointment. I'm clearly not dressed for the doctor. A black-tie breakfast doesn't sound quite believable. We are not ready in our friendship for me to be completely candid with her. What would I say? I used to be in the District Attorney's Office, so I have a deep and unnatural yearning for a crime scene? Or maybe I want to see the Hastings house because they're so rich I might be able to pick up a spare ironing board or claw hammer. Or, perhaps, I could tell her the truth—my life is so empty that checking out a 7,500-square-foot town house with a warming room and twelve-foot ceilings is the closest I can come to having a life.

Of course, it could be that I am a concerned parent. It is not so strange that a mother would be more than moderately curious, obsessively curious even, in the wake of the murders of two colleagues, so to speak. I say colleagues as we are all in the same business of raising our children, working with the same company, Hawthorne. Is there something about these two women that we all missed, something the cops would never think to look into?

My need for information is trumping my protracted and uncharacteristic state of inertia. Another sign that I am getting better.

I just barely make it to the tour. It consists of two couples—one Italian and one Chinese—and me. I imagine the Italian male is a race-car driver and a swim champ. His companion, I am certain, is a model, a jewelry designer, and an EMT. I can't help but stare at him. He is blessed with beautiful auburn hair perfectly combed and brushed back, perhaps with a state-of-the-art Japanese gel or an incomplete spritz of Italy's version of Aqua Net. He appears to be wearing layers of taupe suede, but it looks good on him. She also sports suede—a ridiculously short brown skirt and superhigh brown boots. Meanwhile she is bare-legged and practically shirtless. A large clock pendant around her neck reports that it is currently 3:37 p.m., only five hours and twenty-four minutes off. She carries an enormous purse, into which she herself would have no problem fitting. They are both wearing wedding rings, and from the short time that I have been with them, they have continuously been making out.

I am pretty sure they are married, but not to each other.

The Chinese couple is older than I am by about ten years. They look extremely professional and superexpensive. She has put herself in a tailored eggplant suit that my great-grandmother would have described as "smart." He is in nondescript navy. She is carrying a notebook; he has a teeny-weeny camera.

I have come completely unprepared.

Thank fortune I have Miriam's old size-four Chloé suit— from when she was fat. Never particularly fat myself, my depression has transformed me into a bit of a bone.

"You look like a piece of paper," Peg had said. "Eat a pork chop. Eat eight of 'em. You're looking like the crack addict I just sent to rehab."

We had been playing Monopoly, the only long-term activity that caught my attention. Peg came over every week. She always chose to be the dog.

"You be the battleship," she insisted when I went for the thimble. "You're too tough for that measly little pawn."

I knew what she was doing: assigning me a tough role in the game hoping that real life would follow. "I wish they had a feather piece," I whined unattractively.

"Why don't you just go without any piece?" Peg said at her most exasperated. "It would certainly reflect your physical appearance. I can hardly see you."

"I think you look divine," Miriam said one day later when I mentioned Peg's worry about my weight. *Divine* was her favorite word that month. The weather was divine, the salad was divine, and now her depressed-to-the-point-of-starvation friend was divine. "You can wear couture."

To be fair, I could see from her expression as she uttered these words that she, too, didn't think I looked so damned lovely, that she, too, had given more than a moment's thought to my current state of svelte. But there's no question that another part of her meant it.

Miriam loves couture. She loves wearing it; she loves saying it. She talks about the designers as if she were on a first-name basis with them: Yves, Oscar, Diane. No matter where we are, she looks as if she were on a magazine shoot. She does her grocery shopping in palazzo pants and velvet shoes, which I guess isn't too difficult if your groceries consist of Diet Coke and Tic Tacs. She loves to dress up.

"It's fun," she explained to Paul when we ran into her once at a baseball game with one of her suitors. She was the only one in Yankee Stadium in an Armani tiered dress.

"I would have worn trousers," she confessed to us a little while later, "but we are going out for a cocktail afterward."

She always has a light tan, which enhances her already beautiful face, as does full but tasteful makeup. She positions her curls in a way that permits her to display the season's best earrings.

"I love to smell good," she told me when I had a coughing fit from standing next to her at a bar to celebrate the end of my first-year exams.

"What is that? I can't breathe."

"Guilt. It's Mathilde Agnucci's new perfume. I thought it would be a good law school fragrance."

"Guilt is what you should feel when you use it. That is awful." I was never a fan of Mathilde Agnucci—her perfume or her clothing. Miriam often wore her signature asymmetrical dresses at parties.

"Really?" Miriam had every reason to be surprised since

I'd never mentioned my distaste for all things Agnucci before. "I just thought the aroma was so unusual."

"It is," I said with a bluntness previously known only to those over ninety. "It smells like rotten lilies and fermented wine." The smell sticks with me to this day.

"Okay. No more Guilt." Miriam returned to her standby: Opium by Yves Saint Laurent.

Paul might have found Miriam's devotion to beauty silly, but I knew it was a large part of what had kept her going during her horrible, virtually unparented childhood, and I had admiration for it. If being a skinny knockout allowed her to grow up whole—okay, nearly whole—then I was determined to simply enjoy her beauty. The devotion to being a stick was harder to swallow—so to speak. Though Miriam had once gained a little weight. It was when I was pregnant. She briefly jumped from a size zero to a size four. I hadn't even noticed, but she was utterly shaken by it. She splurged on a Chloé suit and a couple of Valentino "pieces"—her nomenclature, not mine. After she took control of her expanding physique, she dropped off a bag for me.

The day Paul and I split up.

"You're going to need these now that you are back on the market," she had scribbled on the bag for all to see.

I had initially scoffed when I opened her gift, but in the last two days or so I had pictured myself clad in the little gold number running into Steve Mykonos. For now, I am grateful that the bone-colored Chloé suit matches my Carlyle address, although it is undermined severely by my tan Easy Spirits. But alas, Miriam didn't grow too fat for her Manolos and I must always remember where I came from.

Serena Fowlkes tells me that she is pleased to meet me, but

midsentence I can tell she is not pleased at all. Although she is encouraged by the upper half of my habiliment, her buoyancy quickly gives way to despair. My outfit screams trying too hard.

"My husband is so sorry he can't make it. He's on the phone with Milan." Oops. I think yesterday I said he was *in* Milan. Or was it Geneva?

"No worries, no worries," says Serena. She is over me. I can come along for the ride, but she is going to be selling to the others.

The five of us admire the lattice wrought-iron gates that guard the house (not well, obviously) from the riffraff. Serena unhinges a latch while cheerily addressing her two couples and bragging about the fine workmanship. The imposing stone staircase heading to the front door is substantial, and all I can think of is how difficult it would be to carry a stroller up there.

But we don't go in that way. We are escorted down a demi-step through the service entrance, a modest two-door entranceway. Serena pulls out a formidable key and places it in the lock. Click. We are inside. My heart is pounding. Some of my questions will be answered.

The Chinese couple is also excited. But for different reasons. He says something to his wife. She is looking at him suspiciously. He keeps talking, almost yelling at her. She is shaking her head no.

I wonder for a second if they, too, are looking into Beverly's murder. Something has sparked a conflict and I can't imagine it's the house—we haven't seen anything yet. I wish I knew more Chinese. I should be paying more attention to Molly's favorite TV show, *Ni Hao, Kai-Lan*.

"May I answer a question for you?" Serena has removed

her Burberry coat to reveal a handsome herringbone suit. Her body, broad-shouldered with a disproportionately muscled set of calves, is not thoroughly feminine. She looks as if she played field hockey once upon a time. She sounds chirpy yet condescending more effectively than any Tribeca restaurant hostess I have ever seen.

"Oh, sorry." The wife looks genuinely contrite. "My husband insists that the lock is a Hadley lock." She pronounces *husband* "hosband." "I tell him that this is not possible. There are only six Hadley lock in the United States."

"I am lock designer in China," the husband chimes in. "I own forty-two lock factory." He is beaming.

His wife bows her head, perhaps embarrassed by her husband's self-praise.

"Why, yes, Mr. Chao. It is a Hadley lock. One of the six in the United States that is still being used."

The Italians separate long enough to take a breath, which Serena interprets as curiosity about the Hadley lock. She turns to the Italians and says, "Malvern Hadley developed a lock at the turn of the last century that was considered unusually magnificent and virtually impossible to pick. It became most fashionable for early-twentieth-century property owners to protect themselves with a Hadley product."

The Italians smile at her and start making out again.

"I'm so sorry to have omitted that information," she says to the Chaos, realizing that they may know more than she does.

The Chaos don't say anything.

"You must have to deal with a lot of details," I say, trying to fill the silence.

"Yes, many details." Serena is looking at my shoes.

It's settled. Serena and I will never be friends.

We head through a narrow hall, which is surprisingly modest. The walls are bare and the thin, flat-white paint has evolved into a color that Benjamin Moore could only call Enola Gray. An oak coat-tree is at the tip of the hall, which thankfully opens up into an enormous kitchen. The kitchen is a mix of glorious appliances and discount seventies décor. The stove is Viking, both refrigerators are Sub-Zero, and the cabinetry is sub-Formica.

The Chaos excitedly open the unimpressive cabinets and start yelling at each other. I try to figure out what they are saying.

"Assisi dishware," Serena informs the Italian couple.

Even the Italians are impressed. They stop mauling one another to give the plates a caress.

I try to envision Beverly serving dinner to a crowd. "Bitsy just loves monks," she would have said. "She has a strong spiritual side. We bought these plates for her."

The Chaos start opening drawers.

"I'm afraid the flatware isn't quite as impressive." Serena's laugh is fake. "It's only from Tiffany."

The not-funny joke is lost on the foreigners, and Serena has established that she doesn't deserve a supportive chuckle from Ms. Cheap Shoes.

Appliance after appliance is top-shelf. A massive Kitchen-Aid, a smaller KitchenAid, a Krups toaster oven in addition to a Dualit toaster. Beautiful dishware, shiny pots, and sumptuous dining linens occupy the drawers and cabinets in the uncharacteristically roomy kitchen. But the bargain-rate counters, kitchen tables, and cabinetry are not lost on any of us.

"The owners are not ostentatious people," Serena assures us.

Not ostentatious people. Serena evidently wasn't present at

Bitsy's third birthday party. It was held at Voilà, New York's hottest nightspot. Beverly rented it out for the day and flew in a magician from Croatia. Nor did Serena attend the show-and-tell where Bitsy proudly walked her classmates through the floor plan of her ski chalet in Gstaad. And neither Bitsy nor Three had mentioned to Serena that Bitsy carried an Hermès backpack to and from school every day.

"There's a lot of pressure on people like us to keep our economy moving," Beverly had told Clayton's flabbergasted mom.

I remember that Beverly is dead and look around trying to re-create the scene in my mind. It isn't easy, as I only know that her body was found here in the kitchen. Was it moved here? I look on the floor for any evidence of blood. Nothing. It is easy to clean vinyl.

Another narrow hall is at the back of the kitchen. Again, there is little décor. The floors are taupe, wall-to-wall industrial carpeting with matching, only significantly dirtier, taupe walls. Off the hall are three small maid's rooms, more taupe carpeting.

"As you can see, the property provides more than generous servants' quarters," Serena tells us.

The Chinese couple nod eagerly. The Italian man is standing behind his "wife" with his arms around her waist. He is giving her a tummy rub.

We go in the first room. A small twin bed against the wall is covered in white sheets and a blue-striped blanket. Mr. Chao opens the small closet to see nothing inside except for two maid's uniforms, a no-frills ironing board, and an iron.

We check out the other rooms. Nothing but a small shopping bag with some clothes in it.

Mr. Chao tells Serena that he is eager to see the rest of the place. Confident that he is the only one on this tour with any purchasing power (the expedition, I have concluded, is part of an elaborate sex game for the Italians), our fearless leader hurries us up a narrow staircase to the main floor. She opens the door, and we enter one of the most beautiful great rooms I have ever seen. And definitely the biggest. The four mahogany and gold-silk sofas, accompanied by six armchairs, do not even fill the space.

"Such exquisite detail," Serena announces as she caresses the couch's mahogany crest rail. The Chaos head over to an eighteenth-century French commode veneered with Chinese lacquered paneling with a red griotte-marble slab. The Italians snuggle in one of the five ribbon-backed Chippendale chairs. My attention is on the walls. Three are adorned with rich red-and-gold-dominated tapestries framed by wood paneling. The fourth houses a huge family portrait: Three, Beverly, and Bitsy. Surprisingly, Bitsy is portrayed as an older version of herself. Perhaps the artist thought a young Bitsy would not give the work the gravitas the Hastingses were paying for. Now the picture is haunting as Bitsy at seven will never be seen by her mother.

My eyes well as I think of how often I picture Molly as who she will be one year from now, five years from now, as a teen, in college. It's part of the joy. And as terrible as Beverly was, she deserved to see her daughter grow up.

Except for the portrait, nothing suggests that a child lived in this residence. I think of our unremarkable living room, scattered with books, one-third of a tea-party set, and well over two hundred Cheerios.

The town house is five stories high. If I had this kind of a room, I would most likely forbid Molly to set foot in it. Like the Hastingses, I would simply hang a picture of her on the wall to remind myself that I had a daughter.

The Italian couple screams, "Oh." In unison. I'm afraid to look. It's okay. They are both eyeing a chaise longue next to the window. Mrs. Chao is taking copious notes. Mr. Chao is nodding his head. Serena looks as proud as if she had decorated the room.

"It speaks for itself," she says as she strokes a herd of golden elephants on the crystal coffee table.

Didn't she just tell us that the couple isn't ostentatious? We walk around the room for a minute or two before we head into the dining room. The walls are black lacquer set off by clear shelves enhanced by cobalt-blue lighting. I feel as if we are in a jewelry box.

The Chaos are staring at the glass dining table.

"The owners here have taken a risk, but you may not want to do the same," Serena says, implying she would not do the same. "The décor merely gives us one idea of what to do with the space."

Mr. Chao runs through a doorway. I follow him. We are in a medium-size room with a small refrigerator, smooth Labrador-granite countertops, and highly detailed cabinetry.

"The warming room?" I ask Serena.

"Yes," she says, exasperated as if I have been asking useless questions all throughout the tour.

Unlike the kitchen, the warming room is beautiful. The deep browns of the granite are offset by the light-cherry cabinetry. A series of small lithographs depicting leafy vegetables hangs over the sink. The earth-toned floor tile looks as if it were imported from a Tuscan villa.

Mrs. Chao touches the wall and says something to her husband.

Serena, accustomed to a satisfied crowd, tells us, "Yes, as you can see, the owners have thought of everything. The taste here is exquisite." She repeats it for dramatic salesmanship. "Just exquisite."

The Chaos nod, as do I, though by now no one is paying any attention to me. We head over to the massive staircase, an anomaly in this cramped city. We ascend, oohing and aahing every two or three steps at the indulgence of the great room as we keep seeing it from a different angle.

"This is the children's floor," Serena says once we have landed and entered through the closest door.

She wants to make sure the Chaos are listening. She is certain they have children. The Italians definitely seem as if they have no kids. At least, none that they know of. I remind myself that on the phone I told Serena that we were childless—not that she would care.

"How many childrens?" The Italian man addresses her for the first time.

"Just one child," she says, then makes a grand arm gesture signifying that they are planning for more.

Shame on you, Serena. I understand why she omits the part about the murder, but there is no reason to actively resurrect Beverly here.

Serena pulls us quickly into a powder-blue room with a piano, a harp, and a shelf filled with wind instruments. The Chaos are exchanging comments with apparent alarm.

"The owners would be open to negotiating the selling of some of their pieces if you so desire." Serena beams. "As you can see, they have exquisite taste."

Exquisite.

Serena and I clearly took a different class in Chinese.

We head into Bitsy's room. With the exception of "The Princess and the Pea" canopy bed, it has a little bit of duty-free-shop look to it. As soon as we walk in the door, we stare at a huge shelf of Lladró clown figures. There isn't a toy in sight.

"This child, she doesn't like toys?" the signor asks.

"Gaaaah!" Serena laughs as if on cue. "No, she absolutely adores toys. Let me show you."

We head into the next room, an enormous playroom filled with toys. I see Beverly's latest nanny, Carmela, playing on the floor with Bitsy.

"Hi, Molly's mommy," she says. "What are you doing in my house?"

I freeze.

Serena looks at the five of us, trying to ascertain who might be Molly's mommy. Now, if I were a truly horrible person, I would tell Bitsy that I had no idea what she was talking about. While tempting, I believe this girl has been through enough.

Besides, Carmela totally recognizes me.

Without any elegance whatsoever, I turn to Serena and say, "I have a meeting. Thanks so much. We'll be in touch." I present the Chaos with my best artificial smile and bounce down the gigantic staircase. I leave through the front door. It is, after all, right here.

I wish I had seen more of the house. I might have gotten more sense of what had happened to Beverly. I don't know whether the killer was foolish enough to leave any evidence, but I did learn a few important things. Beverly's body was in the kitchen—not the warming room. This means that the killer most likely entered through the downstairs entrance—he didn't break in. Excuse me. Or she didn't break in. The lock was a

Hadley. Mr. Chao was amazed by its condition. It would be unlikely that it was picked. It would be even less likely that the Hadley had been a replacement lock: Three, in the depths of sorrow, shopping around for an antique lock after his wife was murdered. Unless of course he killed her. Then of course he wouldn't have had to pick a lock. But I know in my heart that Three didn't do this. So now I am back to wondering about doors. As for the one here upstairs, I check it as I close it behind me. It doesn't look suspicious either.

Could the killer have come in from this floor and found his or her way downstairs to kill Beverly? The body was found in the kitchen. Was it moved? What was she doing in her kitchen anyway? She clearly didn't decorate it for her own enjoyment. She made it clear on several occasions that she didn't like to cook.

At last year's Hawthorne bake sale, she proudly told Bitsy's teachers that she didn't know how to turn on her oven, and if they had any questions about what she could donate to the school, the best person to talk to was Velma. (Velma was three cooks ago.) And the rest of the bottom floor was dull, undecorated, and impersonal. Beverly would never go down there for any social interaction. It was clearly a place for the help. Could Beverly have been stabbed by—

"Hi, Molly's mom." This voice is far deeper than Bitsy's. Coming toward me is Steve Mykonos.

"Hi, umm . . ." My stomach is aflutter.

"Steve." He's smiling.

"Hi, Steve. Aren't you supposed to be dissecting frogs for kids or something?"

"I do believe they are a little young for that. We're more likely to admire a live frog."

"That doesn't sound like as much fun to me."

"So you'd prefer seeing a dead frog to a living one?" Steve challenges.

"In my science class, most certainly. I want to get my money's worth."

"I see your point, but death is too confusing for these kids right now." He is talking about the murders.

"Oh, of course you're right. I didn't make that connection. Bad mommy."

"I'm always making that connection. It's on all our minds."

Is this the part where I tell him that I was just snooping around the Hastings murder scene? We both pause. I don't know how to say good-bye.

He speaks. "I know this is awfully forward, but would you like to grab a coffee with me?"

"You mean now?"

"Sure. Now's as good a time as any, unless you have something to do?"

"No, I'm good." My morning is wide-open since my real estate tour was cut short.

"Great. I know a little place that happens to be right here."

And there it is, two steps to my left. Caffè Piccolo—"little coffee." So little that I've never noticed it. "I didn't know this was here."

"You and everybody else. It is the city's best-kept secret. Far superior to the silt they give you at the Better Bean."

Though I am partial to the silt, I keep my mouth shut.

We head inside, where it is more like a cave than anything else. The walls are stone, not the smooth-worked stone of the Hastingses' warming room, but more like the stone that offers residence to a mega-colony of bats. It is dark. And it would have been cold except for the huge fire burning in a fireplace at the far wall. The modest counter has a few muffins and scones, and a coffeemaker and an espresso machine are behind it.

I see a chalkboard, which lists the usual coffee and espresso drinks, tea, water, and bread products.

"I'll just have a coffee," I say. After working in the DA's office and being married to a cop, there always seemed to be something silly about paying an extra $2 for foam.

"Do you want a muffin or anything?" Steve asks.

"No, thanks."

He leans into my neck and whispers, "If you're nice to them, they'll give you an egg sandwich. They've got a kitchen in the back."

"I'll take an egg sandwich," I hear myself saying. They don't cook at the Better Bean.

Steve signals the barista and says something in a language that's clearly not Italian.

"Greek," he says, reading my unfamiliarity. "I guess you're not a speaker."

"Not modern Greek. A little of the older stuff. You never know when you might get stuck at a dinner party next to Pericles."

"True. By the way, the guy who's making your sandwich is named Pericles."

"Really?"

"No, just teasing."

I ignore for a second that his comment is unfunny. Instead I focus on a lesson I learned when I was single. If a man tells a woman he was teasing, he was flirting. Steve Mykonos is definitely flirting with me. I can't deal.

Yet.

"Molly really loves school this year. She's a great kid." He slides a chair out for me. "Whatever you're doing, keep it up."

I guess lying in bed all day, weeping, and watching TV is really working for me. "I can't take all the credit," I say demurely. "It takes a village."

"The village is doing its job."

"The village is lucky to have such a good kid."

We eat our egg sandwiches.

"Molly's father seems like a good guy." Steve is probing.

"He's a great father."

"But not a great husband?"

"No. He was a decent husband. I wasn't exactly wife material," I say with a generosity of spirit I don't feel.

"Meaning?"

Wow. Steve is aggressive. "Meaning Paul married a smart, successful, can-do woman who morphed into a woman who apparently could do very little." And then he himself morphed into a douche bag when he cheated on her.

Not exactly what you want to say to a hunky guy.

"You seem confident to me," Steve says, confirming my long-held belief that men, despite their proficiency in science and math, are not so good at reading people. "Maybe he wasn't the right guy."

Oh, he's still flirting. "Maybe."

We are once again silent. My egg is gone, and I have nothing to do but speak. "I had a hard time when Molly was born."

"I hear a lot of moms say that."

"Really?"

"Yeah. All of the alpha women in New York City give birth and are suddenly forced into a role of passive domesticity. The husband doesn't want them to work, they don't want to work, or they want to work and they feel guilty."

Steve has obviously thought about this. I don't tell him that Paul wanted me to work. He was proud of me.

"I thought I wanted to work, but I felt disconnected from the people in my office. I didn't know how to talk to them once I had the baby."

I can't believe I am telling Steve all this. He is the first man that I have spoken to about any of it, but he seems genuinely interested.

"I've heard that, too," he offers. "No one wants to hear about your kid crying all night or having a cold. They just think it's a reason they will have to cover for you."

How does he know this? "Excuse me, but have you been married or do you have a girlfriend with a kid?"

"No, I've just heard bits and pieces here and there. Plus it seems so obvious."

"Maybe you went into the wrong field," I say with admiration.

Steve smiles at me. "I think of compassion as a hobby rather than an occupation. Plus, you're easy to talk to. You seem open."

"I'm getting there." He grabs my hand for a second. I'm not sure what he's up to, but I find it exhilarating. I gulp. "I guess I should be getting back."

"So soon?"

"Don't you have work to do?"

"I'm off today. Science isn't an everyday course requirement at Hawthorne."

"Yet," I warn him. "No. I mean, don't you have to learn about the world?"

"I do"—he pauses—"but I was having a good time."

"I guess it's good to get away from thinking about things like force and particles all the time." I have no idea where I find the words *force* and *particles*.

"There's a joke in there somewhere, but it's way too early for me to make it."

Early? In our relationship, perhaps?

"I hope you're going somewhere wonderful. You look fantastic." I remember I haven't changed out of the Chloé. "Can I walk you somewhere?"

"No, but thanks."

I run out of Caffè Piccolo.

Steve's questions bring me back to my relentless sadness. Just after Molly's birth, I was so tired, so worried, so lonely, and yet so much in love with my little baby. No one got it.

When Molly was just over a year old, she started walking. Marching, really. Doctors had told me that her development might be delayed until she was three, possibly four years old, due to her early birth. I was relieved by her progress but always fearful of setback.

"That child needs to go to the playground," Estelle, a nanny in our building, had told me when she saw Molly weaving through our lobby.

The playground. I hadn't thought of that. How foolish. Of course I should take Molly to the playground. But what if she fell on her head or broke a bone or ate something toxic?

"I'll take her," Estelle offered.

But of course Molly couldn't go outside for extended periods. No ozone was left. My dermatologist told me that given my skin sensitivity, my children would be at risk.

"Does the baby's father have any skin cancer in his family?" he had asked me.

"I'm not sure," I had answered, wondering if the doctor thought I was an irresponsible wife for being ignorant of these matters.

"You should find out."

It took me weeks to find out. I wasn't about to tell Paul about my melanoma, but I owed it to my kid to find out the family history. One night when Mary came by to see her granddaughter, I asked her why she had become a pathologist. Did she have any family experience and all that? No, she just liked it. And Frank had no family history of skin cancer either.

"We're a heart-attack family," she said. "Both my parents died that way, as did Frank's mother. His father was killed in a car."

"Great," I said.

She looked at me.

"I mean great that your medical field has you despite your . . ." I couldn't even finish the sentence. My foot had gotten so far down my throat, there was no room left for more words.

"No. We are lucky in that respect."

She ignored my gaffe. This of course made me want to confide in her. She had remained warm even when Paul was moving upstairs and had told me that she would always consider me her daughter. While I believed that she believed what she was saying, I couldn't trust her completely. After all, her son had betrayed me.

I relayed all of this to my dermatologist, who told me that I just had to be a tad extra-careful with Molly.

"That's so nice of you," I said to Estelle, "but Molly isn't that sort of kid. She has health issues."

"That kid?" Estelle was laughing. "That is a healthy baby girl. You take her to the playground and she'll have the best day of her life. I'll take her by myself if you want. I have a half hour before my Eli needs me.

"No, thank you. That is really nice."

"Free of charge," Estelle said, misconstruing my unwillingness to accept her offer as frugality. "I like babies. They don't talk back. Eli is getting a little too mouthy."

There was no possibility I would give this woman my child. I didn't think she would steal her or anything. I had seen her in the building, and she seemed competent and nice. Really competent and very nice, but she didn't know Molly and her needs.

"You just tell me," she said. "I work in 12E. 'E for "Eli,"' I say to my boy. You give me that gorgeous baby and you get yourself a big nap."

I can't say I wasn't tempted. I had seen her with Eli from 12E. A stocky five-year-old, he had a squeaky voice and a cowlick. He made it clear he was smitten with Molly. When he'd lost his first tooth, he forwent the tooth-fairy booty and presented her with his incisor.

Estelle had grabbed it from him. "You can't be giving your bones to a little baby."

"But she's sooooo pretty."

"You let the tooth fairy give you some money, and then you buy her a present," Estelle instructed.

"Goody. I'm going to buy her a really cool gun."

She'd smiled at me and patted him on his head, briefly taming the little bundle of hair that refused to lie straight. Estelle was in tune with this kid, but she didn't know Molly.

The solution was for me to take Molly to the park. And so I did. I have never liked New York City playgrounds. From time to time, a story in the paper or a segment in the news appears about a renovation or about an architectural feat at one Manhattan playground or another. Safety may have been a problem in the past, many of the articles remark, but no more. The parks are filled with entirely new bolts and screws, which I kept reminding myself of when I took Molly to our nearby park on First Avenue and Sixty-seventh Street.

As we entered the gates, I assured myself that my daughter would have no interest in doing any of these activities. She was more of a talker than an athlete.

But when we got there, Molly's energy doubled. She bounced up and down in her stroller and waved to every single person we passed. She squealed with delight when she saw a pigeon. The other one-year-olds looked at her as if to say, *Do you live in a cave, you've never seen one of those?*

She was in awe of all of the playground's activities, staring at the children burying each other in the sandbox, eyes fixated first on the splinter-filled, lead-paint-bleeding seesaw and then on the shiny, boiling-hot slide.

But she couldn't contain herself when we came to the swing. She started screaming, "Daddy." That was just about the only word she knew. She called everything Daddy.

"Daddy, Daddy." She was bouncing harder and clapping harder and pointing.

"Your kid wants to go on the swing," a pasty-faced boy with a head of bright red hair informed me.

"Oh, no, she just likes to watch."

"Me. Me. Me." Molly was pointing toward the swing and shouting.

"Looks like she wants to go on the swing to me," he said.

"Mind your own beeswax," I said.

"I could push for you," he said, unstirred.

I yelled at him in my head, *For the love of God, would you leave my family alone!*

But I lost. I took her out, placed her gently in the little chair, pulled down the latch, and started pushing with about one inch of give. The chain squeaked.

It's broken; she will break, I thought. I looked around at the babies next to me. Their chains squeaked louder, as they were pushed harder. Two babysitters were chatting with each other, and another mother was talking on her cell phone. No one else had caught on to the safety hazard.

The squeaking showed no mercy.

I kept telling myself that the Parks Department didn't have the resources to hire someone to oil swings with any frequency.

Did they have the funds, though, to ensure safety? The squealing got louder. I could feel the blood pulsing through my ears. Molly let out a huge scream, and everything went blank.

I woke up in the emergency room at New York Hospital, where my daughter was born.

Where was Molly? The swing!

"My baby," I screamed. "My baby. She was flying so high on the swing."

"Your baby is fine," a round-faced, round-bodied nurse said to me. "That woman over there has her."

And there she was. Estelle. The nanny from 12E was holding Molly. They were singing the alphabet song, and Molly was hitting her nose. She looked happy.

"Your daughter is fine," said the nurse, who looked like a giant snowman.

"But the swing. She fell from the swing."

"No, ma'am. She didn't fall. You fell. You passed out."

"Oh, no. You must have the wrong chart. I saw her fall." *Did I see her fall?*

"Molly," I shrieked.

"Daddy." She started clapping. Estelle carried her to my bed. "Daddy."

"You okay, Mrs. Alger?" The nanny's familiar voice was comforting.

"What happened to Molly?"

"Molly and I have been playing and singing." Molly was gleefully sucking on a tongue depressor. Estelle leaned in to me, "I told her you was asleep."

"But the swing?"

"The swing?"

"When it broke. Don't they want to take her for an MRI?"

"Molly didn't fall off the swing. She's fine. And the swing didn't break. You passed out."

Why was Estelle covering for the Parks Department? I saw her fall off the swing. I was sure of it. The swing went up, and a lot of noise, Molly was shrieki—

Okay. It was confirmed, I was officially a raving lunatic.

"Do you have any medical conditions?" Nurse Snowman was back.

"No." *Only that I am obviously insane.* But the nurse was certainly not entitled to that piece of information.

"Are you currently on medication?"

"No." If I were, wouldn't that mean I had a medical condition?

"Are you pregnant?"

"Definitely not." Now, that's a medical condition. "I probably didn't eat enough breakfast." In truth, I hadn't eaten any breakfast—or any dinner the night before.

"Are you under a lot of stress?"

"No."

"Are you sure?" I could have sworn I saw her looking at my ringless hand.

"Yes." Who was she to talk to me like this? "I fell."

"The doctor will see you in a minute."

Estelle returned with Molly and put her in my arms.

"Where's Eli?" I asked.

"I took him to his mama's office. She hope you get better."

"Thanks," I said, feeling sheepish.

I hardly ever saw Eli's mother. She had been solicitous of me after Molly was born, telling me how cute she was. She offered some of her baby equipment: a high chair, a diaper table, and an ExerSaucer.

"I don't think the baby industry needs any more money," she had said in a mock-conspiratorial way.

I was grateful for her kindness but I didn't have the energy to follow through. After several attempts to befriend me, she downscaled her amiability to mere politeness. And now her babysitter is asking how I am feeling.

As I scripted an apologetic monologue in my head, a sturdy fifty-something woman, wearing a lab coat and glasses with a chain, walked in. She introduced herself as Dr. something or other and asked how I was feeling.

"Embarrassed but fine," I told her. "Now I just want to get Molly home."

"I know the feeling. But they want to make sure you are good to go." Then she said as an aside, "We could get in a lot of trouble if we sent someone home too early. There could be blood and lawsuits."

"Don't tell me that." I chuckled for the first time since I had given birth. "I learned that my first week in law school."

"Oh, a lawyer. Hmmm. I'll do extra tests."

"Not a lawyer anymore. You're fine. I did criminal stuff

anyway, so unless you're euthanizing me or committing insurance fraud, you're safe."

"Criminal law. That sounds fun and exhausting."

"You are right on both counts." She was easy to talk to. A lot better than the judgmental nurse.

"So you're on maternity leave?"

"Not sure," I told her.

"Gotcha."

We both paused.

"I'm afraid if I go back to work, something will happen to Molly. She's sick."

We both glanced at Molly in the hall. She was belting out the ABC song and choreographing a dance to it.

"She looks fine to me."

"Oh. Yes. Well. I shouldn't say she's sick. She was premature and it was touch and go for a while. Sort of. I'm not sure how touch or how go, but it was bad. And you know how it is. You never know when disaster could strike. I mean, before Molly I was pregnant. I thought it was perfect. And then, boom, miscarriage. And then a few weeks ago, I found out I had cancer. Melanoma." The doctor looked concerned. "But it was fine. I'm fine. They caught it early. I had a small operation. No chemo or radiation or anything. I'm not on anything for it if you need to know, but I told that to your nurse."

"But that can still be traumatic."

"Sure. Whatever. It was a reminder to me that anything can happen. One day you're fine; the next you have cancer. We're all at risk. You know my husband's—I mean ex-husband's—brother was killed when he was a little boy. He was playing. *Playing*. You have to be vigilant. I need to be vigilant, and I can't risk anything by going to work. Something could happen." I was talking a mile a minute. "Before she was born,

I never thought like that. The pregnancy was perfect and then, boom, vasa previa—"

"Vasa previa? Never seen it—only heard of it. You're lucky."

"Really lucky. So you see. I know that anything can happen. Even if it looks like all is going well, it can be really bad. Vasa previa, melanoma. I'm not that superstitious, but these things always come in threes. I have to worry about it all the time."

"The worrying must be exhausting."

"Oh, it's really exhausting. You don't know."

"I take it you don't sleep."

"No, I sleep all the time."

"How many hours do you sleep?"

"Oh, only when Molly's asleep. Maybe fourteen or fifteen hours," I said, as if it were normal. "Sometimes more if she's at her dad's."

"Good to have the break, right?"

"Right. Although I sometimes check on her. He lives upstairs."

"Because of her health?"

"Exactly. Paul, that's my husband, ex-husband. It's hard to get used to the labels. We just split. He wanted me to run back to work. He's a cop. I had worked in the DA's office. He had a fantasy that we were a team."

"And he didn't understand the pressure you were under."

"I'll say."

Nurse Snowman walked in with some charts to show the doctor.

"I have great news for you," my new friend said. "Everything looks good. You and Molly can go home."

"Wonderful. Another relief."

"Kate, your life seems overwhelming right now. The ex that doesn't get it, a baby who is transforming into a toddler? Would you like to talk again sometime?"

I found myself saying yes, and then it occurred to me. "Are you a shrink? I missed that."

"Among other things. I hope that doesn't bother you?"

It would have bothered me if I weren't stark raving mad.

"If it makes you feel any better, I was an obstetrician earlier in my career. I know a lot about this stuff. And whether or not you feel comfortable with me, I think you really need to talk to someone who has an idea of where you're coming from. I or someone else might give you some tools to help you delight in motherhood. I think we can get you there."

My eyes filled with tears. To my surprise I said, "I think I could do that."

"That's great. You can make an appointment with my receptionist Giselle on the third floor."

"Okay. I have only one embarrassing question."

"Go ahead."

"What's your name?"

"Judy. Judy Schmitt."

I knew her name. It was the psychiatrist I had made the appointment with before I found out Paul was cheating.

I'm breathless as I run up the fire stairs to pick up Molly. This is Paul's day to collect her from school as I have a standing weekly appointment with Dr. Schmitt. After a year of three days a week in treatment, we whittled our sessions to once a week. She told me this afternoon that she was amazed at my progress.

"If I didn't know better, I would say you were happy,"

she'd said to me when I arrived showered, wearing a little makeup, an ironed shirt, and even a belt.

"Naw." I attempted casual. "Two friends from Molly's class have died."

"Is that right?"

"Yeah, it's freaky and creepy and frightening." I was not feeling remotely freaked-out or frightened.

"What happened?"

"They were murdered." I wondered if she found my response way too calm.

"How does this make you feel?" Therapy-speak for "keep going."

"I don't know. You just said I seem happy. I'm not happy, but I'm not paralyzingly sad."

Dr. Schmitt remained silent.

"I mean, is that weird? Should I be crying? I was all fragile about giving birth, but suddenly I'm brave in the face of death?"

"Do you feel you might"—Dr. Schmitt paused here—"be next?"

"Oh, no, nothing like that. But why am I not more, you know, psycho about this?"

"Maybe you're done with psycho?"

"I don't feel done."

"Don't worry. You can keep coming back here."

I felt a sense of relief.

"Do you want to talk about these murders?" she asked.

"No need. With those victims, the only through line is the school. Beverly and Johanna both have kids the same age in the same school. But there's nothing else really similar about them as people."

"You have said that the families at that school are wealthy."

"Yes, but there was no money taken at either scene."

"Hmm."

"Maybe the killer hates the school." I laughed. "Not the women, per se."

Schmitt remained quiet.

"But I could understand if Beverly and, say, Phillippa were murdered. They are both horrible snobs, and I don't like them. But Johanna Crump seemed perfectly fine to me. Except for the kid—Caleb—awful. But then again, I have a girl and maybe Caleb was just temporarily awful. Bitsy isn't so bad. There are definitely worse kids. Also, who kills parents because they have bad kids? I keep getting back to the moms. They aren't that bad." I was thinking aloud, rambling. "I am missing something, I know it."

"Missing something?"

"Yes." I waved her off as I was in deep thought. "Missing something that links them. Unless it's just someone killing Hawthorne mothers willy-nilly."

"Does that scare you?" Schmitt was trying to keep it a therapy appointment rather than a police investigation.

"No, that's not what it is." My voice had a hint of irritation. I had already told her that I wasn't scared.

I spent the rest of the session going through similarities between Beverly and Johanna. I had pulled out a fresh index card.

"With the exception of the kids being the same age and the same grade in school, nothing."

"As long as it's not scaring you." Dr. Schmitt looked at her watch. Our time was up.

Needless to say, I didn't tell her about my trip to the mansion.

As I face Paul's apartment now, I consider once again whether I have missed out on a glaringly obvious clue.

"*Nada,*" I say to myself. I need to do more digging.

I knock on the door. "Paul, it's me," I say as I bang. I'm a minute late. I'm never a minute late.

I knock again. "Paul?"

I'm nervous. Could he be punishing me for being sixty seconds late and have taken Mo—?

"Coming." Willa. "Coming."

She opens the door. Her blond hair has been thrown into a casual ponytail, and she is wearing a cute orange hoodie and a pair of old Levi's that accentuate her grasshopper legs and lack of belly fat.

"Hi, Kate," she sighs. "So sorry. Mol and I are in an intense game of Zingo! She says she'll be right out."

Mol? She says she'll be right out? "Okay." I feel my blood pressure rise.

Out of nervousness, I look in Paul's refrigerator, and I'm comforted by what's inside: an impressive array of deli meats and cheeses, two jars of peppers—one hot, one sweet—a tub of mayo, Pommery mustard, Food Emporium–brand canned pitted olives, and iceberg lettuce. The ripened tomatoes and bags of hero rolls sit out on the counter.

If Paul has an addiction, it's a good deli sandwich on a roll. When we first started dating, I noticed that he would go through long periods without eating.

"Is there anything I should know?" I had heard about men with eating disorders and body dysmorphic disorders, and I knew to tread carefully.

"Yes. You should know that sometimes I forget to eat."

"You sound like the models who lie to magazines to justify their unnaturally low weight and end up dead or weighing three hundred pounds two years later."

"Do I look skeletal?"

We were lying in bed. He has, or should I say had, as I haven't seen his abdomen in a while, the makings of a six-pack.

"You're kind of perfect." I wasn't just saying that. He was. He was thinnish and muscular without looking like a gym bunny.

"I eat like a snake. I will go twenty-four, thirty-six hours without a thing, and then I'll become ravenous and—"

"Eat an innocent bunny rabbit?"

"Exactly, or an entire pizza." At the time, Paul kept no food in the fridge. There was a bottle of tonic water and a third of a stick of butter, but nothing else. "I buy the food when I'm hungry."

I spent a good deal of time with Paul at deli counters, listening to his detailed instructions on how to make a sandwich to men wearing shower caps and clear plastic gloves. He switched around his deli meats, sometimes going for turkey or low-fat ham; other times selecting *soppressata*, roast beef, or a cutlet of some kind. He loved Muenster, mozzarella, and provolone, but eliminated them if he hadn't slept enough, as he claimed they give him gas.

"The important thing, the single most important thing," he instructed the deli man and then me, "is a nice healthy slathering of mayo."

After we had been together for a few months, I surprised Paul by loading up my refrigerator with all of his favorite sandwich fixings.

"This way you don't have to rely on the store-bought sandwich," I told him as he admired his new gift.

He pulled me into him and kissed me. "Can you do all this to my kitchen? Better yet, why don't you move all of this stuff when you come to live with me."

That was how Paul asked me to move in with him.

———

I espy his laptop on the coffee table. Maybe I can use this Willa/Mol conspiracy to my advantage.

It's not as good as the notebook, but it will do. I turn the computer on, and I type in Paul's password: MAY171980. It is the date and year his brother was murdered. He will never change it no matter how much the cyber-crime task force admonishes him. I click on his hot-cases file. I am presented with eleven selections. *Mommies* is at the top. I click there. There are two files: Hastings and Crump. I go with Hastings and look for anything relating to yesterday's mission. It's a bunch of notes in Paul's shorthand.

F dr open. This means that the front door, the one on the main floor, was open.

D/s locked. The downstairs door was locked.

No ev. bdy mved. No evidence that Beverly's body was moved.

N.p. No fingerprints.

Neyore. I know this one. That was code for "no evidence of robbery." Back in the day, Paul and I divided home invasions into E.o.r.'s and N.e.o.r.'s. Paul had delighted in invoking Winnie-the-Pooh in his law enforcement career. His brother, Mark, had been a big fan.

Hub bad. Here, I'm not sure. Hormones have affected my memory. This either means that Three had a bad alibi or he is bad for the murder, meaning he most likely didn't do it.

B-in? n.l. Break-in not likely.

Thank you, Paul, for marrying me and letting me into your mind.

I scroll down a couple of lines and see a note: *Trace Katie e-m. asap.*

Katie?

I'm Katie.

E-m is definitely *e-mail*. Is he referring to an e-mail I have written or one about me? Does someone think I did this? Why is this an ASAP? Is it urgent? Why hasn't he said anything to me, Katie?

Could there be another Katie? Stranger things have happened, but I say we stick first to the less strange.

He hasn't said anything about this for the same reason he didn't tell me about his extramarital seminar. He's a liar. And he doesn't have my back.

"Hello?"

Paul. I exit the file and shut off the laptop, not remembering whether it was on or not when I started snooping.

I slide into Paul's line of sight. "Hey," I say. I must commend myself on doing a fantastic job of hiding my irritation.

"Hey."

"Just got here." I know I sound defensive.

Willa bounces out of the room. "Kate, sorry to make you wait so long. Mol insisted on a rematch."

"I won, I won, I won," Molly tells me, running in.

Paul shoots me a look.

"It wasn't long at all." I laugh artificially. "Two and a half, maybe three seconds."

I long to ask him about the Katie e-mail, but I will have to find some other way. I turn to my daughter. "Molly, sweetie, it's warm enough now. Do you want to go to the park?"

Dr. Schmitt has helped me be okay with taking my daughter to the park.

"The park, the park, the park. You know what *park* rhymes with, Daddy?"

I can hear Paul sucking in his breath. "No, butterfly, what does it rhyme with?"

"*Park* rhymes with *shark*." She is beaming.

Paul and I are thinking the same thing: *park* rhymes with *Mark*.

He turns to me. "You okay?"

"Why shouldn't I be?" I hear the way I sound and kick-save with a warm smile. I realize I'm smiling way too much and standing about two inches closer than I have for the past three years. Am I imagining things or is he looking at his computer? "Great." I turn to leave, realizing my mood might not be appropriate under the circumstances.

"I'm here if you need me," Paul says.

Oh, sure thing there, pal. You are my rock.

"She knows," Molly instructs him. "C'mon, Mommy, I wanna show you the seesaw."

I take Molly down the stairs. We are all in agreement that the stairs are faster than the elevator. Maybe I can get the Katie e-mail from my computer. Alas, I even have trouble logging on to YouTube. No, I'll have to get back into Paul's house.

As we walk into our apartment, the phone is ringing. I look at the caller ID.

Private.

I don't think I know anybody with a private number. Even my law enforcement friends keep their numbers visible. Miriam used to keep her number private on the theory that it made her look mysterious. I didn't understand this strategy. But she explained it to me: "It just seems so desperate to show everyone your number."

"I don't get why that is desperate."

"Because it's like, 'Look at me, I'm calling you.' Don't you see? The private number is more mysterious."

"No. On the contrary, it seems sneaky not to reveal your number. The default position is self-identification, so any attempt to change that seems like you are hiding something."

"Oh, no. Guys don't think that way," Miriam assured me.

Then four days later I received a call from Miriam. Her number was on the caller ID.

"What happened to the private number?"

"I was watching Bobbi-Ann Johnson on *Perfect Day Perfect Life* and she said having a private number seemed sneaky."

"Good for her."

So who could this sneaky person be on the phone right now? I pick it up.

Dial tone.

Bobbi-Ann Johnson was right. Sneaky.

Maybe it's Steve. He's young and single. Would he even call me? We did just see each other. He could easily get my number. I am listed in the phone book and in the Hawthorne directory. This year's, that is.

Last year, Bree Medina, the ineffectual but pretty assistant to school director Irene Druvier, made a whopper of a mistake on the phone and address sheet for Molly's class. The number she listed for Molly and me was Consuela's Family Pizza. I didn't have the energy to call the school and make a fuss. Besides, I didn't see myself as the kind of mom other moms would call for conversation. I was way too depressed. Besides, all the important school correspondence and birthday-party information was done by e-mail. The address and phone offering was a vestige of a prior millennium.

The mistake bothered Paul. He'd called and asked if I had contacted the school about their error.

"No," I had said.

"Did you notice?" He got all police officer with me.

"Yes."

"Are you going to correct it?" Paul could be controlling.

"No."

"Do you want me to?" When it suits him, Paul forgets that we are divorced.

"If I wanted you to do it, I would have done it."

"What if one of the parents needs to speak with you?"

"That's why I have e-mail."

"Katie, you aren't good at checking e-mail."

He was right, but I wasn't about to concede. "I don't want to make waves in the school. If people start asking me about my calzones, I'll ask for a new sheet."

A few months ago, Paul slipped Bree a note before school started, and she corrected her mistake. But her incompetence remained intact. This year she switched Aimi's and Beverly's addresses.

Within hours of the mail delivery, Beverly was at the school. "This isn't acceptable."

"We'll take care of it." Irene spoke to her as poor Bree was sitting in a corner picking under her nails with an undone paper clip. Beverly could do that to you.

"These lists are published," she bellowed, irate. "This isn't just for the school. And as you well know, my husband and I live in a town house, not some nouveau riche apartment. This is not the impression we wish to give."

"I understand."

I don't, I wanted to say. I wanted to ask what she meant by "published." Why would anyone care?

Irene seemed to find some sense in what Beverly was saying, though she was clearly trying to get her out of the office.

I didn't see any sense in it at all. For one thing, while Beverly's town house was spectacular, I was certain that Aimi's apartment was pretty snazzy as well. She is immensely rich, well traveled, and would consult with an art director before putting a stamp on an envelope.

Of course, Beverly's tantrum worked. In the next day's mail, we got our new class list with Beverly's and Aimi's addresses in their correct places.

"Phew," I said to myself as I threw it in the garbage. It wasn't as if I would ever need to know exactly where these women lived.

I picture the Hastingses' home, and my mind flashes to Paul's notes. The door to the bottom floor, the servants' quarters, was locked. There was no evidence of tampering. The Chinese family said so. The lock was old and special, and in good condition. Once again, I doubt that a lock would have been broken or picked, and discarded, only to be replaced by a masterpiece.

No way. Three didn't have that kind of energy.

The door upstairs was open, but the body was downstairs.

Could the killer have barged in the front door, forced Beverly downstairs, killed her, and then come up? This makes no sense.

And the body wasn't moved. Those forensics people are always correct on that stuff. One thing I learned as an assistant district attorney: if you're going to kill someone, kill 'em where you want them to be found.

It seems likely that the killer came in from downstairs, closed and locked the door, killed Beverly, and ran upstairs and outside.

Why upstairs?

That's where all the stuff is.

But nothing was taken.

My reverie is interrupted when the phone starts to ring again. Boldly, I pick it up before the caller ID kicks in.

"Hello."

"Kate?" It's Steve.

"Who's this?" Nothing wrong with his thinking I have a handful of gentleman callers.

"Steve. Steve Mykonos. From Hawthorne?"

"Oh." I have to stay cool. Maybe he is calling on official school business. "Is everything okay?"

"That depends. Would you agree to have dinner with me Friday night?"

The phone beeps through. "Can you hold for a second? . . . Hello."

"Katie."

"Hi, Mom. I'm on with someone."

"A boy?"

"Are we twelve?" I say, irritated.

"Your tone suggested that we are."

"Mom."

"Katie. I don't want to keep you. I'm coming to New York City for a week. I have a post-traumatic-stress-disorder conference next Tuesday, but the cheapest day I could fly is Friday. Would you two like company?"

"Can you babysit?"

"Sure, but wh—?"

"Thanks, Mom. I love you so much." I click back to Steve and blurt out, "I'd love to go out with you."

"Mommmeeeee. The park's going to close." In the flurry of phone calls, I had almost forgotten about the park.

"Got to go," I say to Steve.

I get Molly into her jacket, me into mine, and grab a granola bar, then the phone starts ringing again. Once. Twice. It's probably Mom trying to get more dirt on Friday's plan. I pick up the phone.

The caller hangs up.

I look down. Private caller.

"Mommy."

"Coming, sweetie."

I remind myself that I will soon be going out with Steve. My first official date since Paul left me.

I'm excited and bored all at the same time. Molly is still at school, and I find myself with nothing to do and no one to call. Once I had a thousand friends. I had my friends at the DA's office, my law school friends, and my undergrad friends from Columbia. My college friends have all gone in completely different directions over the years. One is a schoolteacher. Another is in advertising. Still another owns a pipe business. When we are together, it sounds like a career forum:

"Oh, you're an editor. What's that like?"

"I knew you'd be a good administrator, but who knew you'd be running the seventh-largest foundation in the United States?"

Many of my friends moved out of New York. Nancy owns a bed-and-breakfast in Maine. Judy is still in New York at her advertising firm, but she had twins a year and a half before Molly was born, so her friends now tend to be other parents of kindergartners. Mavis and her partner Kendra split and get back together continually.

It's hard to keep up.

Then there are those three years of inexplicable sadness that killed my career, my marriage, and, I'm afraid, most of my friendships.

So I can't just make a quick phone call to Judy, Nancy, or Mavis and suggest we run out for coffee and a pedicure. It has to be something big and organized. That's how we communicate now.

So that explains Miriam. She can be exhausting, but she's always game. And she knows how to look good.

She answers the phone on the first ring. "Hi, babe." She must think it is someone else.

"Miriam, it's Kate."

"I know."

I let it go. Miriam loves to sound as if she were a character out of *Sex and the City*.

"I need your advice. I'm having a fashion emergency."

Miriam squeals. "I don't have any more fat clothes. So you are going to have to buy yourself something."

This is a good start.

"I don't mean to say you're fat," she backtracks. "I just have a different standard for myself."

"I have a date," I blurt.

"A what?"

"I know. It sounds like a foreign word, but I have an evening planned with a member of the opposite sex, and I have no idea what to wear."

Miriam doesn't even ask me about the date. She's in work mode.

"I'd like to try to wear something I have."

"You kill me, babe."

"It worked with Paul."

Miriam ignores this comment. Clothes are her métier. Even when we were kids, she loved to dress up and dress me up.

"Let's see. Is this a first date?"

"Yes. It's with a scientist type." I decide not to tell her the entire truth.

"Ooh, sort of Peter Parker and you are Mary Jane."

"No. He's totally not a superhero."

"That's what Mary Jane thinks when she's with Peter."

I don't argue with her.

"But I don't think you'll want to wear a dress. That seems desperate." Miriam always wears a dress.

"That sounds right. Can I wear my black pants?"

"Yes, but I say you spice it up with something. Do you have anything in petal?"

"Is that a color or a style?"

"You totally crack me up. It's like pink."

"No, I'm totally not a pink person."

"I think you are, Kate. I say go for it. But let's see. Maybe something cerise or cranberry."

I start to get heart palpitations. "Maybe I should just wear my black cowl neck."

"Maybe you should just wear an 'I'm a missionary' sign. Kate, honey. Times have changed. You aren't in the Paul fairy tale. I'm an expert at this."

"I'm not ready for cerise."

"Do the black sheer that I gave you from the fat bag. I promise. It will work wonders. And then call me with every juicy detail."

It occurs to me that Miriam hasn't asked me for any of the predate details. But that is how we connect. On the other hand, I realize she is exactly right about the outfit.

"I will," I tell her. "Though it's hard to focus on the date with all of these murders." I am dying to bounce some of my theories off her, even if it is Miriam.

"Yeah, well . . ." She trails off. I can tell she isn't listening. We have left her comfort zone. "You just focus on the outfit."

Notwithstanding my comfort in the date attire, I feel unfulfilled. I grab my MetroCard and purse and run out to get the No. 6 train downtown. Katie from the Block cum Nancy Drew, on my way to City Hall, my stop for years and years. I head into the DA's building, 1 Hogan Place. I can no longer go in the employees' security line. I have to stand with the defense attorneys and all their clients, the ones who aren't in jail.

I am impatient in the rickety, old elevator to Peg's office on the eighth floor. The smells—Chinese food, mothballs, and dust—bring me back to my first day here as a summer intern. Most of my first-year law school buddies had been angling for jobs at law firms, but I saw a career as an assistant district attorney as a way to right the wrongs of the world.

During my first year of law school, I was able to pay some of my law school tuition doing research and administrative work for a professor, Rick Whelan, an evidence scholar and a foremost expert on exceptions to the hearsay rule and, more important, a dynamic teacher. For the most part, Whelan put my organizational acumen to good use, placing me in charge of his files and the revamping of his office. Every now and then he would reward me with research tasks, which, more often than not, meant reviewing his work to make sure he was relying on good law.

I was thankful for the job and the money. More significant, I was grateful for Whelan's connections. When I told him I wanted the district attorney internship, he called his buddy Margaret O'Neill—everyone calls her Peg, he told me—and said he had a stellar and winsome candidate for the office.

I interviewed with the internship coordinator, talked about

my interest in fighting for justice, delivered a writing sample, and was offered a position right away.

My first day of work, I came up in this elevator all by myself, an uncommon occurrence during the morning business rush, but everyone else insisted on crowding into the elevator that took off seconds before mine. I didn't understand their impatience until the elevator reached the seventh floor and started making noise. It stopped a millisecond after that just before hitting the eighth floor. Sounding as unpanicked as I could muster, I picked up the emergency phone.

"Yup," a bored-sounding voice of ambiguous gender said.

"I'm stu—"

"Elevator two, wait." He/she interrupted me, sounding unimpressed.

"How long?"

But she had hung up.

Unsure of what to do, I pulled out a copy of Whelan's evidence textbook. I hadn't taken the class yet—it was for second- and third-year students, but I had read the book so many times and reviewed so many of his articles that I felt it would be unnecessary. I loved the rules of evidence. They made so much sense. I shared his zeal for scholarship on hearsay, though I was ultimately drawn most to the intellectual discourse on legal relevance. I liked it all, and even though I could practically recite his treatise by heart, I found something new each time I read it.

"You're not going to win any extra credit around here for looking like a scholar," an older, attractive woman with her bun held together by a pencil said to me.

The doors had opened.

Embarrassed, I stood up. "I wa—"

"Peg O'Neill," she interrupted. I would learn later that her raspy voice was the product of years of smoking.

"Hi, nice to meet you. Kate Hagen."

"Great name. Let's go to work."

I was confused. I knew from Whelan that Peg was on the executive staff in the office. Interns were being mentored by junior people.

Peg sensed my confusion. "We decided that a senior person would get one of the interns. You're the lucky one. All the others were scooped up in elevator one."

"Well, thanks, Ms. O'Neill, I'm really just awestricken."

"The name is Peg. And you shouldn't be awestricken just yet. You haven't seen me do anything. Wait till you watch me in court. That's when awe strikes."

"That would be great, *Peg*." I inadvertently screamed her name in my attempt to follow her directions.

"Hurry, we're late."

"Late?"

"We've got to question a suspect."

"Really." I had never come face-to-face with a real criminal before.

"Really. I need you. We're trying to get evidence and it appears you have the book." She was staring at Whelan's tome. Then she winked at me.

I hastily put the book back in my briefcase, a faux-weathered-leather thing my mother had sent me just before the job started, and we headed into an interrogation room. It was more sterile than I expected, and small, maybe fifty square feet. Most of the room was taken up by a brown Formica table. The walls were a dull white, and the rug was a dirtied bright blue stained with coffee and gum.

Peg and I were the first to arrive.

"What was the crime?" I asked Peg, slightly afraid that I would use the wrong lingo on my first day.

"We have a suspect coming in who was accused of raping a woman just hours ago. She is still at the hospital."

Rape. In my mind I recalled the elements of the crime. Sexual penetration of another person without his or her consent.

"You know what rape is, right?" she asked.

Without thinking I said, "It's awful."

Peg laughed. "Too bad that's not the legal definition."

After that a police officer, Michel Dasteng—Mikey, I would later call him—came in and said, "He lawyered up."

I froze. I couldn't remember what the implications of that were. Lawyering up was something they talked about in Criminal Procedure, a second- or third-year elective. I put my head down, hoping Peg wouldn't ask me anything. I was lucky because a second later another officer opened the door for a forty-year-old, whey-faced man in a navy suit accompanied by another forty-year-old, less-sallow-faced man in a gray suit.

"Which one of you is the lawyer?" Peg asked.

"Very funny," the pasty guy said. "Phillip Yargosy." He handed both Peg and me business cards that read THE LAW OFFICES OF PHILLIP YARGOSY. "Let's get this cleared up," he said to Peg.

"I would like nothing more," she answered. "I have a pile of cases that need tending to."

I stayed silent, holding a pencil and a legal pad on the table, primed to take notes.

"What can you tell me?" Peg asked.

"I can tell you this is a case of mistaken identity. My guy did nothing."

"Really, tell us about that," Peg instructed.

"I don't know what you're talking about."

"We've got a twenty-seven-year-old victim at New York University Hospital with vaginal tearing, a bloody lip, and a broken nose, who was just raped in the men's room at the Just Inspirations store in the Citicorp building. Ring any bells for you?"

"You got the wrong guy. I swear. I wasn't even near the Citicorp building. I work at the Lucas West Men's Clothing Store six blocks away. I was there the whole day, doing inventory."

"Your colleagues have said there was about an hour where they didn't see you, and we've got you on a videotape walking into Just Inspirations."

"My client says he was doing inventory," Yargosy said, "and there are about twenty thousand men in this city who look exactly like him. Including, dare I say, me?"

He was right, I thought. The suspect looked incredibly familiar. There were five of "him" in my law school class.

Yargosy continued, "If that's all you got, you might as well go back to all your real cases."

"Just a second," Peg said. "I have a crack assistant here with me—who happens to be a scholar on evidence. She doesn't just write about it, she secures it."

Peg looked at me. I looked at Peg.

Despite my apparent composure, I felt sheer panic.

"Well?" Yargosy looked at me.

His client, sitting a little too close to me for my own comfort, was also looking at me. In an effort not to panic, I took in a huge deep breath and started to cough.

Guilt. That smell. That smell. Rotten lilies and fermented wine. I would know it anywhere. I had my evidence. I rifled through the legal pad to obtain a fresh new page and scribbled a quick note to Peg. "Suspect stinks of women's perfume. Get him to say he was only around men."

"So let's be clear," Peg said, "no sexual relations today with someone at the Just Inspirations?"

"No, ma'am," the suspect said.

"Could anyone have misconstrued any physical contact with a woman as sexual relations?"

"No. In fact, I work in a men's store and I wasn't even near a woman."

"No women in the store?"

"No."

"Are you sure? Some men's stores carry a small line of women's apparel and fragrance."

"Not us. We don't carry any clothes or fragrance."

"You don't?"

"Our clients aren't partial to it. This is a very conservative group."

"So you don't wear fragrance?"

"The boss has a policy. So no."

"Great. What if I asked if you submit to a testing of your clothes?"

Before his lawyer could say anything, the suspect laughed and said sure. He handed us his sweater.

Officer Dasteng pressed a button on his cell phone, and the other officer walked back in. There was a handoff of the sweater between the two officers.

"What is this about?" Yargosy demanded.

"Your client is drenched in, in . . ." Peg looked at me.

"Guilt. No offense." I turned to Yargosy. "That's the name of the perfume that's all over him."

And that was my first day at work. More important, it was the start of my friendship with Peg, my rock.

So here I am now, heading back to my old job, seeing the old rock, and taking a risk in elevator two. I've been stuck in it three times since that first day. Paul and I were in there for fifty-five minutes once. When I was pregnant, he told his friends that the baby was conceived in elevator two.

"As long as he or she is not born there," one of them had responded.

This time, Peg is in her office.

"Asking for your old job back? Go to Sue in HR. I'll see you Monday."

"Very funny, Peg. I just stopped in to say hi."

"Hi. I'm busy." Clad in a teal, formfitting wool dress with a Peter Pan collar, Peg has not even lifted her head to look at me. She is staring at her computer with a perplexed look on her face. Her desk is completely bare with the exception of a thin pile of papers. Her floor, on the other hand, is wall-to-wall research: legal reports, treatises, periodicals, and, I'm sure, way too many memos from eager young assistants who wish to impress her. It is likely that an old one of mine is still buried underneath—the woman hasn't cleaned her office since the prior millennium.

"As long as the desk is clear, the head is clear," she says of herself. Her husband, Marty, a neat freak, warns her that if she doesn't manage the mess, someone is likely to get hurt in it and sue her and the city. He has the cases to prove it. Marty is a litigator.

She refuses to speak to me during work hours, just as she refused to indulge my maternity leave. "You were in a bad place," she told me a couple of months ago. Her tone betrayed her disappointment in my inertia. To be fair, Peg had been patient with me since my change in affect, but her forbearance has long been coming to an end. She prides herself on her proactiveness. When she was twelve, her mother died after a long battle with cancer, and Peg was forced to raise her four sisters and brothers. She mourned for one day before she became the matriarch of the house.

"I didn't have a choice," she always says. "How could I explain the stages of grief to a four-year-old? The little guy needed me, and so did his older brothers and sisters. I had to make do."

That's Peg, the queen of one foot in front of the other. When *The New York Lawyer* did a feature on her, the reporter was genuinely surprised by Peg's background. "I'm just so impressed," she had said. Off the record.

"Don't be," Peg said. "You would have done the same. Anyone would have."

But that isn't true, I now know. I certainly didn't. In my early days at the DA's office I heard the few Peg detractors refer to her as cold.

"No compassion," Geralyn Zeiders whispered to Len Mushnik when Peg chewed out an assistant for failing to show the defense certain files they were entitled to see. "It's a mistake anyone could have made." When Peg overheard this, she asked Geralyn to speak to her and said, "That's the kind of mistake that leads to a rapist raping yet another woman. Now who has no compassion?"

While Peg doesn't shower her loved ones with hugs, kisses, and I love you's, she always shows up. She came to the NICU every day to see Molly, she came with me to get my operation at Sloan-Kettering, and she stood next to me when I signed my divorce papers. She refers to herself as the queen of action. "It speaks louder than words."

Also queen of the adage, she repeats her favorite to me today. "'The devil makes work for idle hands.' Now you're fine. Get back to work."

"Plenty of moms don't go back to work," I protest.

"You're not plenty of moms. You're Kate 'Needs to Have a Job' Hagen. Don't make me lecture you anymore. It's unbecoming."

"Speaking of unbecoming, I have a date on Friday."

"A date? Why didn't you say so?" Peg shifts herself so that she is facing me.

"Name?"

"Steve."

"Does he have a last name or is he like Liberace?"

"Mykonos."

"Isn't that where you went on your honeymoon?"

"No. We went to Crete."

"Does this Steve do something?"

"He's a teacher."

"You mean a professor?

"If you want to believe that Molly is being taught by a professor."

"He's a nursery-school teacher? You're jonesing for a nursery-school teacher?"

"Not a nursery-school teacher. Sort of. He teaches science at Hawthorne."

"I could teach science at Hawthorne. 'Kids, look up in the sky. That big, round, bright thing is called a sun; at night it's called a moon.' "

"Very funny, Peg. You'd have a bunch of kids with damaged retinas. By the way, if it makes you like him better, he's getting his doctorate at Columbia."

"Of course it makes me like him better. I'm all about superficial things like achievement. Let's Google him."

Let me say here that Peg is amazing at her job. She has tried more than forty cases over the years and won thirty-seven convictions. She is the pride of the DA's office.

But Peg likes her gossip.

When Paul and I started dating, she needed a minute-by-minute account of our first moments together.

"What did he say and what did you say?" she would grill me every time I got off the phone with him. And then, after each date: "What were you wearing and was there delicious awkwardness?"

Once we were engaged, Peg faked despondence. "I'm going to have to watch *General Hospital* again. I need my romance. You guys have become officially boring."

Years later, after I found out that Paul attended a "seminar," Peg tried to console me.

"You should be happy," I had said to her. "We're not boring anymore."

"Kate," she had responded, tears in her eyes, "you know I loved you boring."

Now she's whistling to herself as she types into her keyboard. "Okay. S-T-E-V-E M-Y-K-O-N-O-S." Her feet are doing a jig under the table.

"Not a lot. Oh, here. He's published an article, 'Nanowire Heterostructures in Micro Fluidic Systems.' Lordy, I just fell asleep."

"Be nice . . ."

"On the bright side, the structures are hetero."

"And yet microfluidic."

We both laugh at our sophomoric behavior. It's the old Kate and the old Peg.

The phone rings.

"Peg O'Neill." She listens, then hangs up the phone. "Oh, darlin', I have to go. We've got a string of jewelry-store robberies that need to be investigated. Not that I'm trying to tempt you."

I won't admit to her that jewelry-store robberies don't grab my interest in the same way that mommy murders do.

She's still talking. "But you're not off the hook. I want every detail of your date."

"Very funny."

"Give your baby girl a big, huge kiss from her aunt Peggy."

She ducks out of the room, and I stand as if I, too, am going to leave. I navigate my way through Peg's "library" and over to her desk. She's still logged on. I recall how guilty I felt when I checked Paul's computer.

Yet I still live with myself.

After all, if I'm actually assisting in the administration of justice here, there's nothing wrong with an extra set of eyes on the case. That it is illegal is a mere technicality that I will over-come when the mayor rewards my crime fighting with a key to the city and a ticker-tape parade. I test the waters a bit and type *Hastings* in the search box. I get some notes. Hmmm, *husband bad* and *no evidence break-in*. These are not that different from Paul's. But there's nothing here about the Katie e-mail. Is it pos-sible Paul knows something he's not telling Peg? Maybe I'll go for the Crump murder. I type in *Crump*. Bingo. Much more here.

Housekeeper discovers body at 10 a.m.

Husband away (?)

Bathtub full—body inside

lungs filled with water and vomit

ruptured eyeballs consistent with electrocution

excessive blistering on hands and feet though joule marks low—consistent with electrocution of 240 volts or lower

240 volt hair dryer in bath—housekeeper: Vic always used hair dryer in the bedroom

body—green color

Coroner—time of death 9:00 a.m.—most likely electrocuted in bathtub and died in bathtub

No break-in

No robbery

Acc. housekeeper—house normal looking

Vic had asked for extra vacuuming that day w/ no explanation

Peg's notes are clear, but nothing strikes me as I read them. Except for the vacuuming. I love to vacuum, so I can't judge. Maybe the housekeeper was a less-than-stellar vacuumer, and Johanna had to give her a song and dance about how she needed extra simply to get a decent job.

The time of death is helpful: nine a.m. Johanna died on the morning of Beverly's funeral. The service was at eleven and therefore provides no alibi for any of us who were there.

I scroll to the next page, seeking something far more interesting. Something about the Katie e-mail. Nada. But, what's this? A little notation: *Hawthorne connection?* This, of course, is my big question. And then: *Phillippa von Eck=record.*

Phillippa von Eck equals record. Phillippa von Eck has a record. Our Phillippa *Town & Country* von Eck. I forget about the Katie e-mail. This is better. I am about to do a search for Phillippa when I hear Peg's voice.

"I need someone to go to court for me."

Thank you, Peg, for your booming loud voice. Her kids used to call her Bad Sniper because they always knew when she was about to discover them rifling through her pockets for change or eating from her hidden stash of candy. At the office we always mocked her attempts to cover up the mouthpiece on the phone when she was having a supposedly private conversation. For someone in law enforcement, she is surprisingly terrible at being sneaky.

I press EXIT, and I'm back in Steve Mykonos's dissertation.

"You're still here." It is a fake reprimand. "I'll tell you what, come back to work for me, and I'll let you sit at my desk all you want."

"Peg, I just wanted your advice on what to wear." Turns out I am quite good at being sneaky.

"Something the guy is used to ripping off," Peg says. "I know, how about a Pamper?"

"Do you want me to go out or do you want me to live as a recluse?"

"Go. Of course. But let an elderly lady have her fun. Your sad act cramped my heartless biting style. A game of Monopoly here and there just isn't enough."

She's right. After living with my self-absorbed depression, she is entitled to as many jabs as wishes.

She watches me as I stand there, then waves me away.

"Go home. Watch a soap opera or catch a sale. Isn't that what you unemployed people do? As for your date, dress like a strumpet and call me as soon as you get home—whenever that may be."

I leave Peg's office dizzy with happiness. I have a date with Molly's hot, hunky teacher, and I'm making serious progress on my investigation. Now, I know full well that this investigation is just for me, but I am still truly excited. Phillippa von Eck has a record. Phillippa von Ick. That's what Liane had called her. She might be a murderess in addition to being awful. She killed Johanna and Beverly, but why?

I'm getting ahead of myself. She did time. She's a rich kid from New York City. She could have smoked too much pot or had a Winona Ryder problem. Every city kid I ever met in college bragged about stealing lip gloss and lingerie. It's hard to think that this would lead to murdering moms.

But it is an interesting development. I hurry back home on the subway. I have a lead, and I know just how to follow it. Liane. But this requires a phone call—not our simple e-mail exchange. Before I take my coat off, I grab the class list from the bulletin board. It's the old one, the one that has Beverly living in a nouveau riche condo. I dial Liane's number.

"Liane Tulsch." It's her cell phone.

"Liane, it's Kate Alger. Molly's mom."

"Kate, is everything okay?" I think she notices the change in means of contact. No e-mails.

"Absolutely. I guess I've never called you before, but . . ."

Oops—I haven't thought this through, and I can't very well blurt out anything about Phillippa, so I say the first thing that pops into my head.

"I had coffee with Steve Mykonos yesterday." Is it a good idea to be trading confidences with her?

"Well, aren't you quite the cougar," she says with a touch of unkindness.

This is strikingly different from our usually pleasant exchanges. It never occurred to me that she wouldn't approve. So I tone it down.

"It was nothing really. We happened to be in the same coffee shop," I lie, "and he sat with me for a minute. But an old lady like me can dream . . ."

"Don't underestimate yourself." Liane is a tad less cool.

I laugh. I feel I should be careful. I know how I will raise this. "I don't want to say anything to him that might undermine Molly's future."

"What do you mean?"

"I know it's silly, but if I am going to send Molly to a

competitive ongoing school I want to make sure that her teachers think well of her family." I head over to my desk to pull out my index cards. I write Phillippa's name in block letters. Seeing it in writing gives me the creeps.

"That does make sense," Liane agrees. "Sometimes the family is the reason the kid gets in or doesn't get in."

"Well then, you have a leg up. Don't you?"

"Not really. I went to an all-girls school."

"Oh, yes, with Phillippa?"

"Yes, but she left Upton for high school. She couldn't handle the academics. Her parents shipped her off to the Winthrop School in ninth grade. They boasted to everyone who would listen that Winthrop had the most impressive field-hockey team in the Northeast corridor. P.S. Phillippa never played field hockey."

"Guess you guys didn't exactly keep in touch?"

I'm fishing. I hang up my coat, and while I'm at it, I straighten up the closet. Just a little.

"No. I was so happy to see her go. But like the snakes on the Medusa she keeps coming back."

I am brightened by Liane's allusion to a Greek myth and feel that we are karmically intended to be friends. "I guess you need Perseus to get rid of her." I gather all the wire hangers.

"Too bad Perseus is just a story," Liane sighs. We are back to being buddies again. "Gotta go. I would love to grab a coffee with you." She pauses. "That is, if you aren't already having one with Dr. Science."

I can't figure out her voice. "That would be great. Anytime. I'm flexible. Nothing on my plate." Except solving a couple of homicides and having my way with a man who knows his microfluids.

I hang up. Liane has given me a seedling of information. Winthrop Boarding School.

After I dump the hangers in a trash bag, I start to review my index cards, but am interrupted by the shrill sound of my doorbell.

I open the door and Miriam is standing there. The doormen never ring her up.

Some people are continually annoyed by members of their family, and, as I said, Miriam is essentially family.

"Well, hello." She brushes by me as if she is the leading lady coming onstage at the crucial moment. Her hair is in its natural state, tight curls that straight-haired girls pay thousands of dollars a year to attain. Not Miriam. "I'm an actor. An ingénue," she says, pushing it. "If I were playing a character or Little Orphan Annie, I would take ownership."

She is a character but a gorgeous one. Today she wears a bright blue cashmere Fabriglioni sweater dress that clings and highlights her skinny body to her advantage, with thigh-high, brown suede boots. I have never seen the outfit before, although this is often the case as she uses shopping as a replacement for eating.

"Hi, Miriam."

"I just had to tell you."

"You're in love."

"I didn't want to talk about it. You know, since you have been soooooooo alone. But now that I know you are back on the market, we can be all girlie and tell each other everything."

In truth, Miriam hasn't seemed to hold back at all on her exploits since my marital demise. I have several unpleasant visions competing in my head right now of her copulating with various COOs.

"So, ask me." She thrusts some candied cherries in my hand.

"What is his name?"

"See, I knew you knew. You could tell by my face, right? Everyone says when you're in love and having ridiculously good sex that you can tell."

I don't want to tell her that the only topic she speaks about is sex. Her face, as always, is very pretty.

"So?"

"Yes."

"Aren't you going to ask me about him?"

I'll bite. "Tell me everything." I put the candied cherries in the refrigerator, certain that they will remain there through Molly's high school graduation.

"His name is Evan. He's an entrepreneur. He owns a business. You would love him."

I pull out Molly's clean laundry and start folding it.

"What kind of business?"

"His own business."

"Miriam, the suspense is killing me. What's the business?"

"I'm not really sure. Something with money and investing."

"Is he a hedge-fund guy?"

"No. Not that."

"Is he an investment guy?" Is it possible I am missing a sock?

"No."

"What, then?"

"It's about money," she concludes.

Oh, good, here is the sock. "How did you meet?"

"Well, I was out with my girlfriends from the gym. And we all said we should go for margaritas and split an appetizer because margaritas are so fattening."

I looked at her.

"Okay, Kate, *I* was the one who insisted on splitting the appetizer. But I had just seen this thing on the news where they said they were eight hundred calories each and I thought, 'Wow, I'm only drinking *that* at my wedding.'"

I debate whether I should iron Molly's cotton jumper, but conclude that my time is better spent solving the mommy murders.

Miriam is still talking. "So we're sitting there drinking margaritas—"

"And enter Evan?"

"You kill me, Kate. By the way, love Molly's dress. Love. I bet if I hadn't drunk the margarita I would fit into it. Anyhow, we were at Ola Mexica, and I had just taken a sip of the most delicious margarita you could imagine. And I see this guy looking at me."

"Evan?" I straighten up the kitchen, certain to put Molly's class list back on the bulletin board.

"Totally. So. I stared at him in my best flirty flirty, and he told the bartender he wanted the same drink so he could have the same 'light' as me."

"Cool."

"But isn't it? I mean, that is such a compliment, don't you think, that someone wants my 'light'?" She pronounces the *t* as if it were a word unto itself.

"That's wonderful."

"I love it that that's how we met."

"So then what happened?"

"Well, we drank for a while and my girlfriends told me to go with him because it is so once-in-a-lifetime to have this kind of chemistry. My God. He wanted my *light*."

"And then?"

"He said he wanted to take me home."

"And?"

"You will be so proud of me. I told him I had to get up early for a shoot. And he said that he wanted to take me out the next night."

"And?"

"And we went out. And it was great. He said something again about my light. I know you think I'm crazy. I wish I could have taped it so you could hear the way he said it."

"When did this happen?"

"It will be exactly four weeks tomorrow."

"Wow, Miriam, you've been holding out on me." Usually she calls me within hours after the act.

"I know, but this thing with Evan feels sacred. I kind of wanted to just enjoy him and us by myself, you know?"

"I do. Anything else to tell me then? I don't want to intrude."

"It's all good. All good. Everyone always says that when you're with 'the one,' you know it. I knew it within seconds."

Come to think of it, Miriam looks more relaxed than I have seen her in a long time. "That's great." I really am happy for her.

There are two short knocks at the door followed by two long ones.

"Someone's at your door."

"It's Paul," I tell her as I roll my eyes. Then, with manufactured kindness, I holler, "Come on in."

"That's hilarious. You guys have a secret knock?"

"He lives right above me and we have this daughter to raise."

"Hi, Katie. Hi, Miriam. You are looking well."

Miriam winks at me and whispers, "It's love." She raises her voice. "Hello, Paul."

"Did I interrupt anything?" He's being as phony as I've been lately.

"Just some girl talk," I tell him as if we were close. It is difficult for me to get through a conversation with him unless it pertains to Molly. But the only way to find out about this Katie e-mail is to get back to his computer, which means getting back into his apartment, which means sucking up to him. So if I have to play the Lucy Ricardo and Ethel Mertz game, then so be it. "Is everything okay?"

"I was going to ask you the very same thing." He turns to Miriam. "Two of Katie's friends have been killed."

"How awful," Miriam says as if she were hearing this for the first time. She most likely has forgotten, as this is not about her.

"Not my friends," I correct him. "People I know. Molly's friends' moms."

"Oh, yeah. You did tell me that. How are you?" Miriam asks.

"Katie is in no danger," Paul says.

How the hell do you know? I give him a winsome smile. "I'm fine," I say to Miriam. "Maybe slightly unnerved." And maybe more than slightly nosy.

"But I think Molly's okay," Paul contributes.

"Why wouldn't Molly be okay?" Miriam asks.

"Because her friends' mothers have been murdered." Paul has become terse. "It can be hard on a kid."

"Does she know?" Miriam asks.

"Yes, she knows," I say. "But not the whole thing. She thinks that the kids' mommies had accidents and that it's bad, but she doesn't quite get the concept of death, let alone murder."

"That's a relief," Miriam says. "I bet she'll be fine. Molly is a great kid."

"Thanks."

"Hey, I've got to go, but it was so great, just talking. At the important times, you're always there for me."

"Anytime," I say.

"Do you want me to come over and do your nails and makeup before your big night?" She winks at me.

"Nah." I blush. "That sounds very advanced."

"If you change your mind, I'm here. Ta-ta." And then she mouths "Good luck" to me as she exits. For a moment, it appears that Paul looks stricken.

"What's with the important time?" Paul skips over my friend's reference to my big night. Okay, so he isn't stricken. He's fixing himself a sandwich. His sense of entitlement is fascinating and annoying all at once. I want to say, *Don't cheat on me and then eat my food.* Instead, I keep quiet and smile all pretty so I can get a glance at his notes.

"She's in looooove." I wink at him, trying to get an invitation up to his place.

"Again?"

"But this guy has lasted a month."

"A month." He's chewing. "You know, I love your tuna. Has he spent time with her during the month?"

"Do you need something?" I scowl, forgetting that I am supposed to be winning him over.

"I'm checking in on you."

"I'm fine. Look, I'm making pie." That's me, Betty Crocker.

"I don't see pie."

"I'm at the beginning part where you get all of the stuff together."

"What kind of pie?"

"Just pie." I, meanwhile, have no idea if I have any ingredients for pie. I might have flour and sugar, and then who knows? Maybe some Abilify or Lexapro to give it that extra kick. "Don't you have people to arrest?"

"You're right. I thought I'd be nice and check on you. And I was hungry."

"Why are you being so nice all of a sudden?"

"I know that you're fine. But in times like this, maybe I realize how precious life is, and that you are irreplaceable—" He pauses. "To Molly. A mother is irreplaceable."

"And I'm the one with all the cold cuts."

Paul looks wounded. I remember my goal here. "That was really nice. Thanks so much." I manage a smile.

He leaves, and I actually do start making a pie. I have nothing to put in it, so I melt a few of Molly's candy bars from her Halloween stash and make a fudgy filling. It's delicious, and I'm sure far more caloric than the margaritas at Ola Mexica.

The phone rings. I pick it up.

Another hang-up. I think about mentioning this to Paul but don't want to give him the satisfaction of thinking I need him.

It's Friday, the night of my big date. I'm at Molly's school, anxious to pick her up. My mother will be at my house in an hour or so, and she is aflutter about taking her granddaughter to the botanical garden to see the conifers.

"It's very special," she told me, "to show children things of nature for the very first time."

I'm in Irene Druvier's office gathering information on summer programs for toddlers when I see Steve. My guy, I guess. At least for tonight. I am fairly certain that I am not imagining a look that he is giving me. That *we've got a secret, a really fun secret* look. As I start to give it back to him, I see Howard Montgomery's mother also looking at him in a slightly inappropriate manner. I've never seen Mrs. Montgomery with her coat off. She tends to have a preppy look, but today she has shed the headband and the Belgian shoes for an amply heeled pair of jet-black pumps and a crimson wrap dress. For once she isn't trailing Howard with an inhaler in one hand and an ERB study guide in the other. Today, she's carrying *No Ordinary Genius: The Illustrated Richard Feynman.*

It appears that Howard's mommy has a crush on my crush.

I am tempted to ask her if she is into him. Okay. Now I am officially insane. We are a bunch of bored women. A gorgeous man is roaming the halls. Who am I kidding? We are all looking at him.

And yet, tonight, he is mine.

But Mrs. Montgomery is still watching him. Maybe this is a sign for me. Stay away from the stud. Maybe I will enjoy the memory of our flirtatious banter and move on to something more realistic. I can cancel. I'll leave a note on my way out.

"Mommy." Molly comes running into the office. "I saw you. Isn't that funny?"

"Very funny. Let's get you home so you can go with Grandma to look at the conifers."

"Can me and Grandma bring Willa to see the confers?"

"Let's see," I say, meaning no.

"Please, Mama, please. I think Grandma would love Willa—she's so pretty and nice. Please, Mama, please."

"We'll see."

I am irritated. It's bad enough that she likes Willa, and it's frankly worse that she finds her pretty.

"Me and Daddy think Willa is the prettiest lady in the whole world."

"For your information, it's Daddy and I."

"You think she's the prettiest lady in the world, too, Mama? Me, Mommy, and Daddy all think Willa is the prettiest lady in the world. And Grandma will think so, too."

"I'm sure she will."

I try to tell myself that it's okay for Paul to think Willa is the prettiest lady in the world. She is ridiculously pretty and Paul is a douche bag.

"Grandma's going to love Willa. She knows so many things."

This conversation is not heading in the right direction.

"Dr. Steve." Molly is screaming at Steve. "Dr. Steve. Me and Grandma and my pretty babysitter, Willa, are going to look at confers. Can we learn confers in science?"

I mouth the word *conifer* to Steve. I feel suddenly seductive.

"Of course we can, Molly," Steve says with his head cocked.

There is no way I'm canceling my date.

As we leave the building, I see Bitsy walking a few yards ahead of us holding Carmela's hand.

"Mama, it's Bitsy. Look."

"Molly, we have to hurry. No time for Bitsy. Grandma is waiting."

"Bitsy, Bitsy, Bitsy," Molly is chanting. "Is that a new baby-sitter?"

Bitsy turns around. "Mollllleeeeeeeeeeeeeeeeeeeeeeee. Mollleeeeeeeeeeeeee."

"Is that your new babysitter?" Molly asks again as we catch up to them.

"Yeah. 'Cause my mommy died."

My eyes fill with tears, and I catch Carmela's eye.

"Your mommy was at my house," Bitsy tells Molly.

I am prepared to deny this, but Carmela did see me.

"Your mommy wants to buy my house. That's what the lady said," Bitsy explains to Molly.

"Mommy already has our house," Molly tells her.

"Maybe she wants mine."

Molly starts crying. "But I love my house. I don't want your house." Had Molly ever been to Bitsy's house, her tears would dry right up.

"It's okay, sweetie. Mommy isn't buying Bitsy's house."

"Promise," Molly says.

"I promise."

I am grateful for these tears as they provide me with a way out of explaining to my daughter why I was at Bitsy's house. I smile at Carmela, wondering if, under Three's control, she will have more longevity with the Hastings family than her predecessors did.

She smiles back and gives a sympathetic look toward Bitsy. I wonder if she knows how difficult Beverly was as a boss. Again, I entertain the possibility that one of the staff killed her. The body was found downstairs with no sign of forced entry. Beverly needed a reason to be down there. The only thing I can think of is a staff issue. But Johanna Crump is dead. And they didn't share babysitters. This is so weird.

Maybe the Crump death is a completely unrelated act. The murder was committed differently. But isn't that too much of a coincidence? The victims, dead within days of one another, have children in the same nursery-school class. Although, from

a forensic perspective, and goodness knows this isn't my specialty, there are no real similarities in cause of death. Beverly
was bludgeoned multiple times and Johanna was electrocuted.
Could one have been personal and the other a red herring?
And why connect them by their children's schooling?

Molly and I have arrived home. Alfred calls upstairs. There
is a delivery for me, he exhales. Should he send it up, he wants
to know. Normally, I wouldn't think twice about this. I am not
expecting a delivery, but they do come here from time to time
without my knowledge. Presents for Molly, usually.

"Is it addressed to anyone in specific, Alfred?" I ask.

"You, Mrs. Alger. It looks like a food." His voice is slightly
more nasal than usual.

This is weird. Or am I being paranoid?

"Would you like someone from the building to bring it up
to you?"

"That would be great, Alfred."

I can tell Alfred senses my nervousness. After all, he was
the one who told me about the second murder. And, let's face
it, the man must know of my mental instability the past few
years.

I stare at the phone. Immediately I think I should call Paul.
What would I tell him? I have a surprise package coming up. I
am a Hawthorne mother, remember, and the other two were
murdered in weird ways. But this could be an explosive.

I don't want to call Paul. I would rather die, truly, than give
him the satisfaction. Besides, he's not the only one experienced
in law enforcement. I have put seven murderers, five rapists,
and all sorts of gun toters behind bars. All without a gun of
my own.

The truth is, the delivery is scaring the bejesus out of me.

The doorbell rings.

Okay, this is it. I grab a penny. If it lands on heads, I'll put aside my death wish and call Paul; tails, I'll deal with it. Heads. I go to the phone.

The doorbell rings again.

I am pathetic. I inhale. I cannot and will not call Paul to intercept a package. If I am on the list of targets, I will die with dignity.

I open the door. It's my mother.

"Phew." I gulp. "I thought it was someone else. Did you see anything weird?"

"Katie. Are you okay?"

Just then our porter shows up and hands me the package.

"Thanks, Julio." I sound calm.

"You're welcome, Missus Alger," he says, smiling.

He may be the last person we see before we die.

"Katie, what is the matter?"

I am clearly acting strange and am scaring my dear mother. "I'll tell you in a minute." If we're still alive.

The box has no return address, but a typed label has my name on it: KATE HAGEN. Hmm. My maiden name. A school killer would probably know me by Paul's last name. I open the box. It is from La Roué Chocolatier. My favorite chocolates.

Is there any possibility these are poison?

I open the card. There is a typed message: *In case tonight doesn't go well, this may be a good consolation gift. If it goes well, I want all details—Miriam-style. XO Peg.*

I laugh, more out of relief than anything else.

Relief that we didn't blow up.

Relief that I didn't tell Paul.

"Katie, give me a hug."

I hug my mother while butting my head into her sternum

just as I did when I was a little girl. I can be this way with her and no one else. Although I trust Dr. Schmitt, our relationship is clinical and dry. I have told her the depths of my despair while sobbing on her couch, but if I saw her in a restaurant, I would shake her hand.

Even Peg, my "urban mother," as my real mother refers to her, doesn't evoke this kind of physicality. When I first started working at the DA's office, I followed Peg around all day and night like a little duck. For a while I even started to dress like her. I put my hair in a bun and ditched my pantsuits for little dresses. Peg has a slight Texas twang, which I adopted as my own, referring to my law school buddies as *y'all* and omitting at times the *g* at the end of words. My interest in order tied in nicely with Peg's pragmatic, results-oriented demeanor.

My mother, on the other hand, is all process. She refers to herself as a work in progress: a WIP. She tends to refer to me in the same way. And Molly is her grand WIP. I like being my mother's WIP, though I tend to regress every now and then.

Regression is part of progress, my mother always says. While Peg has held my hand throughout my depression, divorce, and inertia, she is waiting for me to get back on track. My mother has no such expectations.

"You are on the right track," she says. "You're on your track."

That's why my mom is my mom and Peg is my friend and former colleague.

I have time before my date. I need to get into Paul's computer. Just seconds ago I didn't want to lose my dignity by calling him, but this is different. I'm not coming from a place of need;

I'm coming from a place of nosy. Besides, he's off work today. Maybe I can offer him a midday glass of wine. He used to like that when he had a day to himself.

I grab a bottle from the fridge. It's been sitting there for a long time now as I have never had the occasion to drink. I grab my completely old and inefficient corkscrew and two glasses. I figure if I go up with the wine like a dime-store Mata Hari, I can helplessly ask him to get it ready with the old corkscrew while I do a quick computer search.

Not enough time. I grab a cluster of organic dusty grapes. Paul will wash them. He can't stand grape dust. He loves a clean grape. That should give me a little extra time. I hum a little tune in my head. "It's All Right with Me" pops into my head. I've always been a Cole Porter fan and I even forced Paul to be the same.

I wonder if Steve likes Cole Porter.

I knock Paul's secret knock.

He's at the door. "You okay?" he asks quickly.

"Of course. I'm fine."

"This isn't a good time." He's acting strange.

"Oh." I show him the wine and the grapes.

"Not now, Katie." He slowly closes the door on me.

I walk away.

He opens the door a little. "I'll call you. Let's talk later."

I leave without saying anything. I am frazzled. How dare he not let me in? What if there were an issue with Molly? Not that there is, but he doesn't know that. A little nervy—not to mention thoughtless on his part.

I was certain I would find out what was in the e-mail. Now I'm stuck in Cole Porter mode.

Only it's "Ev'ry Time We Say Goodbye."

What an ass!
Paul, not me.

When my mother sees me opening the door with a bottle of wine in one hand and a cluster of dingy grapes in the other, she puts on her therapy face.

"Anything I should know about?" she asks.

"No, it's not what you think it is."

"What do you think I think it is?"

"You think Paul hurt my feelings."

"I do?" She sounds genuinely confused. "I thought you ran out to buy something to bring on your date. But, now that you bring it up, were you just at Paul's?"

"Mom. I really don't want to talk about this."

"We don't have to."

Steve and I are on our date. So far so good. I didn't have him pick me up at the apartment because Molly would have been enormously confused. My mother, curious to look at him, was disappointed with this arrangement.

"Can't you take a picture of him with your cell phone or something?" she asked.

"Maybe you should date," I said.

This is a terribly sore subject with my mother. She knows that she should date, and she knows why she doesn't.

She has a deep-seated fear that she will put a lot of effort into a relationship with a man who'll disappear, she has said to me a number of times over the years.

I understand. I think therapy worked to the extent that my

mother is completely over my father, but she still can't get beyond the lack of closure. If he had just written a postcard saying *It's not your fault—I'm nuts*, or even *It is your fault*, she might be able to get involved with someone. But he disappeared.

"If it weren't for you, I would think I imagined the union," she'd once told me.

She doesn't seem sad, but she knows that her life could be richer if a romantic element were present.

"Just for some companionship," I had urged her right before I got married. "Paul and I will vet any guy you have interest in. Not all guys disappear."

Of course mine sorta did.

But here I am now, sitting in Fornax, which is Latin for "furnace," across from one of the best-looking guys I have ever seen. He is wearing a caramel-colored turtleneck sweater, which underscores his dark eyes and skin. The sienna-hued interior of the place is warm and cozy, and the lighting is dim, a relief given that Miriam forced me to wear her ultrasheer black blouse instead of a safer, less sexy black wool sweater.

"Cool place," I tell Steve. I am tempted to move a piece of his hair that has just fallen in front of his eyes.

"I thought you'd like it. I remember you told me you were into astronomy."

I look up at the ceiling. It is so blue it is almost black, littered with small patches of white outlined in a bright blue. And there I see it. "You know about the Fornax constellation?"

"Only by complete coincidence. I knew there was a constellation called Fornax Chemica because it looked like a chemical fuel heater or furnace to—"

"Nicolas Louis de Lacaille," I jump in. My interruption is

prompted less by my desire to show him what I know than my excitement at his knowing some of the same stuff.

"You pronounce it better, anyway," Steve says.

"Boy, are you thoughtful."

"It was fun to plan it."

"To planet?" I ask. "Did you plan that?"

"Which would you prefer I answer: yes, I am an earnest geeky sort, or, no, that was a mere coincidence?"

"They both have a certain appeal."

We are flirting.

Steve orders a bottle of wine. "Should I not have done that? Do you like wine?"

"I love wine." I leave out the part that it has been four years since I've had a full glass.

Steve is good at chat. He is careful not to say anything about anybody at school. He does not gossip. That's what he had told me at the coffee shop. This makes me like him even more. He is a man of character, I think to myself. Like Paul.

Or like Paul was.

I stop myself from analyzing the ethics of Paul's betrayal of me. I have prosecuted his actions in my head, with Dr. Schmitt, my mother, Peg, and even Miriam way too many times. I refuse to do it as I eat my lamb couscous with a man who represents possibilities.

"I was a little nervous about asking you out," he says.

Oh yeah, says a voice in my head, but I remain cool and coy. "Why?"

"Weren't you a lady lawyer?" he asks in a silly, old-fashioned manner.

"And that would make you nervous why?" I am in mock-cross mode.

"You'll always have the last word."

"I'm not a last-word kind of gal."

"What does that mean?" He remains playful.

Truth is, I have no idea. I haven't been on a date in so long.

"What made you become a physicist?"

"More significantly, what made you become a lawyer?"

"I love order. I know I shouldn't say that to a physicist." I recall the many allusions to our predetermined entropy.

"People who love order are in all jobs. There's got to be something else."

"I like order coupled with fairness. I, too, took science as a kid. And I remember in fifth-grade lab class doing an experiment with a Bunsen burner and some chemicals. We were required to do a report on what happened when the chemicals were heated."

"Let me guess, you blew up the science lab."

"No, the story is far more boring. I executed the experiment perfectly, but when I got back my lab report, my teacher, Mrs. Carpenter, had given me a C."

"Why?"

"Because when I reported that the chemicals had separated, I spelled *separate* S-E-P-E-R-A-T-E."

"Ah, didn't you know the rule that there is a rat, A-R-A-T, in *separate*?"

"I do now, but I didn't know then. No one did. It wasn't until after we got our reports back that I noticed that all of the other kids had spelled it incorrectly, and many of them were given A's."

"Maybe their findings were more thorough."

"No, Professor, they weren't. When I brought this to Mrs. Carpenter's attention, she said that she was tired of seeing the mistake, and by the time she got to mine, she wanted to make an example of me."

"Harsh."

"Harsh? I cried and screamed. I wrote a letter to her, which I photocopied and gave to the principal, laying out her flawed reasoning."

"Did you get a better grade?"

"No. She said, 'Tell it to the judge.'"

"And?"

"There is no and. I realized the world wasn't fair and I decided to try to do my part."

"By throwing people in jail."

"No. That part is fun."

Steve is easy to talk to. He seems genuinely interested in the anecdotal minutiae of my life, and I am more than happy to disclose these details. The wine is making all of this easy. Without thinking I reach across the table to brush his hair away from his eyes. I let my hand linger on his cheek for a few seconds more than is justifiable. He grabs my hand and starts kissing it.

He leans into me and whispers in my ear, "I am going to pay this check and then I'm going to take you to bed."

Without hesitation I agree, although in the back of my mind a voice is asking me about Molly. Lo and behold, another voice reassures me that my daughter and her grandma will be fine.

Steve gets up and leads me out of the Fornax and into a building across the street.

His apartment.

I can't believe I just had a sleepover with a man as good-looking as Steve Mykonos. I go through the details in my head, but it is hard for me to savor one single moment of our date. The whole evening was like a dance, and not surprisingly the soon-to-be-Dr. Mykonos is a good dancer. More surprisingly, I was not so bad myself, although I have to hand it to my companion's leadership skills. When I first got divorced and entertained vague notions of future sexual encounters, I grimaced at the thought of awkward bra removal and stilted discussions about birth control. Yesterday, just before our date, I dreaded that Steve, smooth, toned, and young, would find me dry and rubbery. If it got to that point.

It did, and he made me feel beautiful and fun.

"You are a vacation," he said to me as he peeled my stockings off.

I couldn't believe his energy. I couldn't believe my energy. I made up for three years of abstinence in one night. I could see myself encouraging my mom to end her dry spell. It's like riding a bike, I would say, except you can't get hurt.

You can't get hurt physically, I remind myself.

My night of love coupled with Steve's alarmingly weak coffee leaves me spent when I get home. However, I've got a double murder to solve. Since Paul is a dead end for me now, I make myself a triple espresso, plant myself at the computer, and do a quick Google search for Phillippa. She is on a thousand committees and gives money to all sorts of charitable ventures that involve art and design. I see nothing about the Winthrop School, though. I narrow my search to look for Phillippa and Winthrop. Nothing. Maybe Liane was mistaken when she said that Phillippa attended Winthrop. It is not characteristic of Phillippa to withhold money from a learning institution.

I look at some of the other articles that provide cursory information on her, and they mention Phillippa and Hawthorne, and Phillippa at Clayton Mortimer's Women's College. Nothing about Phillippa at Winthrop, but Liane was so certain she had gone there. I check out the Winthrop School site. It's beautiful. It's in the Berkshires, so every picture is flooded with tall trees and mesmerizing cloud formations. Somehow, I can't see Phillippa in that venue, although she was quite a bit younger.

I troll around the computer hoping to get something on Winthrop that would lead me to Phillippa. *The Berkshire Source* has a piece dated November 2009 about a married couple, Norm and Betty Chamberlain, who had recently retired after thirty-five years of teaching at Winthrop.

"We can't imagine what life holds for us," Betty was quoted as saying, "but our time at Winthrop has been precious."

Thirty-five years. They must know Phillippa.

I look at the article. They live somewhere in Westchester. I call information. "I'd like the number for Norm and Betty Chamberlain, please."

Within seconds I am connected.

Ring.

Again, I am unprepared, and afraid of exposing my excitement.

"Hello."

Hi. Do you know anything about Phillippa von Eck's police record?

"Hi, this is Kate Rorschach with *New York, New York* magazine. I'm doing a story on the future of boarding schools, and I came across a lovely piece about you. I was struck by your thoughtful comments on teaching, and I wondered if I might be able to speak with you." Nothing wrong with laying it on thick.

"What magazine did you say you were with?"

What magazine did I say? I gulp my coffee, hoping that it will magically provide me the answer. Oh, yes. *"New York, New York."*

"Heard of it. We don't get it. I'm more of a *New Yorker* kind of guy."

Of course you are, although I am relieved. He will see no record of Kate Rorschach.

"As I was saying, I am doing a piece on boarding schools, and I think the article would benefit so much from any insights you and your wife might have. I was wondering if I could interview you?"

"We don't get into the city much."

"Oh. I would come to you." Do reporters really do this? "I could come by your home or, if you would prefer, take you out for coffee."

"Go out for a coffee?" Norm sounds irritated. "We have perfectly good coffee in our house. You will come here."

I have a fun and relaxing weekend. Between the coffee and the naps, I recover from my X-rated evening. Paul comes by on Saturday night for our big family dinner. Whenever my mother is in town, we all eat dinner together for Molly's sake. I feel guilty that she doesn't have a sibling, and my mother feels bad that Molly doesn't have a maternal grandpa.

"We have to make the most of our teeny, tiny family," I tell Peg.

"It seems off to me, but whatever works for all of you. Who am I to judge?"

"You're Peg O'Neill, one of the most judgmental people in the world."

Paul is always game for nights like this. It gives him more

of an excuse to check up on me. He is watching my every move, waiting for another swing incident. He will not be getting it this weekend. I make chicken with figs, which everyone loves. Even Molly, although she says she doesn't like figs or chicken.

"She's got the right spirit," my mother says.

"And I love the cuckoos," Molly's word for "couscous," and possibly Paul's word for me.

Paul brings a bottle of wine, a small bottle of grape juice, and an even smaller bottle of wheatgrass juice. "For Virginia."

"I'm having the wine, too," my mother admonishes Paul. "It's my big family celebration as well."

We steer clear of the tough topics: the murders, the dating, and the divorce. Instead, we focus on Molly.

"I like this almost as much as I like traffic lights," she announces.

Paul and I laugh.

"I expect her to say that on her wedding day," I tell him.

"And her wedding night," he says, and I almost spit out my food.

"It's great to see you laugh, Katie," he says with apparent sincerity.

How amazing that the person who leaves you the most heartbroken is the one who can make you feel this good. At least for the length of the dinner.

I sip my wine.

"Can we play a game?" Molly asks the whole table.

"Of course," my mother says. "What do you want to play?"

Molly widens her eyes and looks at me and then at Paul. Molly points at Paul. "He knows."

"I didn't say we could play."

"But Grandma did, Daddy, and Grandma is our guest."

"She sounds just like you," Paul taps me gently on the wrist.

"What's the game?" my mother asks.

"It's . . ." Molly pauses, looking at me. There's nothing I can do. My mother gave her the go-ahead. "It's Name That Bad Guy."

"What on earth kind of game is that?" my mother asks.

"Yes, Paul," I say, laying the ghoulish burden where it belongs—on him. "Please refresh us as to the rules of the game." I love watching my ex-husband squirm.

"So," Paul responds with slightly forced aplomb, "one person, It, thinks of a bad guy and—"

"And everybody has to ask for hints and they guess," Molly interrupts. "Daddy's really good at it. Aren't you, Daddy?"

I open a new bottle of wine and pretend it's champagne, so that I can toast Paul's discomfort.

"Daddy. You're good at it. Right?"

"Yes," he murmurs.

"What's that?" I say. "I couldn't hear."

"Yes, I'm good at it."

"Yeah. Okay. I'm It," Molly declares.

My mother looks at me for guidance. I am too drunk to figure out a way to tell her that murderers aren't part of the game. "Charles Manson," she says.

"No." Molly laughs. "Grandma's bad at this."

"Ted Bundy?"

"No, Grandma, you're cheating. There's no criminal Ted Bundy."

"We stick with things like stealing," I tell her.

"Do you give up?" Molly screams.

"No, I want some hints," Paul whispers.

" 'Kay. The person was really, really bad."

"As bad as the person who made up this game?" I ask.

"The person was a man," Molly says.

"I could have guessed that." From my mother.

"No, Grandma, plenty of bad guys were ladies. Bonnie was bad."

"Bonnie and Clyde," I remind her.

"And Lindy Ferlin, she was bad, too."

"Lindy Ferlin," Paul throws in. "She's the one who became a bad guy because she didn't go to bed when she was told."

"Oh, that Lindy Ferlin." My mother laughs. "I was thinking of the Lindy Ferlin who was taken away by the authorities for scaring children with stories about criminals."

"Do you give up?" My daughter is jumping while she says it.

"No, if we're going to play, let's play," Paul says. "Is the person American?"

"Yes," Molly says. "He's American, and he's dead, and he's really, really bad."

"Was the person a bank robber?"

"Yes, Daddy. You give up?"

"No, I don't give up. Are you sure he's a robber and not a counterfeiter?"

"No." Molly looks disgusted. "He's not Frank Abagnale, because Frank Abagnale is alive."

"Let's see." I try to recall which criminals Molly knows.

"You give up? It's Specs O'Keefe."

Of course, Specs.

"Of course," Paul says, "Specs."

"Who's Specs O'Keefe?" my mother asks.

"You don't know who Specs O'Keefe is?" Molly asks.

"I'm guessing he's not related to Georgia O'Keeffe."

"Or Michael O'Keefe," Paul says. "He used to be married to Bonnie Raitt."

I realize that I am not the only one of Molly's parents who's drunk.

"The Brinks robbery," Molly tells her grandmother.

"Ah," my mother says.

"Grandma, you should know about it. You were alive then. It was 1950. Did you know Specs O'Keefe?"

"I'm afraid not."

"I say we change the subject." I really want to end this discussion of crime, especially when the biggest Bad Guy of all is attacking our community.

"Okay," Molly says, "Grandma, can Mommy and Daddy and I come to your house?"

"Of course, sweetheart. You are invited anytime, but I would prefer if I were there when you came."

"Because you want to see me?" Molly asks proudly.

"Of course, and because I want to show you around my house myself." My mother refills our wineglasses.

"But I know where everything is. We always enter through the back door because the front door is swollen like a boo-boo and impossible to open. And also because you secretly want everybody to come back and look at your vegetable garden. Inside, you have a cool kitchen, but it's all wood and Daddy is worried that your house will explode. Will it, Grandma?"

"No, sweetheart."

"You have a TV from the old days. It's shaped like a box and doesn't have colors." Molly has suddenly transformed into a savant. "Your living room has a really cool leather rocking horse and a big old grandpa clock that hasn't worked since 1994, and there's pictures of Mommy from when she was a baby, but she was so fat, and a big girl like me." How does Molly know this? "Your floor is too cold, so we all have to wear slippers when we go." Molly is describing my mother's house with extreme accuracy. "You eat off of plates you made in your kilm."

"*Kiln,*" Paul corrects her. "There's an *n*."

"Which one is *n*?" Molly asks.

"The *n* sound, as in nutty little girl," I say. Then I find myself looking at Paul as if to ask, *How does she know this?*

"But then it would be called nilm," Molly continues.

Paul winks at me.

"I'd be happy to show you my nilm, Molly," my mom says.

"Virginia, please." Paul cups Molly's ears with his hands. "That sounds PG-13."

"Nilm should be a place where Dr. Seuss characters travel to," I throw in as I notice my wineglass is again empty.

"Or a scientific measurement," my mother says.

"A Greek letter," Paul offers as he raises his glass to me.

I feel my face grow warm.

"Daddy tells me about Grandma's house. It's our goodnight story," Molly says.

I picture Paul picturing the house I grew up in. He is looking at me.

"Quite a storyteller," I say to him.

"I just tell the truth."

Sometimes.

"Daddy's favorite room is the basement, because that's where he stays when he goes to Grandma's house. Right, Grandma? And, Mommy, where do you sleep?"

Paul and I were still married the last time I was home.

"Molly, can you be a big girl and help Grandma clear the table?" my mother asks. Molly jumps up and scurries out of the room, her sippy cup in her hand.

"My mom is great with the kick-save," I say.

"Indeed," Paul says, playing with the remnants of dinner left on his plate. "This was nice. You are a great cook."

"My repertoire needs expanding."

"Take the compliment, Katie."

I nod at him as I play with the imaginary food on my plate.

"You're a great mom, too."

"Thanks. You're not half-bad at the father job." I grab my plate and then his and head into the kitchen.

I remind myself that I am being nice to Paul because I want information. I can only wonder why on earth he's being so nice to me. But I find that I'm smiling.

"What's so funny?" Molly misreads me.

"Nothing, sweetheart. I was just thinking of you and the nilm."

Sunday morning, Molly and I make a papier-mâché statue of my mother dressed as Athena, goddess of wisdom. In turn, my mother makes me a kitchen-friendly herb garden.

"You seem like you could take care of it now," she says.

"Mom, even in my darkest hours Molly was cared for. I can handle a couple of chives."

"I don't want you to handle them. I want you to enjoy them."

She's right. Chives are best enjoyed homegrown.

I have to give the woman credit. She has shown remarkable restraint in not asking questions about my Saturday-morning return from Steve's.

"You look more yourself," she says as I am passionately polishing cabinet fixtures.

"By *myself*, do you mean tired, hungover, and dirty?"

"No. You are obsessively cleaning, which, for you, means happy and at one with the world."

I consider this. I am sort of happy. I just spent fourteen hours of my life with a beautiful man sharing good food, good conversation, and passion that I didn't know was in me.

"I think I may see a smile."

"Have I been that bad?"

"Yes, but you're making progress."

I see her eyes light on the bra strap hanging out of my purse.

When Peg calls me, I tell her that I am pleased to report her chocolates weren't necessary.

"Tell me everything," she says.

"Not my style," I remind her as I soak the dishes, "but he made me feel really good."

"Are you in love?"

"Totally not."

"I knew it. Too neat?"

"I don't know. Too neat. He's too young. He's Molly's teacher. He's—I don't know, he's—"

"Not Paul?"

"He's obviously not Paul. That's a good thing." Peg isn't willing to fully embrace my fury at Paul. "But he's obviously not something else. I can't put my finger on it. He's not serious. He's not a serious person."

"I thought he was some kind of scholar."

"He's a serious scholar. He's just not a serious person." My nose tickles as the bubbles rise from the sink.

"He's not Paul." Peg will always be a big Paul fan. Not so at first, when I introduced them to each other over lunch at an upscale Japanese restaurant. She gave him a really hard time.

"Some men can't deal with really successful women, did you know that?" she accused him after they shook hands and he alone said nice to meet you.

"I am well aware of those men," he said.

"This one is going to be a star." Peg talked about me as if I couldn't hear.

"I sure hope so."

"You say that, but when she gets regaled at events and dinners, will you be happy to sit quietly and clap?"

"Peg, this is so inappropriate." I was mortified. Paul and I had gone on only six dates, and she was already transforming him into the castrated husband.

"No, she's protecting you. I get it." He then turned to her. "I can tell you this, Peg. My father is the dean of Cornell Medical School and my mother is a pathologist. My father had always wanted to be a doctor, and he is very good. But he is a better administrator. He has a gift for medical education. Practicing medicine is his passion. My mother on the other hand is perhaps the most well-regarded physician in her field. She has published more than four hundred articles on surgical pathology. She's been honored more times than I can count. And my father, knowing that his wife is better than he is at the thing he loves doing more than anything else in the world, is simply proud of her. Those are my role models."

Peg was practically crying. "You got me. But you better not be full of shit because after lunch I will go home and google your parents. If you told me a false word, I will make this little romance here very difficult for you."

But Peg knew he had been telling the truth. She even paid for the meal: high-end sushi. At our wedding, Peg joked she wanted to give me away. "That mother of yours is pretty great, so I'll be your dad." Within months, she was treating Paul like a son, the way she might treat David and Matthew when they reach their thirties. "He's an excellent man."

Peg had a more difficult time accepting Paul's betrayal than I did. For weeks, she refused to believe he had cheated on me. While I was hurt by her stubborn stance, I knew she wanted what was best for me. Given our work and age dynamic, I may have put her on an unrealistic pedestal from which she had to come down.

"I usually have a nose for this," she said. "He didn't seem like that."

I reminded her that she'd been so impressed with the aspect of Paul as husband of a successful career woman, she never considered his reaction to my being a failure.

"You are not a failure. You're on a detour," Peg had said, despondent over the split. "But maybe you can work it out." She remained hopeful. When it became clear that no working out would be done, she decided that I should find a guy who was Paul minus the cheating.

Steve is not Paul, but he's not completely different. Like Paul, he has a lot of stuff. His minuscule one-bedroom apartment is bursting with collector's items: two old typewriters, a vintage steam calibrator, a Sans & Streiffe microscope, a shelf of stamp albums, and a Mexican-machete collection.

"I'm a collector of things," he'd announced when he'd seen me studying his objects.

Peg and I hang up. And there it is: the overly familiar knock at the door. Do I tell Paul that it's not a good time and slam the door on him as he did to me? Maybe I should revoke his privileges and force him to call me every time he wants to pop by.

I answer the door. But first I splash a little cold water on my face.

"Hi," he says enthusiastically.

"Hi," I say without affect.

"I didn't mention this the other night in front of Virginia and Molly, but I'm sorry about the other day. I was just conducting some business."

Oh, really. I was conducting business, too. With a hot physicist. "No worries," I say.

"I thought you always said *no worries* was code for 'how dare you.'" Paul laughs. He's right. I did and do. It is a phrase employed by passive-aggressives all over these United States.

"I've grown out of that." I'm seething inside.

"Really."

"Really."

We share an extended silence.

"So, you're okay?" he asks.

"Why wouldn't I be?"

During these pauses I want to yell at him and ask him why he thought so little of me that he would cheat on me. Sometimes I want to ask him why he didn't help me more. And when he leaves, I want to cry. Always. But now, I have a distraction, his computer. Actually I have two distractions. The computer and Steve.

"Great," he says awkwardly. He's sounded like this since we separated, as if he's hoping that my voice will be filled with forgiveness.

More silence. He reaches his hand to my face. For a nanosecond or millisecond—whichever is shorter—I forget that this is the man who betrayed me.

"You have . . ." He is gently touching my cheek.

Shit. My face is wet. I mop it inelegantly with the back of my forearm. "I'm cleaning."

"Cleaning." Paul raises an eyebrow.

"Cleaning." He is sort of smiling. "What?"

"You really are okay."

Now he thinks everything is fine. Good for him. We transition into a change of subject by another awkward silence. I have to keep my eye on the prize.

"What brings you to these parts?" I say it a tad seductively, hating myself only a little.

"I was checking in on you, but I don't think it's necessary. You seem, as you say: great. You seem relaxed." Paul, I am noticing, does not seem relaxed.

"I guess so." But I don't want to seem too relaxed. I want his computer.

"Great. I just want you to know that your well-being is important to me." So that's why you slept with another woman while I was your wife.

"That's really kind of you. Your well-being is important to me too." Can I see the computer now?

"Just be careful, Katie," he says. Am I hallucinating or is he staring at the bra strap still hanging out of my purse?

"So, I'll see you." I shut the door.

The computer thing is not happening right now.

Molly, my mother, and I plan a touristy Sunday in the city. Miriam, clad in fur from head to toe, encumbered by a medium-size orange tree, comes by just as we are leaving.

"Where are you going?" she asks.

"We were going to take Molly to the special winter carousel event in Central Park and then to the zoo."

"But I brought you this tree. Isn't it just perfect? I saw this and I thought of you."

I must admit the tree is pretty impressive. "Miriam, the tree is marvelous," I say, choosing a word she has been saying as of late. "Maybe you can come by later so I can thank you properly. My mother is here and we have a whole urban-outdoors day planned."

"But couldn't we welcome the tree?" Miriam asks, petulant.

"I want to go fishing." Molly echoes her tone.

My mother, without thinking, has told her that people fish in Central Park.

"Maybe," I say. *Maybe* is my word for *no*.

"*Maybe* is your word for *no*," Molly says.

"I'll take her fishing," Miriam says.

For a moment I picture Miriam in her fur, grabbing a wriggling fish with her teeth. Then I do a double take.

"You want to take my daughter fishing? It's way uptown, you know."

"I know," Miriam says, "but I thought we could be best girlfriends and fish."

"Do you know how to fish?" Molly asks.

"Miss Molly. You can take the girl out of Colorado, but you can't take Colorado out of the girl," she sings as she rearranges her ermine muff. There is some truth to what she is saying; Miriam, my mother, and I spent many summer days fishing for trout in Gore Creek. She has never once brought up this memory before, and I wonder why the sudden interest in Molly.

"Just so you know"—she turns to me—"my relationship is still fabulous. Knock wood!"

Oh, that's why. "Does your entrepreneur have kids?"

"No, but we may want them."

Really?

"Really?" my mother asks.

"We've talked about it. On our first night together, in fact.

He was with a woman before, a single mom, with a kid, and he got really attached to her."

"The mom?"

Miriam gives me a sinister look. "No, the kid. He carries the picture around. Well, I just think that is so sweet."

"It is really sweet," I agree. "So you want to borrow Molly?"

"Oh. I don't mean like that. I just thought it would be really cool to get to know her. I mean, how does a four-year-old think?"

"They like cookies and fun," my mother says.

"And pretty ladies." I'm thinking of Willa.

"I like traffic lights and confers," Molly says.

Miriam asks her how to spell *confer*.

"I don't know how to spell. Look at it in the computer."

"Did she just tell me to look at the computer?"

"That's what Daddy says he's going to do when he doesn't know anything. He looks at the computer. The computer knows how to spell. That's what my daddy says."

Funny, I want to look at Daddy's computer.

"Molly, can I get a picture of you next to the tree?" Miriam whips out her bright pink cell phone.

"No," Molly answers.

"That's not nice, Molly. Miriam wants a picture of you." I turn to Miriam. "To show the boyfriend?"

"Oh, no," she says disingenuously. "Don't you just love the tree?"

Miriam walks over to the windowsill in the kitchen. She picks up Molly's class picture from her first year at Hawthorne and studies it. "Can I have this one?"

"No, that's my class," Molly scolds her. "That's all my best friends."

"When was this taken?" I have no idea what Miriam's agenda is.

"Close to a year ago. It was her class picture from last year."

"So I bet you guys don't even look the same."

"Yeah, we do," Molly says.

I shake my head so that she can't see me. "Some of the kids look different. Last year Tess had Little Orphan Annie hair, only dark, and this year her mom has let her grow it out."

"Tess looks completely different," Miriam says. "Are you worried that Mommy will forget what you looked like?"

"Mommy won't forget. Mommy has more than fourteen pictures of me." Molly has just learned to count to fourteen.

"Molly, let her take the picture."

Molly stands up, flings her arms out, and shows all of her teeth.

"Try to look more natural," Miriam instructs her.

"Miriam, she's letting you take the picture."

"This works," she says. "Okay. Got to go."

"Aren't we going fishing?" Molly asks.

"Your mommy said no," Miriam says quickly. "I'm glad you love the tree. Isn't it great?"

After Miriam leaves, Molly asks me, "Did you really say no, Mommy?"

"No, sweetheart. Miriam just wanted to show your picture to her new boyfriend. She wants him to know she likes kids."

"But she doesn't like kids," Molly says.

"We all act crazy when we're desperate," Mom explains.

"What's *desperate*?" Molly asks.

I pick up Molly from school. Paul dropped her off this morning. I wonder if I will see Steve. I notice Liane coming down the stairs as I go up. She doesn't look herself. Her silk shirt is completely wrinkled, her unkempt braid doesn't do her long hair any justice, and she's not wearing her signature earrings. Instead of looking casually chic, she looks casually homeless.

"Hey there," I call to her.

"Oh. Hello."

She sounds cold. This is the second time in one week. Did I misjudge Liane? I was so sure she would be my mom buddy. Like the ones you see in commercials musing about fussy eaters and persistent stains. But I can't tell if she is acting weird or if I have lost all social senses. The me of five years ago would ignore her coolness, chalk it up to something going on in her own life, and suggest a new coffee date. The new me is damaged.

Steve is in the preschool office helping incompetent Bree work the fax machine. He is wearing perfectly pressed khakis and a blue pin-striped oxford shirt. I try to meet his gaze. I have a quick vision of him throwing me on Ms. Druvier's table and taking all my clothes off with his teeth.

"Mommmeeee." Molly snaps me out of it. "Mommee," she says again, as I haven't responded quickly enough. "I have something for you." Her pink coat is falling off. She rearranges it and checks her pocket. She looks confused for a second and then digs into the empty NYPD backpack she'd insisted her daddy give her. She pulls out a crumpled ball of paper and hands it to me.

"For me?" It looks nothing like the reams of paint-splattered construction paper projects she comes home with.

"Uh-huh. Open it." I unfold it and read, *My apartment tomorrow? 6? (p.m.).* It is signed *S*.

Steve gave Molly this love note for me. How bold!

How unprofessional!

How sexy!

Thank goodness Molly doesn't know how to read.

He walks by me again. I nod at him, not certain where this little romance is going. I was being honest with Peg when I said I wasn't in love with the guy, but I'm drawn to him.

"Katie?"

Paul. What is Paul doing at school? I feel resentful when he's here. I know he's a parent, but it's one of the few places I don't associate with him. We are rarely here at the same time. We joined the school after the divorce was final, and I am starting to make a life here that is completely unrelated to Paul. I have a friend. I have a love interest, a like interest—an interest. I don't want to feel the combination of pain and anger here.

I can't help looking at him. Habit and curiosity often trump mental health. Is he scruffier than usual today, or is it that he is scruffy compared with Steve? I crumple the paper and put it in my pocket.

"Did I screw up the schedule?" I ask him, even though I am certain that it is my turn to pick up Molly.

"Oh, no. Nothing like that." Paul puts his hands in his pockets. For a second, he seems not like himself. He looks uncomfortable. Aha. Could it be that he saw me looking at Steve?

I feel smug. You're not the only one who's sneaking around behind closed doors. You may have Willa, but I have Adonis. Does he have Willa? My mother isn't convinced. She claims that Paul isn't into young pretty things.

"Was I never young and pretty?" I'd asked her.

"That's ridiculous," she'd snapped. "Of course you were. But Paul was into you despite your fabulous looks and youth. He would definitely be more interested in a woman of substance."

"What if Willa is a young woman of substance who happens to be hot?"

"I spent an afternoon with her. She is delightful. She is pretty. But a woman of substance she is not." I must admit that my mother's assessment provided me with some pleasure.

Paul scoops up Molly. "I just wanted to surprise my girl."

Ms. Druvier emerges from her office. "Detective Alger. Mrs. Alger." Like the pope, she doesn't recognize divorce.

"Hi, Ms. Druvier," Molly sings.

"Well, hello, Molly."

There is a pause. I have noticed that Ms. Druvier, despite her lengthy tenure as school director, is not always sure what to say to the children.

Paul looks at me. He's not here to see Molly. He's not here to see me. He's here on business.

Molly and I leave. She is insisting that we go out for hot chocolate. Bitsy, apparently, has hot chocolate every day—sometimes even twice. She has been talking about it at school, bragging about it.

"I told Bitsy I never had hot chocolate," Molly said.

"I think you are too young for it."

Molly is a spiller. She can have the hot chocolate when she goes to college.

"Bitsy says that she never had any hot chocolate until her mommy died. Now she has hot chocolate all the time. I told her that I wanted hot chocolate with my mommy before she died. Can we have hot chocolate?"

I guess I can deal with a few spills.

We get home, and Miriam is in the house, sitting on our banquette, wearing a pink Valentino suit, and holding a patent-leather Yves St. Laurent clutch on her lap.

"Hello, old friend," Miriam says. "Your mom and I have been having a lovely time."

My mother has a glazed look on her face.

"I have got to go," Miriam tells me.

After she leaves, I say to my mother, "Did she want a free counseling session?"

"I'm stumped," my mother says. Miriam's the daughter Mom keeps from the neighbors, but she's a link back home.

"Why the interest in Molly?"

"I don't know if it's Molly per se," she says. "She says she's in love. Maybe she really does want children."

I can't imagine Miriam with a child. She ran away when I was having Molly. Paul had called her when Molly was born. She was on the short list of people to call. I thought she could put her self-absorption on pause while she met my kid. Instead, she left for Los Angeles on an "emergency" within twenty-four hours of Paul's call.

"I have to take care of something," she had told him gravely.

A few days later I got a long-winded e-mail from her telling me that we were best friends and that she wanted to be there for me, but she had gained too much weight. She realized this when she had to buy size-four clothes, which was just not acceptable. She would go to her favorite L.A. spa.

They know how to take care of this stuff here, she wrote. *It's just that with these seven pounds, I may as well kiss my career good-bye.*

"What career?" Paul had said. "What kind of friend does this? A spa?"

I agreed with Paul. And the e-mail did not exactly smack of the truth. "I'm thinking lipo."

"I'm thinking wacko," Paul said.

Miriam would not have been much help had she been here,

but her sudden departure was jarring. Admittedly, once she returned, she looked terrific. And I can't forget that she sent me a couture layette. She must have put on a bit of weight as I recalled how she looked before she'd gone to the spa, but it was hard to assess given that I had gained about a thousand pounds. Now, Miriam was back to her near-beautiful/near-emaciated self. But the work never seemed to resume.

"Grandma, are you ready?" Molly asks.

Molly has emerged from her room in an orange party dress, black-and-white-striped tights, and blue crocs. Grandma promised to take her to the traffic-light exhibit at the Museum of the City of New York. Molly has been looking forward to this for weeks.

"Are you sure you don't want to come with us?" my mother asks. "I don't think it's good for you to sit around with nothing to do."

"Oh, I think I'll be fine. You guys have fun."

"Grandma, can I put on some of your lipstick? I want to look pretty."

"Sure." My mother pulls out an organic Chapstick and applies it to Molly's lips.

"Beautiful," Grandma says as she nudges her granddaughter to look at herself in the mirror.

"Beautiful," Molly agrees as she twirls in front of the mirror.

"You sure you'll be all right?" my mother asks.

"Fine. Don't I seem fine?"

"You seem fine. Maybe a little on edge.

"Go," I tell her.

Five minutes after Molly and my mother leave, I throw on my coat and head to Grand Central to meet with Betty and Norm.

I take a train to Croton Falls. It is a seventy-six-minute ride. When we spoke on the phone, Norm told me there was a taxi stand right outside the station.

"Don't dawdle, though. If you don't grab a car right after you get out, they figure you're not interested."

I hurry off the train and grab a taxi. The driver is a fleshy, translucent-skinned fellow who is smoking the last centimeter of his cigarette.

"Where to, ma'am?" I can't tell if he is speaking through a mechanical larynx or if those are his original vocal cords.

"Two sixty-three Palmer Road."

"You up from the city?" He lights another cigarette.

"Yes, I am."

"Good for you. Get some fresh air."

"I agree." I squelch my urge to cough.

"What are you doing up here in the countryside?"

I'm trying to figure out if Phillippa von Eck killed Beverly Hastings and Johanna Crump. "Just visiting friends."

"You'll never want to leave. We've got everything here you have in the city. We've got stores and a movie theater." He pronounces it thee-ate-er. "They have a gourmet store in the town, too."

"Good to know."

"Yup. You seem like a nice young lady. Don't let the city corrupt you."

"Uh-huh." I am eager to leave his car.

"You married?"

"No."

"A pretty thing like you should get married. You don't want to die alone."

I am shtupping my daughter's hot nursery-school teacher if it makes you feel any better. "Good advice."

"Glad to help out." The car stops. "Here y'are."

I bolt out of the car. Norm and Betty live in a sea-foam-colored home. Together, they are waiting for me in a white, screened-in porch. The two are sitting on a wooden bench holding hands, drinking lemonade—as if in a commercial for AT&T or a discount life-insurance company. They exude care and concern, even from several feet away.

They stand up. Betty is wearing a tan safari jacket and white pants. She looks as if she studied makeup application under Carol Channing, though the lipstick is in the vicinity of her lips. Norm sports a bright orange polo shirt, khakis, and enormous white sneakers.

"Ms. Rorschach?" I recall Norm's clear voice from our phone conversation.

"Kate. May I call you Norm?"

"Please do."

"And please call me Betty," his wife says in a sophisticated 1940s movie accent.

"Thank you, Betty." I adjust my navy pin-striped pantsuit, wishing I had opted for a more comfortable wardrobe.

"Would you like some lemonade?"

"Sure."

"We add a little something."

I'm not sure how to respond. Is this what happens when people retire? They spike their early-afternoon lemonade? I take a sip. Betty awaits my reaction.

"Mint," she says. "People think it's something complicated, but I just mince a little mint and put it in at the end."

I am relieved.

"You thought we spiked it, dintcha?" Norm says, laughing.

I start laughing. The Chamberlains have put me at ease.

"Kate, what can we tell you?"

"I am doing a piece for *New York, New York* on boarding schools, as I told you, and I just wanted to hear some of your insights." It feels horrible lying to these people.

"What kind of stuff?"

"I'd like to focus on character building rather than academics. I know a lot of parents send their kids to boarding school because they believe it will shape them in a way that is community-oriented." I am making everything up as I speak.

"We found that to be the case. The girls at Winthrop, for the most part, saw their classmates as extended family members."

I am not so bad at this. Is that a good thing?

"We both came from day-school teaching situations. The girls who board are forced to figure out a way to live together even if they are not naturally disposed to liking each other," Betty says.

"What we saw is that some of the girls who detested each other right off the bat became fast friends after a few months or so."

"That must have been very rewarding."

"Extremely. I think it's why we stayed so long." Norm squeezes Betty's hand. "We never had kids of our own, and we took these relationships very seriously."

"You guys should write a movie."

"That would be a hoot," Norm says.

"Or a television program" comes from Betty.

Having been a child fan of *The Facts of Life,* I agree with her. "Do you have any examples? You know what they say. The devil is in the details." Is that what they say? What if Norm and Betty are offended by my invocation of Satan?

I should have scripted this on the train rather than daydreaming about the fictional day when Paul learns about Steve and me. Paul will tell me how surprised he is at how quickly

I've moved on. He'll ask me if Steve knows anything about Booker T. Podge and his notorious gang of four and a half. The half stands for his cohort who tried to turn him in to the police and was later found sliced in two. Paul will ask me if Steve knows anything about Risa, the first transgendered individual to be tried for murder. She had been charged for killing her boyfriend when she was a man, but was 90 percent in transition at the time of her trial. The jury was deadlocked: half of them bought her insanity defense and half thought he had been perfectly sane when he stabbed his Realtor boyfriend nineteen times.

Paul's interrogation will conclude as, in a whisper, he inquires whether Steve has taken the time to learn that the bright white dwarf star Regulus is part of Leo. The lion's foot, to be exact. I will tell him that the answer is most likely no to all of his questions, although I can't for certain say that about Regulus as Steve did know about Fornax. But that wouldn't matter, I will utter from my solar plexus, because Steve said the seven magic words to me, seven words that never seemed to occur to Paul: *That must have been hard for you.*

And, as far as I can tell, Steve isn't going to any seminars.

"Loads," Betty says, bringing me back to a question I'd almost forgotten I'd asked.

"Any you would care to share?"

"We often saw that odd girls would get shunned by the group. For example, three years ago, it was brought to our attention that one of our freshmen obsessively applied suntan lotion, even when she was inside. Some of the girls complained of the smell."

"It was Bain de Soleil orange gel," Norm throws in.

"Yes, that's right, Bain de Soleil gel. And people complained about the smell and the color. Others said they were concerned about her. But they really just wanted to embarrass her."

"Betty"—Norm is worked up—"tell her about the toothpaste."

"Oh, yes, the toothpaste. That very girl went through a phase where she ate nothing but toothpaste. We all thought she would die. First from the lack of nutrition, and—"

"Then the fact that toothpaste is potentially toxic," Norm cuts her off. "You have all those warnings on the box. The classmates were merciless. One of them dressed as a tooth with sunglasses for Halloween and wore a big sign saying, 'I am . . .'—we can't give you her name of course."

"Of course. How horrible." I write all of this stuff down even though it is useless to me.

"It is horrible," Betty says, "but then the dean of students called a huge meeting about bullying and all that. The meanest girls in the class ended up in tears and befriended the toothpaste girl. These are all learning moments."

"Learning moments," I repeat as if it were crucial, while writing on my pad.

"They used to have these clubs called junior sororities, and the girls would engage in all sorts of hazing activities," Betty continues.

"Hmm." This may be relevant to Phillippa. She is the sorority-hazer type. "Did the girls drink?"

"Oh, no. The incidents were typically hair-related. One year, the older girls snuck up on their pledges and put Nair on their heads for the entire night. When the girls woke up, they thought they had been soaped and washed their hair. But their hair came right off."

"That sounds criminal," I say, trying to sound as un-law-enforcement-like as possible. "Did they go to jail?"

"Oh, no, it stayed within the school. We liked to handle these pranks. Jail can ruin the lives of these girls forever. The school thought it was in a better position to handle this."

And that's what the parents were paying for. "Did anyone ever go to jail for this stuff?"

Objection. Leading question.

"Only one that we can remember," Norm says. "There was one girl we considered genetically cruel. Nothing in the Winthrop experience could have shaped her. She was engineered to be mean."

I bet this is Phillippa. "Was she one of those popular mean-leader types?"

"Not really. She didn't make friends easily, but she did get what she wanted." Norm is shaking his head.

"People were scared of her," Betty cuts in. "You just knew looking at her that she had power. She was rich certainly, but not the richest girl in the school. She was smart enough—"

I cut Betty off in a most nonjournalistic manner. "Was she pretty?"

"There was something crisp about the entire package, but pretty she wasn't."

"She had bad ankles," Norm announces.

I love you, Norm. This *was* Phillippa.

"Did she graduate from the school?" I probe.

"She did. In degree only. She finished her coursework at home and they mailed her the paperwork."

"Because she had been put away," Norm reminds Betty

"Ah, yes. Now I remember. This girl was incarcerated."

"You mean, like prison?" Phillippa. Phillippa. Phillippa.

"Exactly." Betty was getting excited. "She did something quite horrible. There was a girl in her class who came from farther away than most of the girls did back then. It was mostly

New York, some New England, a little California, and an occasional Texan. Well, there was a girl from Casper, Wyoming, in the class. She was incredibly homesick. And she brought with her a pet bird—"

"Screechy," Norm interrupts.

"Norm. Shame on you. His name was Jingo," Betty addresses me, "but all the girls called him Screechy behind her back."

"Yes"—Norm chuckles to himself—"because he was so, so—"

"Loud?" I offer.

"Yes. Loud." Betty smiles. "The bird was, by all accounts, nettling. And yet, when you saw the girl with her pet, she lit up. It was quite lovely really. Especially because she was not terribly confident."

"She was odd," Norm says.

"She was odd," Betty repeats, "but in an agreeable way. She didn't quite know how to put herself together. Her hair was always a mess, and she didn't have some of the things the other girls had. They all had carried a certain kind of knapsack."

"A Watkin," Norm says.

"A Watkin. That was it. She didn't have one, but she went to New York and must have gotten a Wotkin. W-O-T-K-I-N. With an o, you see. A counterfeit in Chinatown."

"All the girls made fun of her," Norm says wistfully. "Eventually, the girls stopped because she was really quite nice and bright. Except for the cruel one. She refused to acknowledge her."

"The one with the bad ankles?" I am disingenuousness itself.

"Yup," Norm sighs.

"I think she was genuinely offended that the girl came from Wyoming," Betty cuts in.

"I can see that," I add, picturing Phillippa snubbing her nose at a fellow Westerner.

"You can?" Betty asks.

"Oh, we get a lot of that in New York City," I throw in quickly. "Especially in the magazine industry."

Betty seems comfortable with my answer because she continues, "The bird screamed every day, and the cruel girl became less and less tolerant of it. One day, she went into the odd girl's room, snapped the birdcage open, and pulled Jingo out. Then she broke the bird's neck. She dropped the poor thing on the floor and left the room. She neither bragged about the event nor hid it from anybody. Her only comment was 'Finally.' "

"What happened?" I gulp.

"It just so turned out," Norm says, "that the bird girl knew quite a few important people. We had heard that she came to boarding school because of some family upheaval. The upheaval was in fact that her father had just been elected by the people of Wyoming to serve in the Senate."

"And in those sorts of jobs, people have all kinds of connections," Betty chimed in. "Within two days, the police had come to the school. The cruel girl had fancy lawyers behind her, but there was nothing she could do."

"What goes around, comes around, I always say," Norm said.

"You don't always say that."

"You're right, dear, but it sure came around here."

"I'll say," I say. "So she went to prison?"

"She did. For just about thirty days. It was a special kind of prison, but she was incarcerated. And they never let her back in the school. She would be allowed to say that she'd graduated from there if she took the rest of her courses at home."

"And that was only because the family donated an obser-vatory."

An observatory. I must bring up my interest in astronomy with Phillippa if I ever get the chance.

"Do you know what's become of her?" I ask.

"Which one? The bird girl is in fact an ornithologist. She lives in Ecuador and is very happy."

"How terrific," I say.

"And the other one"—Norm senses my curiosity—"I have no idea. My guess is she just became a self-important society lady."

"I always tell Norm she is a serial killer." Betty laughs. "You know, they start with small animals."

I've heard.

On the train home, I think about my meeting with Norm and Betty with satisfaction. We talked for over three hours. They seemed to genuinely like each other. And, for that mat-ter, me.

I felt bad when they urged me to send them a copy of the article.

It is close to six o'clock when I get home. My mother has just called to say that she and Molly went to Noodle Works for dinner. There is no need for me to rush home. I walk uptown from Grand Central, reminding myself how pretty Park Ave-nue is this time of year. I find myself two blocks from the pre-cinct, Paul's precinct.

Suddenly, despite everything, I'm compelled to tell him about Phillippa and the bird. After all, he may have more facts of this nature. Is he even aware of her record? Are he and Peg even comparing notes? He should know about this if the killer is going to be stopped. I find myself walking up the steps into his workplace. No one even questions my being at the precinct. I was a fixture there for so many years and I share a child with a detective. I head over to Paul's desk. He isn't there. It looks as if he's gone for the day. Not because he has achieved any sense of tidiness. In fact, his desk is more cluttered than ever. There are about fifteen pictures of Molly. I am proud to say that I appear in two of them. He has several superhero figurines, three not-quite-empty rolls of wintergreen Life Savers, and an array of mechanical puzzles. His chair is pushed under his desk. That is so Paul. Leave a mess, but place the chair symmetrically under the desk.

I head out the door to go home, and I see Paul from the precinct stairs. He's not with Willa, but he is with a woman. Their forearms are grazing each other. They are walking toward me. She is pretty, with brown, wavy Rita Hayworth hair and lemon-shaped eyes like the starlets of the sixties, high cheekbones, and clear but not completely youthful skin. I'm thinking mid-thirties? She's wearing a mink coat. It's hard for me to picture Paul with a fur lady. Suddenly the thought of him with Willa the Gap girl doesn't seem so bad.

Fur!

More annoying, the coat makes it impossible to assess accurately her figure, but I assume she is thin with curves in the right places.

"Kate, what a nice surprise," Paul says as if we were colleagues.

"To be sure," I declare as if I were working on a law review article.

The woman extends her hand. She is wearing a clunky emerald bracelet. "Ellen Westin," she says.

"Kate Al—I mean Hagen," I exhale. What happened to the

ease of conversation I enjoyed over minty lemonade with the Chamberlains?

"What brings you here?" Paul asks. "I hope everything is okay?"

"I was in the neighborhood." My lie is quick. "Living near here and all. It was such a pretty day. I thought I would walk and enjoy New York. You don't get days like this every day."

The bling decorating Ellen's earlobes looks like the disco ceiling of Studio 54, circa 1986. I feel the tears make their way through my eyes. I don't know why. Humiliation, most likely. Paul is probably feeling validated after most certainly confiding to lemon eyes about my bizarre postbaby breakdown. He got out of that marriage just in time, they will agree as soon as they leave my earshot and take a taxi. Better yet, her driver will take them to a swanky art opening.

As I will the tears from making their presence public, a new emotion takes over.

Indignation.

While he is enjoying her diamonds and furs, I am doing his job!

"I should go. I think Molly is home waiting for me. Nice to meet you, Ellen," I shout. Then I walk as briskly as I can back home.

And instead of engaging in my typical behavior, which includes crying with intermittent self-reminders that Paul is a lothario, that he is insensitive, I focus on how I'll never get to his computer.

I get home. Molly is all fresh and clean. She has taken all of her books off her shelf and placed them in five tall piles in the front hall.

"Molly, are those towers?" I ask proudly.

"No, they are books."

"Great."

"Mama, read them to me."

"I can read a few, but there are over a hundred books here."

"That's okay," Molly insists. "I don't mind. I have time."

I sit down to read the books to Molly. I get through twenty-seven of them before she asks me if it is okay for her to go to bed. At first, her request for me to read to her had seemed burdensome, but after getting through every Dr. Seuss we had, in addition to the trials and tribulations of Puddles the three-legged dog, I feel comforted. Molly needs me. She and I, at least, are a team.

I feel empty. My newfound chirpiness after the Chamberlain visit has given way to a feeling of loss.

"You okay?" My mom is in the doorway.

"I'm great," I say, not feeling great. "I saw Paul today." I pause. "With a woman."

"The babysitter?"

"No, I think you were right about her. No, this was a real woman. Someone substantial. I mean she was old. Old like me," I correct myself. "Not *old* old. And rich. Her outfit and her jewelry cost more than this apartment. She looked like Mrs. Howell from *Gilligan's Island,* a few years younger, with long hair. Paul must be attracted to her money."

"Did that bother you?"

"Of course it bothers me. Everyone is getting killed, and Paul is jetting around like a bon vivant."

"But, sweetheart, you had that nice date the other night. As I recall, I didn't hear you come in until the next morning."

"That has nothing to do with it." I am officially annoyed.

"Paul is negligent. Doesn't it bother you that I'm paying taxes for his salary so that he can run around with some woman while we're being terrorized by a maniac?!" I realize I am screaming.

"If that's what's bothering you."

"Yes, that is what is bothering me." I exhale and unearth the ironing board.

"Again, sweetheart, how about the nice date?"

"He doesn't have any long-term potential." As evolved as my mother is, I can't tell her that that was just great sex. We must speak in euphemism. "There's something missing there." Years lived.

"Kate. You shouldn't fall in love with the first guy you date. It's all right to be attracted to someone, enjoy his company, and know that this is not a lifelong event. You, too, deserve to have fun."

"'It is fun to have fun,' said the Cat in the Hat," I say for the second time tonight.

"Precisely. And you need to read some books that aren't for preschoolers."

It is 6:15 p.m. and I am ringing Steve's bell. We haven't communicated since I got his note yesterday. He opens the door immediately and kisses me lightly on the cheek. He's wearing a forest-green polo shirt under a gray V-neck sweater. His wavy hair is neatly combed except for the one errant clump that falls over his eyebrow, beckoning me to touch it.

"I thought we might grab dinner." He's holding my waist.

I stop myself from saying, *Whatever*. Sure, dinner with Steve is fun, but I was hoping for a roll in the hay.

"Sounds terrific." I was raised right.

We walk a few blocks to a place called Mejor.

"Do you like tapas?" he inquires.

"Terrific," I repeat.

We walk in. The restaurant is warm and cozy. It is made entirely of wood.

"Can I help you?" a Spanish-accented hostess wants to know.

"Could we sit at the bar?" Steve requests. "It's atmospheric."

We sit at the corner of a wraparound bar. Steve pushes two chairs close together and signals me to sit on one of them. "The tables seem a little formal." He puts his hand on my leg.

I like where this is going.

"Are you a meat eater?"

"I beg your pardon?"

Steve smiles. "Are you a vegetarian?"

"I was for about three weeks in eleventh grade."

He calls to the bartender. "One pitcher of sangria and a charcuterie platter." And he says, "I hope it wasn't too forward of me to order your beverage."

"No more so than it was for you to put your hand on my leg."

"I don't see you complaining about that."

"Exactly."

"So, what have you been doing since I last saw you?" he asks.

"You know. The usual." Taking a day trip to Croton only to learn that Phillippa is at the very least a convicted animal killer, not to mention meeting my ex's new rich girlfriend. "How about you?"

"Same here. Teaching, writing. Thinking."

"Thinking is good."

"Thinking about you."

I blush. The bartender gives us our sangria just as the wait-ress comes by with a beautiful array of meats.

"These look great."

"Eat. Eat."

I help myself to a few pieces of pork.

"Don't forget the figs," Steve reminds me. "That's what makes this dish."

"Been here a lot?"

"A lot."

We eat in silence, but I find that the sangria is more delicious than the food. On my way to Steve's apartment earlier this evening, I realized that our conversation topics are limited. I could probably talk to him for hours on end about how hot he is, throw in another fifteen minutes on the subject of our menu, and maybe seven and a half minutes on Molly. Then there would be nothing. But as we drink our sangria, I am pleasantly surprised by the smoothness of our exchange.

I flash for a moment to Paul, arms around Ellen Westin. They look good together. He's handsome; she's pretty. I take another sip. Steve and I look good together, too. I vividly recall my breathless writhing a few days ago. This man and I have chemistry. I take another sip.

"I have a confession to make," Steve says.

Please don't tell me you're married.

"I have a crush on you. I mean huge."

I can live with that. A gorgeous, brilliant, caring man. Fuck Ellen Westin and Paul—I'm slurring the words in my head. I have something better and younger. I'm back. I mean really back. This week I went to Westchester by myself and basically solved the mommy murders. Paul, with his computer and his new girlfriend—I mean, his new *old* girlfriend—is still at square one.

Suddenly, I'm awash in confidence. I'm turned on by Steve. Frankly, I'm turned on by myself. I had Betty and Norm eating out of my hand.

"What I would give to know what you're thinking," Steve whispers seductively.

"I'm thinking Phillippa von Eck killed Bitsy's mommy," I whisper back.

"You can't be serious." Steve is almost laughing.

I know I should keep my mouth shut about this stuff, but it's so pleasurable to talk about it. I feel so capable and at the same time so wanted.

"I think she killed Bitsy's mommy and I think she killed Caleb's mommy."

I want to tell him everything. I know it's the drink, the ambience, the attraction, and I know it is completely inappropriate. That said, I want to tell him about the Hastings home, and about sneaking into Peg's computer and Paul's, too. Especially Paul's. The man who's off gallivanting with lemon eyes, while I'm keeping our city safe.

"I love Molly's sense of humor, and yours is even better." Steve is laughing.

He doesn't get it. He's a nerdy scientist who makes my knees weak. I realize I can't tell him. Not just yet. I'll wait until we are lying in sweat-soaked sheets after several hours of lovemaking. I predict this will be at about eleven thirty.

As far as I'm concerned, Steve can't pay the check fast enough.

"Do you want to go somewhere else to grab another drink?" he asks.

Oh, no. "Can we get back to your place?"

"Your wish is my command." As we walk, Steve encircles my hand with his. "I like this."

This is feeling a little too boyfriend-girlfriend for me, but I'm on fire. I keep my hand in his. We walk in silence.

His apartment feels different to me from the way it did the other night. It feels almost as if someone were here. It may be that I am spending way too much time on these murders.

"Will you excuse me for a sec?" Steve heads into the bathroom. "Make yourself at home."

I try, but the place feels less homey than it did the other night. I go into his bedroom, hoping the reminder of previous events will be inspiring.

I look at his bookshelves. He has way too many reading materials devoted to physics. Half of them I can't understand. Oh, good. I realize that that's because they are in German. He doesn't have much fiction; a few used Shakespeare paperbacks that he probably read in college. He has a collection of America's best erotic poems and Germany's best erotic poems. It occurs to me that he speaks German. I am starting to enjoy myself when I see a shiny object on the corner of the shelf.

It is a jade earring.

I've seen that earring before. It is Liane's. From the pair that was noticeably missing yesterday in school, the ones she made in her jewelry class. She had been so proud of them. I pick the earring up. Her initials are there. This is unquestionably hers. What the hell is it doing here?

Of course, I know what it's doing here.

Liane seemed so happy. I thought she was happy. And now I am remembering that she turned slightly sour after I slept with Steve. And then before that, when I told her we'd had coffee.

I must have known this on an unconscious level. After all, I had been quick to lie to her about the circumstances of the coffee.

"Hello, beautiful." Steve has obviously gussied himself up for this occasion. His hair is freshly combed, which only adds to my distaste.

What can I say? I am completely turned off. Not only is he a boy slut, but he's way too kempt for me. There is nothing I can do. I'm not even angry, frankly. I feel soiled. I grab my things and head out the door, but not before handing Steve back the earring.

"Wait, Kate," he hollers from the doorway, but he doesn't run after me. What's he going to say? Some of the ladies were over for a jewelry party?

I can't grab a cab or a subway. I have to walk home to process all of this. Does Steve have a mommy fetish? Me, Liane, who else? I ponder this question. Howard Montgomery's mother changed overnight from stiff librarian to a MILF. And in the back of my mind, as strange as it seems, I always thought there was something with him and Phillippa, despite her supposed frigidity and her portly ankles. As I recall, she got him the job. Come to think of it, he laughed when I told him that Phillippa was the murderer. He was laughing because he'd slept with Phillippa. A pattern, it would seem, emerges.

A pattern of mommies.

Not as horrific a pattern, but certainly as curious, as the other Hawthorne pattern: the pattern of death notices.

A pattern of murdered mommies.

Different names. Similar circumstances.

Just how similar?

Maybe I could figure out what tied Beverly and Johanna together other than the school. Steve recently got to the school. I found it weird that Phillippa was his benefactor, and even weirder that he was teaching the kids about bears: the specialty of a mother who had been killed. Steve was sleeping with at

least three of the mommies. And most likely Beverly, the erstwhile massage scholar, as well. One of them became jealous.
Perhaps the one who, as a teenager, snapped the neck of a bird
that was in her way. Beverly and Johanna were in her way, too.
What about Liane and me? I guess we're next.

I walk a little more and think of Phillippa in her jealous
rage killing all of us so that she can be with her young ward.

It doesn't seem right. But rage the woman certainly has.
Norm and Betty said so. Yet I would have thought she would
more likely kill moms for living in the wrong zip code than for
sleeping with her man.

She so lacks sexuality.

Maybe I'm wrong. Steve, the pig, certainly thinks so. He
seemed amused when I suggested that Phillippa was the murderer. He was almost taunting me, come to think of it. Just a few
days ago he said that my career in the DA's office intimidated
him. And then today, when I divulge, in my expert opinion, the
identity of the killer, he chuckled.

He chuckled.

Does he know something I don't?

And now it occurs to me, maybe he's laughing at the Phillippa theory because he knows very well who killed Beverly and
Johanna.

It was him.

Okay, it was *he,* if you want to get all grammatical.

I don't know what is more disgusting: Steve sleeping with
Phillippa or murdering my fellow moms.

But why would he kill them?

He's a collector. He said it himself. I had thought it was
sweet. I feel the sangria and the pork rise up in my throat.

He collects women. But sleeping with them isn't enough;
he has to kill them. It's a pathological extension of his collect-

ing. I should have been more suspicious when I learned that he was getting a Ph.D. What academic would want to be around screaming kids all day? To make a little money? Why not tutor college kids in physics or high school kids? The pay is better. I should have been more skeptical. My guard was down. He was so good-looking.

What kind of investigator am I?

I laugh at myself, going incognito to the Hastings home, scouring through Paul's and Peg's computers, fabricating a magazine piece to justify a clandestine trip to Croton Falls.

And then to take my mind off my "work," I sleep with the killer.

Classic.

When Peg finds this out, she is sure to stop begging me to come back to the office. And Paul . . .

Paul.

Paul is not the smug type, but it would probably be satisfying for him to know that while he is dating the beautiful-yet-age-appropriate Ellen Westin, my young stud is going to be the subject of next week's *Dateline NBC*.

I am on Thirty-fifth Street now. I have walked halfway home, a mile and a half, and I still can't process it. I slept with a killer. I was just giggling over pork with a man who bludgeoned Beverly Hastings to death. A man who would leave a child without a mother.

Two children without a mother.

I know how he did it now. This all makes sense. Steve was sleeping with Beverly. I try not to create too clear a mental picture here; I have already come close to vomiting. He would go to her house, but he wouldn't go through the upstairs. To avoid the possibility that Three would come home and see them, they would stay downstairs. Three probably never went downstairs. And he certainly wouldn't enter the house that way. If Three came in the front door upstairs, Beverly could easily shoo Steve out of the house, then run upstairs to greet her rich husband.

And what about Johanna? Maybe they were together. He offered to take a bath with her and declined to join her, opting instead to toss in a high-voltage hair dryer. It was brazen of him to be there right in her room. But Crump the husband seems like a guy who might not notice a hot young guy scrubbing his bride.

Hot young guy.

I am comfortable in saying I am officially over Steve Mykonos.

In fact, I try to envision my single sexual encounter with him, or three, if you are the type who microanalyzes a single date.

Yuk.

Now I really hope Paul never finds out about this. Before, I was worried simply that he would judge me for going at it with Molly's part-time teacher. Think of how a roll in the sack with a murderer would come off.

What confounds me is the motive. Why does Steve need to kill these women? Did they become too clingy? Did he become too clingy? I didn't sense any cling from him at all. And I hardly think Beverly would have risked her hard-earned social station with Three to be with an academic. I didn't know Johanna well. Perhaps they shared an appreciation for the sciences.

Or perhaps Steve is simply a psycho.

Alfred is on duty in my lobby. His bulging eyes betray a look of disapprobation. When I get upstairs, I'll call Peg and tell her about my suspicions. She may mock my terrible taste in men, but her jeers are more welcome to me than Paul's unavoidable disgust.

My mother is waiting for me. The door is open. The television is blaring, a rarity for my mother, who is violently anti-television. "There's so much to see," she says all the time.

I agree, they have almost one thousand channels, but I am certain that isn't her point.

"Thank goodness you're here."

"What do you mean? Is Molly okay?"

"Molly's fine. She's great. We were having such a lovely evening. I was telling her about the advantages of composting at home."

"Mom, you're breathless over kitchen waste."

"No, Katie, you know this is how I gather my thoughts. Ms. Druvier from Hawthorne called. There's been another murder. I've been trying to call Paul. No answer. I've been trying to call you, and then I heard your cell phone ringing. You left it here."

"I know. I'm still not used to going out."

"You should have a system."

"Mom. What happened?" I'm shaking.

"Mrs. Druvier said another mother in the class is dead."

"Another murder?"

"She said not to jump to conclusions."

"Who?"

"She wouldn't say. She only told us to take precautions and—"

"Maybe I inherited my investigative skills from you," I scoff in a manner that is completely uncharacteristic of our relationship.

"I will ignore that. It's a stressful time."

"Sorry." I sound just about as sorry as my daughter sounds after engaging in naughty behavior.

"I didn't think I would be telling you all of this. I figured you would know already. I tried to get Paul's take on it. I tried him at home, at work, and on his cell and I still haven't heard back from him."

"He's probably out with Ellen Westin," I say, forgetting there are bigger problems at hand.

"He would answer his phone."

"She's high maintenance. I know the type."

I turn to the television. Finally, a breaking-news story: SOCIALITE PHILLIPPA VON ECK IS DEAD. WE WILL CONTINUE TO PROVIDE THE INFORMATION AS IT DEVELOPS.

Phillippa von Eck is dead. Dead, they said, not murdered. It's murder, though. As soon as the news desk learns that the vic's kid is a Hawthorne student, they will produce a long-winded piece about the murders. Who will be next? they will ask. They will try to interview all of us, but few will participate. Aimi Wentz might enjoy a small role in the media portrayal of these murders—she has that Los Angeles quality to her. Within a week, they will produce a segment on the suspects and speculate on television about that which I have been speculating in my head: the identity of the killer. But they won't know about Steve—unless he sleeps with the reporter.

So Steve killed Phillippa right before he met up with me. Like an animal, he prefers to kill before he eats.

Is it possible, though, that Phillippa was killed while I was with Steve? Could someone else have killed her—someone other than this deranged sex maniac?

The news breaks into "More on the Phillippa von Eck story—Phillippa von Eck's body was found inside her foyer.

Cause of death—stabbing. The weapon: a samurai sword from the family's famously enviable collection."

A shiver goes through my body.

Neither Edwin nor Woodrow is mentioned. I watch the television as I tackle my spices. I rearrange my spice jars and sort the clearly expired ones from the I-can-get-away-with-its. I was never much of a cook, but my mother taught me that throwing in a seasoning here and there could produce an edible dish, and she knew I would be drawn to the spice library, as she called it. During my dark time, I might have used a pinch of cumin here and mustard seed there, but I had lost the ambition to put anything back in its rightful place.

A reporter is standing outside Phillippa's building with a LIVE CRIME SCENE caption at the bottom of the screen. "We have no motive, but we are treating this as a homicide."

I smell a Pulitzer.

The newscaster goes on to say that two other women in this neighborhood have been murder victims as well.

The reporter does not mention Hawthorne. "The police believe that Mrs. von Eck was killed at six-thirty this evening."

"Six-thirty? They have got to be kidding me," I scream.

"Katie, keep it down. The baby is sleeping."

My mother is right. Except that Molly isn't a baby anymore. True, I don't wish to wake her. This whole thing can't be good for her long-term psychological well-being. If I'm lucky, I'll only have years of bed-wetting.

"You're right." I put down the turmeric so that I can hug my mother. I start crying. "This is very stressful."

"It must be," she says in her therapy voice. "But, Katie, do keep in mind that Supercop lives right above us."

"Can we stop praising Paul?" I whine.

"Okay, then, let's praise you. You built your career in the

DA's office not just on your lawyering skills, but on your investigative ones. You have a sense. You have always said so."

"No, I don't." I am now crying. "I don't have it anymore."

"What on earth are you talking about?"

"I thought it was Steve."

"Your Steve? The little one? You thought he was it? The one you would marry?"

I wipe my eyes and my runny nose with my sleeve. "He's not little. He's young. And, no, I didn't think I would marry him. I thought he was the killer."

"You went out with him to catch him? Katie, that is dangerous."

"No, I went on the date to have—you know, a little action." I'm not comfortable talking about this with my mother, no matter how progressive she is. "I didn't think he was the killer until an hour ago." I'm still crying, by the way.

"So you're having a slight setback. One little intuitive misdirection does not mean you don't have it anymore."

I cut her off. "And before that, I thought it was Phillippa von Eck."

"Oh, dear. I'm going to make you a feel-good drink, and we are going to hash this out."

"Mom, I am definitely not in the mood for one of your sorrel shakes."

"Good, because I'm making you a margarita. I'm not an imbecile."

I laugh and then start telling my mother about my visit with Norm and Betty, about the bird, and Phillippa's record. "I thought that the killing of the bird was the onset of a serial spree."

"Could be." My mother stops for a few moments. "But a serial killer usually derives pleasure from the death of the animal.

Phillippa's pathology seems different. The bird bothered her and she killed it. It wasn't as if she were fulfilling a need to kill."

"I didn't think of it that way."

"That still wouldn't have ruled her out as the killer here. If those women bothered her in the very way the bird did, she may have wanted them dead."

"Good point but completely moot."

"I was letting you know your instincts weren't necessarily off, in my professional opinion."

"Okay, then let me tell you where they were off."

"Steve?"

"Steve," I say, sounding as furious as I feel. "The man is a slut. No, that sounds too petty. He's a sex addict. And I think he's doing it with every mother in Molly's class, plus who knows who else."

My mother doesn't respond, so I keep talking.

"We went to dinner, and then when I was at his house I saw Liane's, Max's mom's, earring on his bookshelf. The woman obviously had sex with him and left her earring there."

"That's awkward. What did you do?"

"I left. I was grossed out. And then my mind started racing. All of the moms in the preschool have the hots for this guy—"

"I have the hots for this guy and I haven't even met him."

I laugh. "I think that is the first time I have ever heard you talk about anyone in a salacious way. You can have him."

"Why did you think he was a killer?"

"I started thinking that he must have had sex with Phillippa."

"Why?"

"He referred to her as Phillippa. No one does that. Not even her husband."

"You do."

"True, but she's not in my life. Correction. She was not in

my life. She was like a nasty cartoon character who appeared at school functions every now and then."

"Maybe Steve saw her that way."

"No. She was his benefactor. He was obviously indebted to her. The whole Steve-teaching-at-Hawthorne seemed weird to me. One day I learned that a science program had been implemented at a nursery school, headed by a mega-attractive guy who seemed to know Phillippa intimately. I was always suspicious. Paul was suspicious, too."

"How do you know?"

"He made digs."

"Could be suspicion. Could be jealousy."

"I'm voting suspicion, but that is neither here nor there. Then I saw Howard Montgomery's mom, who is a perfectly blah-looking, nerdy mom, go all va-va-voom one day when she was picking up her son. It happened to be a day that Steve was at the school."

"And you think she was with Steve and suddenly rediscovered her sexuality?"

"That is exactly what I think." I realize I'm waving a vanilla bean around.

"It could be."

"Now let me remind you, Mom, that prior to Steve's employment at Hawthorne, there were no murders. Suddenly, there are three. This is the only change in the Hawthorne environment that I'm aware of."

"That you're aware of," my mother repeats in a warning tone. "You yourself have said that you are often out of the loop with respect to what you refer to as 'the minutiae' at the school. How do you know there isn't a junior Yogilates class being taught as an after-school? Or a parent-based community-service project?"

"Mom, did you just use the word *Yogilates* in a sentence?"

"I did." She reaches into the refrigerator to help herself to some unpasteurized milk she bought from a black-market Ukrainian dealer.

"Mom, first, I would know if there was Yogilates at the school. For the most part, these victims weren't exactly service-oriented. They wanted their kids to go to Hawthorne because it was essential to their social positioning."

"Still, they know they have to participate in school events. Didn't you tell me that Phillippa hosted the cocktail party? To someone like her, that is community service."

"Good point," I chuckle.

"Anyway, I'm not saying that these women died doing a project. I am just pointing out that there may be all sorts of politics and gossip at the school that you are unaware of."

"True. But I am getting there. Liane . . ." I stop.

Liane. Would she really fill me in on the gossip? I had assumed that the woman was my link to Hawthorne Central, but she was obviously withholding some information from me; for example, she was doing my date. To be fair, I was equally dishonest with her. But I'm depressed and divorced.

Sort of depressed and sort of divorced.

No, completely. My husband and I share a daughter and he spends time with Ellen Westin, and I'm with Tiger Woods minus the golf skills.

"Kate," my mother interrupts me, as I am about to feel mighty sorry for myself. "Perhaps Steve is a sex maniac, but unfortunately he's not the only one. If every sex maniac embarked on a killing spree, this city would be less crowded."

"I know, Mom, and it's not worth discussing because Steve didn't kill Phillippa." His dirty leg was touching mine at the bar at Mejor when she was being sliced up. "Still, he may be the common denominator here. Maybe one of the moms is in love with him and she's in a jealous rage, trying to do away with all of the competition."

"Stranger things have happened," my mother says.

The phone rings. It's Steve. Unbelievable.

"Do I get it?"

"I say, you get it. Get it over with," my mother says.

Doctor's orders. I pick up the phone. "Hello."

"Hi, Kate." Steve sounds breathless. "It's Steve. Steve Mykonos."

I know.

"Can we talk?"

"There's not really much to say."

"I'd like to explain."

"You don't have to, Steve. We made no promises to each other. We only went on one date. I just don't do that."

"I know, but I think we should talk."

"Steve, I can't right now. Not with what happened with Phillippa."

"Phillippa?"

"Didn't you hear? She was killed tonight."

"Not Phillippa, too!" Steve's voice has risen to falsetto.

"I've got to go."

"Well?" my mother asks.

"I can't believe I was attracted to that."

"If it makes you feel any better, sex addicts tend to be very charismatic."

We are at Hawthorne. Last night's events have prompted Irene Druvier to call a special parents meeting. We are all huddled in a classroom, each of us sitting on a teeny-tiny, primary-colored chair, staring at our kids' drawings, paintings, and collages on one wall, and family photos on another. I notice that Beverly, Phillippa, and Johanna are still on the wall. It looks like a memorial.

Mrs. Montgomery sits across from me. She has returned to her frumpy style of dress. As I look around, everyone looks a little dowdy. I'm in a sea of under-eye circles, stringy hair, and mom jeans.

Alas, I'm finally at home with these women.

"There is no need for concern," Ms. Druvier says in a husky voice with a trace of an affected English accent. "But we ask that parents in the school be mindful of people they let in their homes, whether it be your help or your whatnot."

I am dying to raise my hand and ask for her precise definition of *whatnot,* as I am sure that the whatnot here is the killer. But Ms. Druvier continues to speak. Clearly, she knows less than we do and is simply filling the air with her vague words, passing time perhaps.

Yes, passing time indeed. Paul enters, and she breathes a sigh of relief.

I am unable to exhale. I picture him giving Ellen a kiss goodbye as she dropped him off in front of the school in her chauffeured car.

Will you be long? she says.

Nah. I gotta take care of this. It's my kid's school.

Don't be long, Ellen says.

You got it. He pulls her to him.

She pulls an earring off her ear and places it in the palm of his hand and closes it. *So you'll think of me.*

"Fortunately," Ms. Druvier bellows, waking me up from my unpleasant daydream, "we are lucky to have a real live detective in our parent population. Many of you know him as

Molly's dad. May I introduce"—she pauses in the same manner she did last year when she introduced the conductor of the New York Philharmonic—"Mr. Paul Alger."

The parents forget their fear for a moment and greet my ex-husband with enthusiastic applause. I see Liane, but her eyes don't meet mine.

"Thank you, Irene," Paul says, disregarding the parental convention of referring to the school director only by her last name. "At this point, there is no need to panic." He sounds disingenuous, as of course there is reason to panic. One-sixth of the class's moms have been murdered. "But we ask that you be extra careful at all times." He looks so big and powerful right now, standing upright while the rest of us have temporarily diminished our size to accommodate to the seating. This gives him authority and an aura of something attractive. Everyone is hanging on his every word. For a moment, the moms are transferring their lust for the pretty science teacher to the superhero.

This bugs me. Isn't Ellen enough?

"Don't open your doors for anyone other than family members," he continues. "It seems that none of the victims here were taken by surprise. They obviously knew the assailant. I have no better way to say this. Don't trust everyone. Not everyone is your friend."

Liane is finally looking at me. She isn't smiling. Does she know that I know about Steve? He would never have told her.

Steve suddenly appears in the room. I can feel the mom eyes shift from Paul to him.

Paul can, too.

Ha ha, Paul.

"Be mindful, especially of new people in your lives. These murders just happened, so we assume that the assailant is someone the victims met recently or that a recent set of circumstances set off a motive in the killing."

Is Paul referring to Steve? Paul glares at him. As far as Paul knows, he is the most recent addition to the Hawthorne environment, but he has a really good alibi.

Moi!

Irene abruptly ends the meeting and tells us that school must go on. "We, along with the police department, have determined that the children are not physically at risk being here. We have concluded that it is better for them to move forward under the most normal conditions possible. So please send your children to school tomorrow. It is the parents who must be careful."

"Any questions?" Paul asks.

Umm, yeah. Does Ellen wear the mink when you are doing her?

"I have a question," Mrs. Kim says. "What should we do about playdates and birthday parties?"

"I would say, don't go," Paul responds. "We need the parents to steer clear of anything unfamiliar. Our feeling at this time is that the victims have been caught by surprise in the most benign circumstances."

"What about doctors' appointments?" Howard's mom asks. "For the kids."

"I would stay away from the doctor unless it's a medical emergency."

Mrs. Montgomery writes this information down.

"What about doctor appointments for us?" Aimi Wentz asks.

"The same thing," Paul says, sounding a tad exasperated. "Only in a medical emergency."

"What do you mean by a medical emergency?" Aimi asks.

Paul has no idea how high maintenance she is. "Use your judgment," he says sternly.

Aimi, though speechless, gives him a flirtatious smile. My stomach does a quick turn as I, to my surprise, allow myself to recall my own lust for Paul at his most capable. About two years into our relationship, we were at the grocery store, waiting impatiently to buy some deli foods, when I saw him, in one single move, glide over to the middle-aged man waiting at the next register, grab his arms behind his back, and cuff him. Paul whispered in his ear what appeared to be Miranda warnings and motioned me to pay for the food.

When I got out of the store, he was holding the guy, waiting for the cops to collect him.

"You were so quiet."

"I didn't want to embarrass him."

Paul had caught a pickpocket in the middle of his job. Paul informed the victim, a mother with two kids, that she would have to wait for the return of her wallet, as it was evidence.

She thanked him and he gave her a little safety talk.

That night, I couldn't get enough of Paul. Before he could finish making his sandwich, I had pinned him against the refrigerator. Then, later, I mauled him while he was reading the paper.

"You like it when I get all cops-and-robbers, don't you?" he teased.

Truth is, I did. But admitting it wouldn't comport with my feminist ideology, so I didn't answer him. Instead I continued to kiss him.

"You don't have to admit it, but I know."

I stopped kissing him to prove him wrong.

"It's okay," he said. "When I see you prosecuting someone,

all I can think about is having my way with you in the court-room."

"Really?" I giggled.

"Of course. I love watching you be good at what you do. And you love it, too. Don't worry, Gloria Steinem isn't going to kick you out of the club."

"Any other questions?" I am back to the present and all at once resenting my ex-husband for triggering a memory of happier days. He doesn't deserve it.

No one dares ask anything more. "Well, then. I see you're in good hands with Ms. Druvier. We'll let her know of any relevant information as it becomes available. Thank you."

"Thank you, Detective Alger," we all recite in unison, sounding alarmingly like our kids.

The parents for the most part go off in separate ways. I hear Aimi telling Natasha's mom that she doesn't feel comfortable with the instructions.

"Is it an emergency that I see my Reiki guy? Not exactly, but I'm just not right without it. Not right at all. Also, I've been seeing him for over two years. I like Paul, but I have to take care of myself. Otherwise, Tess will be no better off than Bitsy, Caleb, and Woodrow."

"He did say use your judgment," Natasha's mom says.

"You're right, but I felt he was judging me. He doesn't know my medical issues. He doesn't care."

Neither does the killer.

I dawdle in the hallway just outside the classroom next to the school's rather child-unfriendly spiral staircase. As they head downstairs, some moms are chatting a mile a minute. Others are silent. I look to the wall of handprints the kids did just a few weeks ago. They had warmed up the place, I recall think-ing, but now they seem eerie, Bitsy's, Caleb's, and Woodrow's hands splayed on the wall in red paint.

I get downstairs minutes later and see Steve coming out of Ms. Druvier's office. He tries to meet my gaze. I avoid his. There is no point. There is no misunderstanding here. There is no need for an explanation. I am grossed out.

Steve is relentless. As I head toward the school's heavy door, he runs to catch up with me.

"Do you have a minute?" he asks.

"No, I really don't."

He grabs my arm. "Look, Kate, it's not what you think."

"How do you even know what I think?" He starts to an-swer, but I interrupt. "Let me tell you what I believe to be go-ing on, and then you can grade me, Mr. Mykonos."

Steve nods.

"Here it is. You like to sleep around. I don't know why. I don't care why. I don't like it."

"That's it?"

"That's it. We are different people."

"Kate, I know you may not believe me, but it's a whole other thing with you."

I laugh.

"No. Really. I'm not denying that maybe I flirt with some of the moms and it goes a little far, but there was something else with us."

I don't believe him. "I want to end this conversation."

"Look, Kate, I'm not trying to win you back, but I do want you to know, for the record, that I had dropped those other women after we went to Fornax. I was flattered that all of these rich, sophisticated women were interested in a nerdy boy like me—"

"But you realized that you wanted to be around the depressed, poor mom."

"That may be how you see yourself, Kate, but that's not how I see you. You are a warm and loving mother: huge turn-on. You're beautiful: huge turn-on. And you call yourself depressed. I'm sorry, but I don't see it. I see a bright, clever woman with self-irony and self-reflection. Frankly, that's the biggest turn-on of them all."

I'm not sure whether to believe him. In any case, I can't continue this conversation as Paul is standing next to us.

"You okay?" he asks me with more than professional concern. He's glaring at Steve.

"She's fine," Steve says.

Paul takes in a deep breath and puffs out his chest. I've seen this look. It's territorial. "I was asking *her*. Are you okay?"

"Totally," I lie, completely at sea in his dominating presence here. Despite my discomfort, and my resentment that he put on this possessive act when he is the one that has cheated and has clearly moved on, I remember that I need him and that I need to be nice to him. "Thanks for the talk. It was helpful."

Steve is still standing there. I am increasingly uncomfortable.

"I should get home. I promised Molly I would let her freeze things this afternoon."

"Freeze things?" Paul asks.

"Yeah. Freeze things. Yesterday we put a piece of paper in the freezer. I told her she could put one of my old lipsticks in this afternoon. She calls it her science experiment."

"Science experiment, huh?" Paul gives Steve an unpleasant look.

"I've been encouraging the kids to think of ways they can change properties in everyday items. We did ice cubes in the classroom," Steve enthuses. "Your daughter is quite the little scientist."

"She is, is she?" Paul hates Steve.

"Yes, she is. They have science camps for little ones at some of the museums. She just went to see the Garrett Morgan exhibit at the Museum of the City of New York. As you know, she loves traffic lights. I can get you some of the information if you want. I can put in a good word for her—"

"Listen, Steve. I don't know what your game is here. But just stay away from my family. I don't want you giving extra help to my daughter, and I don't need you throwing yourself at my wife."

"Ex-wife," Steve says.

"She's still the mother of my baby girl, and I don't like to see her harassed."

"Oh, really," answers Steve.

"What's the matter with you? I told you to stop bothering Kate."

"I wasn't bothering her. I was talking to her. Frankly, I was telling her how great she is. When did you last do that?"

"This isn't your business."

"It's just as much my business as yours. Your wife sees herself as a depressed has-been. I see her as a beautiful woman who got through a very tough period all by herself."

I am standing with the two of them, listening to this conversation. Neither seems to address me.

"What do you know about my wife's depression?"

"I know that she had a baby, she was depressed, no one helped her. And then, because she wasn't fun anymore, her husband walked out."

I hate to give Steve credit, but he does have a point.

Paul is speechless.

"I told her that she did a remarkable job pulling herself out of a tough situation, despite being abandoned by someone to whom she entrusted her future. Look, I may be some dopey single guy, but last time I checked, marriage vows included sickness and health. Bravo to you for getting the health."

Suddenly Steve is down. Paul has punched him. Right in the nose.

It's unclear what my role is. Do I, the scorned-yet-furious ex-wife, take care of Paul? Or do I, the kindly-but-turned-off ex-lover, take care of Steve? They were perfectly capable of carrying on the conversation without my intervention, but the circumstances have taken a turn. Do I support my ex-husband because we share history and a daughter, or do I tend to the one-night stand I just dumped because he is wounded?

I have to keep two things in mind: Paul betrayed me and has a girlfriend, and Steve is a whore.

Paul looks at me. "Be careful, Katie," he says, and walks away.

"Is he referring to me or to the killer?" Steve asks as he slowly pulls himself up.

"We need to get you some peas." I guess I'm supposed to take care of Steve.

"Peas?"

"Frozen peas to put on your nose. I'm really sorry about this. I think Paul is tense because of the stress of the murders. There's a lot of pressure obviously to catch this guy."

"That wasn't about the murders, Kate."

"Believe me, it was." But all at once I'm not sure if I believe what I'm saying. "We really should get you some ice." His face continues to swell. I am mortified by the whole situation.

"Look, what I said before was true. I understand that I look like a, a . . . ," he stammers.

"A horndog."

"I guess I deserve that. But this job here is like a break from my life. I'm never around little kids, I'm never around rich people. I'm never around attractive women. My field is still full of men. Suddenly, I got here and I was treated like a rock star. I got carried away. I acted badly. Honestly, this is a parenthesis in my life. I'm really just a physics geek who happens to have a crush on you."

I believe him. I'm flattered. "Steve, you really need to ice your face."

"You won't give me another chance, will you?"

"Steve, I can't. I think you're great. I think you're honest. I think you learned your lesson, and I think there's someone else for you."

"Harsh." Steve grabs at his face.

"No, Steve. As you said, this isn't reality for you, but it is reality for me. For all of us moms. These kids. This school. This is what we do."

He isn't listening. I think his face really hurts.

"Look, when your stint here is done, you'll graduate from Columbia, and you'll discover something incredible about microfluids. They will fly you to Oslo, where you win a prize, and on the airplane, you will meet a woman who is warm, self-reflective, and age-appropriate. She will also be rich and sophisticated, as they will fly you first-class, and she will have paid for the seat next to yours."

Steve laughs.

"For what it's worth, you're smart and . . ."

"And hot?"

"Yes, very hot." I can't help but smile at him.

Our gaze is interrupted by a noise just outside Druvier's office.

Liane.

I hurry home, trying to sort out all this information in my head. I am relieved about Steve. Not so much that he isn't a killer, but rather that he isn't a complete slimeball. He's young and stupid.

I am more confounded by Paul's behavior. I don't understand the violence. I have never seen Paul lift a finger at another human being in all the time I have known him. This man constantly confronts violent sociopaths, yet in all of his triumphs as a cop, the only time he ever caused anyone injury was when he jumped a fleeing rapist and twisted his arm. Now, in addition to hurting me perhaps irreversibly, he has embarrassed me.

Steve's face looked pretty bad.

Could Paul think he is the killer? Worse, am I required to set him straight?

I stop for a second.

Someone is trailing me. I feel it.

I turn around—nothing. But I know someone was there.

The last person I saw was Liane.

I'm home. Molly comes running to the door.

"Mama, Mama, I love you, I love you, I love you." She throws her arms around me in a most dramatic way.

"And I love you, too."

Molly giggles and squeezes me really tight.

My mom walks in and smiles. Tears well in my eyes.

"Are you okay?" my mother asks me.

"I am. Very much okay, in fact."

Molly runs back to her room. I lower my voice so only my mother hears what I say next. "Does this mean I'm even crazier than I had thought? Don't get me wrong, I feel horrible for Beverly, Phillippa, and Johanna. Even though I wasn't a big fan of Beverly's or Phillippa's, I would never want them dead. I just wanted them in another city or another school. I was depressed when everyone was alive, but now that they're dropping like flies, I have the energy of a teenager."

"That's the difference between sadness and depression. You are sad for these women and their families, but you aren't crippled by it. You've been climbing this mountain for months now and you've reached the top."

My mother has spoken.

I feel at this moment so blessed to have such a wonderful mother and a great daughter.

"And we are lucky to have you," my mother says, reading my mind.

"Mama, may I play with my Pick Up sticks, now that we are finished hugging?" Molly yells.

"Yes, honeybee."

I walk into my daughter's room, pull the Pick Up sticks off a high shelf, and go back out to my mother.

I tell her briefly about the meeting with Ms. Druvier and Paul.

"What about Steve?" she asks.

"You're right. He is not a killer. I don't even know if he's a sex addict. I think he was like a kid in a candy store, with all of those unhappy women drooling all over him."

"Does Paul know about you and Steve?"

"He knows something. Steve told Paul that he was a shitty

husband. Rather brazen for a man whose job it is to teach your kid how to put marbles in holes."

"And?"

"Paul punched him."

"Paul? Our Paul? Paul punched someone?"

"That was my reaction, and I was there. But he punched him hard."

My mother starts laughing.

"Why are you laughing?"

"Because, sweetheart, Paul is jealous."

"No, there's no way." I might have believed her a few weeks ago, but Mom didn't see him with Ellen Westin. "I think he doesn't like Steve."

"Katie, Paul doesn't like a lot of people. He doesn't punch them. He's no dummy. He sees you a little differently now. You are no longer the depressed, fragile flower he walked out on, but a . . . what's the word?"

"Cougar?"

"No, you are alive."

And I realize now why I forgive Steve. The man is a dog, but he did expedite my resurrection. I pick at a quinoa-sorrel salad my mother has prepared.

The phone rings. Private number.

"No one can kill me through a phone wire," I tell my mother. I pick up. "Hello."

Click. Another hang-up.

"What was that?" my mother asks.

"I've been getting hang-ups the past few days."

"Hmm, any idea who it is?"

"I don't know. I thought it could be Steve."

She starts to say something and stops herself.

"What?"

"When you were out with Steve last night, someone hung up when I answered the phone. I figured it was a friend of yours who didn't feel like leaving a message with a babysitter. So it couldn't be Steve."

"Did you check the caller ID?" I ask, knowing the answer. My mother doesn't even have a cordless phone.

"It's the same phone you grew up with, honey. It's completely reliable," she says whenever I encourage her to get a technology makeover.

I grab the phone and scroll through my calls in the past twenty-four hours. A private call was placed to me at 7:02 p.m. last night. Steve was with me the entire time.

"Not Steve," I say.

"Should you call Paul?"

"What? To tell him that someone has called without leaving a message?"

"Not without leaving a message, Katie, without speaking. Someone has been calling you and hanging up the phone."

"Mom, I can't call Paul every time something scares me. I have to wear my big-girl pants."

"You won't be calling him out of fear, Kate. This kind of behavior is stalking. You know that. Maybe it's the killer. Maybe the killer is targeting you."

"That's ridiculous." As I say this, I recall sensing that someone was following me home from school. "People get hangups all the time."

"Kate, call Paul. I'll call him. I'll tell him I'm scared."

I love my mother. I tell her everything. But I don't know how to put into words my inability to do this. Paul gave up on me, on us, within a short time. He watched me go through something awful and didn't have the faith to ride it out or the wherewithal to help me. I remember the day he left as if it were yesterday. I had told him that given his hours away from home, the marriage was over.

"You know I have always had a workaholic tendency," he said. "Why is it bothering you now?"

He had also tended to take responsibility for his behavior and to be honest even when it might have been unpleasant, but he refused to man up here. A sign that it was over.

"You know you aren't working," I said.

"I'm working a lot harder than you." Paul pointed to the piles of dirty dishes in the sink and the overflowing garbage can.

"And that gives you permission?" I was screaming so loud and crying so hard that the words seemed inaudible.

"Kate. You really need to get ahold of yourself." Paul wasn't crying. He wasn't crazy. He was obviously done. His patronizing tone fueled my hurt and my rage.

I took the deepest breath I could muster, put my tears on pause, and looked him straight in the eye. "Get out." I sucked on my tongue for a second. "How's that for getting hold of myself?" Then I headed to Molly's bedroom, made sure she'd slept through all of this, and curled up on her floor until I knew he was out of the house.

He has moved on. He is even; he's cheerful. And now he's involved. I'm not a prideful person, but I can't, every time something scares me, call a man who let me down.

But my mother already has Paul on his cell. "Grandma here. We have had a bunch of hang-ups on the landline. My daughter seems to have everything under control, but I'm worried."

Paul says something I can't hear.

"No, but it sounds like the caller waits for me to say hello a few times before he hangs up."

I think Paul is talking again.

"Or she. Weird. I get this feeling it's a man."

Paul is still talking.

"No, we don't think this is a suitor." My mother gives me a slightly victorious look.

Paul is talking again.

"Paul, it's not him." My mother rolls her eyes.

He is down here within seconds.

"So you don't know if the murderer is a man or a woman?" I ask.

"We don't."

"Do you have anything?"

"I'm not at liberty to say."

"That means you have nothing."

"Katie, if you're so desperate to be an investigator, just get back to work."

"This isn't about my wanting to investigate. This is about the environment in which we choose to raise our daughter. Your parents insisted that we send this kid to private school because they see it as a safer place, but last I looked there were no parents getting whacked at PS 6. And, if we knew a little about why it's Hawthorne, I could make an informed decision as to whether we should continue to send our daughter there."

"All I can tell you is that there is nothing more or less dangerous about Hawthorne than any other schools."

"You don't know anything." I am angry.

Paul doesn't say a word. I rifle through a stack of old photos to initiate my photo-organization project. I stop on one of me, hugely pregnant, laughing, holding up a half-eaten veal Parmesan hero. Paul is in the picture, too, kissing my belly. I quickly put that in the bottom of the pile and opt instead for a picture of Molly on a swing. The silence is uncomfortably long.

"I'm sorry, Kate."

"I'm sorry, too." I am grateful that there isn't going to be a huge blowout fight.

"No, I'm really sorry."

"Mommy." Molly comes in.

Her timing is terrible. Paul is softening, and perhaps I can get something out of him. I get an idea. "Maybe we should have this conversation someplace else," I say as I give him a Molly-doesn't-need-to-hear-this look. Finally, I can get to the computer.

"Do you want to continue upstairs?" he asks as if it were his idea.

I let him think it. "Good point."

"Molly, your dad and I need to have a grown-up talk upstairs."

"That's okay, Mommy. Grandma and I will have a best-friends talk here."

My mother looks at me, confused.

I try to mime an Inspector Clouseau characterization behind Paul's back, and my mom looks even more confused.

"I'm sorry I wasn't there for you," Paul says to me in his living room.

While I am intent on getting into his computer, I am distracted by his apology. "Whatever."

"What's going on with you and the science guy?"

"That would fall into the file marked 'none of your business.' "

"I don't like him."

"Noted." I disguise my hostility badly.

Paul, oblivious, keeps talking. "Lately, I've been doing a little reading on depression and postpartum depression. I didn't want to think of you as sick. When my brother died, I made a pact with myself to go forward relentlessly. When one bad thing happens, make two good things happen. If I'm sad, I will myself to be happy, to count my blessings. Life is too short. I just didn't get how you couldn't do the same thing."

"Right." I left my anger and hurt downstairs. My goal up here is to get to his laptop.

"I'm really sorry, Katie. I wasn't there for you. I didn't get it."

This isn't the scenario I would have expected here. All at once the room is quiet.

"And I'm sorry."

"I had cancer." Why am I telling him this?

"What?" Paul looks terrified for the first time in his life.

"I had skin cancer. Melanoma."

"Are you okay?"

"I'm more than okay. I'm completely fine. I was a little freaked-out, but we caught it early. Actually, it was Miriam who caught it."

"Miriam?"

"Yep."

"So what happened?" Paul is tripping on his words. "Did you have any surgery? Chemo?"

"No chemo. No radiation. A minor surgery. I am fine."

Paul presses his lips together in concentration. "I wish you had told me," he whispers.

Why? So he could go AWOL for that, too? I don't say anything.

"But you're okay."

"I'm completely okay."

"Where was it?"

"On my arm."

"Can I see?"

I would never have predicted that the conversation would take this turn.

"Okay." I take off my jacket silently. I'm wearing a tank underneath. "There's a little scar where my triceps would be if I were Miriam," I joke.

Paul comes over to my arm and touches the scar. We stand there for minutes. He doesn't let go. It almost seems as if he is shaking. I don't look at his face because I know he's crying. I can't hear him, I can't see him, but I know what this silence is. It's about me, and Mark, and death, and our marriage.

Paul leans into my arm and grazes my scar with his lips. For a single moment, I forget my reason for being here.

How am I supposed to get to the laptop now?

"I'd better get back to Molly." I pull away from him.

As I head down the stairs, I realize that I can't go back to the apartment just yet. Molly will be bouncing on me. And my mother, wearing her therapy and parenting hats, will be asking me all about our conversation. I'm not ready for her to analyze it. I have to process it first.

Paul is sorry. He's sorry for bailing on me. He's sorry for not hearing me. He's sorry I couldn't tell him that I had cancer. A conversation I'd started in my head, I hate to admit it, countless times. I couldn't finish it, though, because I knew that it would never be enough.

And it wasn't. He never said sorry for cheating. He didn't mention it. Maybe he thinks that was implicit in his earlier declaration. Maybe he thinks I don't even know about it and he can get away with not bringing it up.

And so, I am still angry.

Only less so, I determine after several seconds.

Even though it is thirty-seven degrees outside and I am coatless, I go for a walk around the corner. Molly could use an ice cream. Okay, I could use a coffee from the Better Bean, but Molly is a perfect excuse. Ye Olde Dessert Shoppe is five blocks from here.

I walk as briskly as possible against the cold wind. I have a hard time clearing my head; my muddled thoughts keep pace with the murky day. I feel as if I'm supposed to rejoice in Paul's words. Isn't this what people want? Validation.

But I feel somehow as if I have won the booby prize, the YOU SEE? I TOLD YOU I WASN'T COMPLETELY NUTS T-shirt. This is less a moment of victory for me than one of sadness.

What could have been.

And then there's this other problem, too.

Someone is right behind me.

I know it's the same guy who followed me home earlier.

Or girl.

Paul had asked me why I was assuming that my crazy caller was a man. I had assumed it.

Yet I can't help but wonder if my shadow is female.

My mind flashes all of a sudden to Liane at the meeting this morning. She was eyeing me so suspiciously. I was certain it was because she thought I was interfering with her boyfriend. But maybe there's more. Liane befriended me rather recently, and Paul warned us to beware of new friends. Frankly, I think I was attracted to the notion of Phillippa as the murderer for the simple reason that I didn't like her. What if our killer is someone I like? For example, Liane. She's eliminating Steve's conquests so she can have him to herself.

This is so crazy. Yet it makes perfect sense. The killer had to have access to the victims. There was never a struggle or a break-in. All these mommies know Liane. She is the friendly neighborhood Realtor. And she makes a damn good earring. Beverly would have let her in. She could have told Beverly to let her in from downstairs. She could have made up a zillion excuses to gain access to Beverly's home or Johanna's or Phillippa's.

My heart is heavy as I reflect on this. While I never had any trouble in the friendship department in my earlier life, I had failed to forge a rapport in the past four years. Then I met Liane, and I thought we bonded. We weren't best buddies yet, but a close alliance had seemed inevitable. Turns out I may have been befriending the next star of *America's Most Wanted*.

I feel a tap on my shoulder. I scream in my head, primed to tell her that I know everything. I turn around. It isn't Liane at all. It's a stranger.

I fight the wind to keep my hair out of my face and I make out a male face. He's small. Not short exactly. No, not short at all. Not too tall though, but he's slight. He's thinner than he should be and his body is slumped. He's in his early sixties. I'm not scared of him exactly, but I want to know why he has been trailing me.

"What?" I say to him in the same manner in which Lucy speaks to Charlie Brown.

"Are you Kate?"

"That's right," I say after having taken a microsecond to determine that revealing my name is going to have no bearing on my living or dying at the outcome of this discussion.

"My name is Gary Hagen."

I had heard this conversation before. A thousand times.

In my head.

My name is Gary Hagen.

My father.

My mother's estranged husband. The man to whom Dr. Schmitt assigns some responsibility for my battle with depression. Anyone responsible for the depression must be responsible, in part, for the breakup of my marriage.

"Kate?"

"Yes." I don't know what to say to this man. *Hi, Daddy. I potty-trained and then went to law school. Now you have a grandchild. And, out of curiosity, how could you abandon the greatest single person in the world?*

But I don't say any of this. I just look at him, frozen. My actor friends have told me stories about freezing onstage, forgetting lines and scenes they've rehearsed hundreds of times. They forgot phrases that came to them nightly in their sleep or interrupted their enjoyment of movies and books. But once onstage, the words vanished.

I was having such a moment.

"Are you okay?"

Finally I manage a question: "Why have you been calling me?"

He doesn't answer right away, but he doesn't deny it either.

"Why have you been calling me? More to the point, why do you call and hang up?"

"I don't know. I mean, I called you because I wanted to call you and hear your voice, but I had no idea what to say to you."

He has a point here. What is there to say? Sorry seems a little silly, and then again, it seems to be the only option.

"Do you have anything to say to me now? You went to all this effort."

"I wanted to see what you were like."

Well, if you had caught me five years ago, you would have kicked yourself for abandoning us. I was successful, happily married, pregnant, pretty in the way a parent would want for his kid, and darn fun to be around. If he had caught me a year or two ago, he would have seen a shut-in.

"I'm like a person who doesn't enjoy being watched." I notice that I keep walking to the Better Bean, my father in tow.

"Fair enough," he says.

"Have you tried to contact my mother?"

"No. I wanted to contact you first."

"It doesn't work that way." I open the door to the Bean, careful to see if anyone I know is in there. I'm not keen on introducing my daddy to anyone.

"I want to know that you are okay. That your life turned out okay even though I, um, I, um . . ."

"Abandoned me."

"Abandoned you." He doesn't disagree.

"I'm okay."

"You look okay."

"Well, then." I order my triple espresso. "Let's move this to phase two."

He shifts awkwardly.

"We go talk to my mother."

I don't offer him a coffee, I realize. He just agreed to talk to my mother and I don't want to stall.

We walk, and surprisingly he doesn't say much. I imagine he is rehearsing his speech to my mother or planning his quick escape. But I treat him like an uncooperative witness and let him know there is no choice. He has agreed to talk to my mother. As far as I'm concerned, we can't get there fast enough.

We see Alfred at the door. He looks at my father with some recognition. My father nods to him. As do I, I notice.

I knock on the door.

"Oh, Katie, thank God you're back. Paul—" She opens the door.

Silence.

"Oh." She recognizes him immediately.

"Hi, Virginia."

More silence. So much silence, and, finally, "Hi, Gary."

Part of me wants them to fall into each other's arms and smooch.

A very small part.

"You look beautiful," he says to her. I think he's relieved.

"Thank you. You look like you." If this were my reunion with the man who abandoned me thirty years ago, I would be stammering like a schoolgirl, but my mother holds her own.

"That's about the nicest thing anyone has ever said to me." He pauses. "Therapy."

As I finish my triple espresso, I start to make a fresh pot.

"That's the best thing you could have told me," my mother says, so warm and forgiving. A lesser person—say, me—might have inflicted a few punches or even a quick spit shot.

"A lot of it." He is warmed by her encouragement. I put extra water in the machine on the theory that this may end up being a long conversation. "I needed it, obviously. I'm not well. I wasn't well. Now I'm sort of fine." He casts his eyes downward and rubs his fingers aggressively. "I have bipolar disorder. I've had it for a long time."

She could have told you that, I want to say, but I can see that this is a man in pain.

"I didn't know there was a word for what I was. I just thought I was moody. Fussy even."

I give the coffee mugs a superfluous wipe and start pouring.

"Sometimes I was so happy, it hurt my head. When I met you"—he is talking to my mother as if I were not even present—"you were just so, so, so perfect. I couldn't get enough. Remember?"

My mother is smiling in a way I have never seen. I don't know if that is how she smiles at her patients or her lovers, as I have never had the occasion to see either.

"I would stay awake all night staring at you, writing you endless love notes even though you were lying next to me. I filled composition books. Five or six a day."

Mania, I say to myself. I know my mother is thinking it.

"The joy was explosive and overwhelming, but I wanted to maintain it. For some, the ups are the hard part; for me, the opposite was true. When I went to the dark side, I was inert. I was determined not to let you see me this way. You were so even, so lovely."

"She still is," I say.

"I'm quite sure of that. But the darkness in me kept building and building. It got worse after you were born."

That's right. I'm here. I take in a breath.

"Not because of you," he adds quickly. "I was crazy for you. And that made it worse. My responsibility to control myself seemed unattainable. I couldn't do it. One night I thought I would die. I couldn't make myself get out of bed, and when I did, I started crying uncontrollably—screaming even. I wasn't simply ineffectual. I was filled with rage. This part was new. I tripped on a shoe that was lying somewhere in the house and bumped my shin. I wanted to scream for hours and days. Not just scream, but scream at someone. I wanted to scream at both of you. There came a point where I didn't recall not feeling this way. The anger never let up. I thought I would hurt someone. I know this must sound unbelievable to you, but I had to leave."

"Couldn't you have gone to a doctor?" I ask.

"I could have, but I didn't see this as a medical condition. I thought it was my personality."

My mother is nodding.

I shiver in part from the cold and in part from recalling my own reluctance to see a doctor. I know what it's like not to be fully aware of one's condition.

"I assumed a doctor would have kept me from my family. I wasn't in my right mind."

"What did you do?" my mother asks, the question she has been asking all of these years.

"I had no money. I left everything with you two. I hitch-hiked around the country for a while, doing odd jobs when I could find the energy. Sometimes I had no place to stay and the weather conditions made it impossible for me to sleep out-side. I got good at breaking into houses when people weren't home and catching a nap here and there."

I know I should be horrified, but I'm curious. "How did you know people weren't home?"

"Oh. Easy. No car. No lights. A perfectly timed patter of lights turning on and off."

"Security company?" I say as if in on the game as well.

"Exactly. I also have the hearing of a barn owl. I still do. If there's a person in a house, I'll hear him."

"Really?"

"Really," my mother remembers, almost smiling.

"Sure, I've been hearing you two and a little girl—your daughter I might assume. All week."

I shiver. "You've been spying on us."

"Yes. But not exactly spying. I've been here twice. I wanted to see you." He is looking at my mother. "And I wanted to meet you," he says to me specifically. "Both times I chickened out."

"Why didn't you write a letter?"

"I don't know. I'm sorry if I scared you."

I don't have the hearing of a barn owl so I had no idea he was there. But it was the principle of the thing.

"The phone calls scared her," I scolded him.

"Look, I didn't want to scare you. I didn't want to hurt you. I could have let myself in. Remember I can pick locks."

"How did you get by the doorman?" I remember Alfred's look of recognition when he walked by.

"I just walked past him and commented on the weather. He never questioned me."

I quickly make note that Alfred should not be relying on his innately frightening appearance to keep bad people away.

"I would never have picked your lock," my father says. "I have a place to stay in New York. A few years ago, I started volunteering with troubled teens in Ohio. Then I got a job as a youth counselor. That's the right thing for me. An agency that recruits for these kinds of jobs thought I would be happy here in New York. The organization gives me a decent salary and provides me with housing and my own counseling and medical expenses.

"About a month ago I got up the courage to see if I could find out anything about the both of you on the Internet, and I looked you up." His eyes well as he starts to say this to me. "And, this sounds so strange, but I'm so proud of you. You went to good schools; you became an assistant district attorney. I just wanted to see you, I guess. And I lost the courage every time I came near you. And then when I heard your mother, I was overwhelmed with sadness."

"What was it like living like that? I mean, before you got help." This was a question I had often wanted to ask criminal defendants.

"Truthfully, if I was up, it was fun. When I was up, I forgot my pain. If I had the money to pay my way, I would be the guy in the bar who would lead the sing-along, or the neighbor who helped get the barbecue going. I watched kids for people, pets for people, and seniors for people. On the weekends, I'd get all the guys together for a game of touch football. I never seemed to get sleepy. And then, when the depression hit, I would become immobile. I never went out: not for work, not for fun. And then I would run out of money, and I would disappear."

"Didn't anyone see that anything was wrong with you?" I hand him a cup of coffee. He takes it.

"After four years or so, I was working in a small town in Ohio for a young psychiatrist. I did yard work and small home errands for him during the day, and he would see me at nights in the local bars and restaurants.

"One day, I didn't show up to fix my boss's roof. I didn't call him. I never called them. I had, as I always had had before, the intention of going to work the following day. But I didn't go, as I had never gone. And then the next and then the next. Sometimes, the bosses would find me and chew me out, even rough me around a bit if they thought I had taken their money."

My father says this with little emotion, but I can feel his shame. My mother squeezes my hand. She can, too.

"Well, like these others, the psychiatrist came looking for me. But he didn't chew me out. He didn't touch me. He just started asking me questions. And they weren't about why I wasn't fixing his gate or his roof. He wanted to know about my highs and my lows. He seemed to know what I was thinking. He described to me the way that I felt."

Like Schmitt did with me, I think.

"We got to talking, and he told me about my condition. I

didn't believe him at first. But we started a drug-treatment plan. Some worked, some didn't."

"Why didn't you contact us?"

"That I blame on my personality—not on the disease." His atonal voice breaks for a moment and he starts crying. "I have great shame. I have nothing else."

My eyes water a bit. I understand. Sort of.

"I'm a psychologist," my mother uncharacteristically blurts.

"I bet you're good." He is laughing and sobbing at the same time.

"She diagnosed you before your Ohio guy, I think." I laugh, although, come to think of it, I'm sobbing, too.

"Are you . . . ?" He's looking at her. "Are you?"

I know what he is asking. "No, she hasn't remarried," I throw in.

"I don't know if that's good or bad," he says. "Do you live here?"

"No, she still lives in Colorado." I take over, protective and proud. "She's here in New York for a conference. She's watching my daughter."

"So you do have a daughter."

"I do. Molly. She's four. She loves traffic lights."

"I'm a bit of a fan myself." He relaxes somewhat. "Are you still married?"

"Divorced," I say.

"Sorry," he says, as if his leaving had brought about this relatively recent development.

"It's okay."

No, it isn't, we are both thinking.

"Well, then," my father says.

"Well, then," Virginia says.

"That's it?" I say.

My father looks at my mother for guidance. She doesn't say anything.

"Anything else?" he asks.

"Nope," my mother says.

"Nope," I repeat in solidarity.

"So that's it. Can I call you?" he asks her, then looks at me as if to ask me the same question.

"No," my mother says sternly.

My father is hurt. "I understand," he says nonetheless. "I would love to have a morsel of a relationship with you, or you, Kate, or even"—he is crying so he can only mouth the words—"my granddaughter."

"For now," my mother concludes, "let me work this out. In my head. Alone."

We exchange uncomfortable good-byes. My father's hands are glued to the interior of his pockets, and my mother practically pushes him out the door.

"So you don't want to see him?" I ask.

"No. I do. But I just want to wait until these murders are resolved. One chunk of chaos at a time."

"Mom, that is a little dramatic."

"Katie, three people are dead. You know them. It's dangerous."

"I should check on Molly."

"She is at Paul's. She insisted he give her a bath up there. Something about better bath toys."

"Great." I'm smiling, really smiling. "I love you so much, Mom." I give her a big hug.

"I love you, too, sweetheart. It's nice to see you back to your old self."

Out of courtesy, I knock our usual knock, the two short

raps followed by the long ones. There is no answer. I didn't expect one. I turn the doorknob. Paul has kindly unlocked the door so that his ex-mother-in-law can collect her granddaughter and his ex-wife can snoop through his computer.

I tiptoe in. I can hear Molly and Paul singing "It's a Small World" in the bathroom. They will sing it over and over. I turn on Paul's laptop, log in, and start my search for the elusive Katie e-mail.

I see the mommy murders file. Nothing new for Hastings. I see Johanna's file. He seems to reiterate much of Peg's information. There is nothing on the Phillippa killing, just a few links to information on samurai techniques and training resources. Nothing else.

What about the e-mail?

I go through Paul's e-mail. I have to look quickly. If I had more time, I might look for something from Ellen Westin. An invitation to a regatta or a box seat at the opera. That would be awesome since Paul hates opera.

"Everything except for Puccini," he would elucidate.

Their singing is winding down. Stress. Nothing. Mommy-murder scheduling meetings, but nothing substantial, jewelry-store-robbery meetings. Hmm. Maybe this was what Peg was talking about. *Arrgh*. Nothing, Katie. I can't go through this any faster. There is no Katie e-mail, and interestingly, there is nothing from Ellen Westin.

Is Paul keeping a separate e-mail for his new romance?

Then I notice something. A forwarded e-mail. From: *Unknown sender*. To: *NYPD General*. Subject: *Hawthorne*. The e-mail is dated one week ago.

I click on the e-mail. It says, *Kate Hagen is next*.

"Mommy," Molly screams.

"Hi, sweetheart." I shut the power off on the computer.

"Why are you on Daddy's computer? Are you looking for answers?"

"Why are you on my computer?" Paul echoes as he comes out of the room.

"I think, Molly, um . . ." I can't very well say she's mistaken. She saw me at the computer. If I tell her she's wrong, she will lose trust in herself, or in me. "I was looking to see if Daddy received an e-mail I sent him."

"But how would you get into my e-mail?" Paul asks.

"And there's the rub." I give a wacky grin.

"Were you looking through my e-mail?"

"No. I thought I had sent you something earlier, and I couldn't remember if I had sent it to you." The lies are tripping off my tongue. And they make no sense.

"You are making no sense." I can't tell if Paul is going to get angry with me for prying in his e-mails.

"I know." I become quiet. "We just talked about so much earlier, you know." I gulp a bit for dramatic effect. "I wrote you an e-mail, and I don't know if I sent it by mistake. I shouldn't have sent it." I lead Paul to believe that the contents of my fictitious e-mail may be of a romantic nature.

Paul grabs my hand. "I understand, Katie. Our conversation is by no means finished." He's looking into my eyes with such intensity that I'm forced, for the sake of maintaining the yarn about my e-mail, to gaze back at him. To avoid getting caught, I need him to believe that we have reforged our connection.

Yet I find my stomach doing a somersault or two.

"Let's go, Molly," I say. "Let's get some clothing on you. Daddy has to go to work, and Grandma is probably waiting for us with a special surprise."

Molly lets me throw her clothes on. Paul has turned on the computer. He glances at me. I can't read his look. Is it come-hither or I'm-onto-you?

We are back home. Should I tell my mother any of this? If I mention Paul's apology and the intimate glances, she might get into therapy mode and start to assess where we both are: his pain, my pain. She'll ask how I feel. I will tell her I don't know. I can't possibly tell her that I felt a surge of attraction just minutes ago.

You're jealous of this Ellen Westin, she will say. *These feelings often accompany chaos. People are dying. Look at all of the people who rushed to get married after September 11.* Or she might press me on my mental state, my poor judgment with Steve and Phillippa.

And she doesn't even know about my misjudgment of Liane. I saw nothing in Paul's files to suggest he was onto her, but it seems as if he is onto nobody.

"Kate Hagen is next," I whisper to myself.

That's why Paul has been so secretive.

And Peg, too.

That's why Paul has been coming here, why he is hovering. He's guarding me, the mother of his kid.

That's why he's so "sorry," and why he glances. I had considered for a second that there might be electricity, but there is no electricity. He's staying close to me to protect Molly, and to catch the killer.

Which, I remind myself, is why I stay so close to him.

Thank goodness I didn't make a fool of myself. Thank goodness I met his gaze for a minimal time. How silly of me to have my heartstrings tugged for even a millisecond.

There is also the matter of Ellen Westin.

"Kate Hagen is next," I say louder.

The e-mail was written a week ago, after Johanna was killed.

And I wasn't next.

Phillippa was.

Could another person have killed Phillippa, someone who wanted her dead and took advantage of the "serial situation" in the parent community? Her death does seem a little odd. Being murdered with a samurai sword is drastic . . . funny almost. But then so do all of the murders: a bludgeoning, an electrocution, and a samurai sword. There's a bit of a Clue-board-game aspect to all of them. Why couldn't the killer have simply shot these women?

It's hard to acquire a gun without leaving a trail if you don't know the right people.

No outside weapons were used in any of these murders. The killer wouldn't know how to acquire them.

Because the killer doesn't have criminal connections.

Kate Hagen will be next.

Kate Hagen. Not Kate Alger.

The killer didn't use my married name. At Hawthorne, everybody refers to me only as Alger.

Everybody except Liane.

Feminist Liane, who happens to hate guns.

The evening passes by rather quietly. My mother spends most of the time going over her notes for the conference. Molly is in bed quite early. Before she falls asleep she whispers to me that she likes it best when she is with her daddy and me at the same time.

"And Grandma, too," she says just as she falls asleep.

I am behind a bush watching the Greek goddess Athena playing with her chum. They are shooting arrows at a tree, danc-
ing and laughing. The sun is bright, and even in my sleep I feel
blinded by its piercing rays, which have taken over the whole
sky.

"You are no match for me, Pallas," Athena jokes with her
friend, as she runs to a stream to collect arrows for their next
round of shots.

"We shall see." Pallas laughs. I laugh, too, but I am invisi-
ble and inaudible to them.

Athena removes an arrow from her quiver and places it in
her bow. As she pulls the arrow back, I see only the sun in my
eyes.

"You forgot one. Let me get it for you," her friend calls. But
Athena has already pulled back her string. A shadow presents
itself for a moment and I see Athena's arrow go forward in slow
motion. I call out, "Pallas."

But to no avail. The arrow hits Pallas in her back and
pierces her heart.

Cut to Pallas's funeral. It is in St. Christopher's Chapel. Even
in my dream I recognize it as the same setting as for Beverly's
funeral. They are eerily the same. Only Phillippa isn't there. But
Paul is there, the other Hawthorne moms are there, and I'm
there. I am staring at the stained-glass window that portrays the
story of Sarah, Hagar, and Abraham.

I wake up.

My sheets are soaked in sweat.

My mother comes running into the room. "Kate."

I'm shaking.

"Kate, are you okay?"

"I'm fine, Mom. I just had the weirdest dream about Athena."

"The goddess Athena?"

"No, the hooker Athena. Of course the goddess Athena."

"Kate. Don't speak to me that way."

"You're right, Mom. I'm sorry. Anyway, it was the story of Athena and Pallas."

"I thought Pallas and Athena were the same."

"Sort of. The story is that Athena killed Pallas. Sometimes Pallas is a woman, sometimes a man. Sometimes it is a maid, sometimes it is her friend. I prefer them as friends. Female friendship is rare in Greek mythology, so I prefer that interpretation."

"Not much of a friendship."

"Oh, no. Athena killed her by accident. That is the tragedy of it. And as a tribute to her dead friend, Athena assumes her name."

"What a horrible story," my mother says.

"All of those stories are sort of horrible. That's their allure. Weird that I dreamt it."

"Why?"

"The story never did anything for me. I mean, you hadn't heard of it and I used to ramble on and on about this stuff when I was a kid. Of all of the hundreds of myths I used to consume and discuss and ruminate upon, the story of Pallas and Athena wasn't one. There's just not that much there. A woman killed her friend by accident. No revenge. No monsters. No storms or wars."

"Which begs the question, why did you dream it?"

"I'm sure it has something to do with these murders."

"Even you are getting spooked," she says.

"In my dream, Pallas was Beverly Hastings."

"Really?"

"Okay, not exactly. But her funeral was essentially Beverly's funeral; same music, same church, same stained glass, same guests. I'm wondering if this is meaningful. Maybe it's a heavenly clue, but I'm not sure what it means." I look at my mother. "You think I'm crazy for seeing this as a prophecy?"

"No, not crazy."

"Do you think it's a prophecy?"

"I think it may be something your subconscious is trying to send to your conscious conscious. You may be holding on to something you don't know you know."

"Is that what you're giving your speech on tomorrow?"

My mother laughs. "Let's try to think about this. There's a murder."

"Technically, it's a homicide," I say. "In a murder the killer has intent to kill. In this story, it's an accident."

"Sure," my mother dismisses my legal expertise. "So the killer in the dream is Athena. Does that resonate for you?"

"No, I'm a fan of Athena. She's the goddess of wisdom and fairness. I identify with her." I pause. "I've got it," I abruptly break in.

"What?"

"I killed everybody. It was an accident and now I remember. That's what the dream meant. I should take myself to the precinct and turn myself in."

My mother doesn't say anything.

"Mom?"

She still doesn't say anything.

"Mom, of course I didn't kill anybody. You know I'm kidding."

"Of course," my mother says, although I know for a microsecond she was wondering where it all went wrong. "Do you have any ideas?"

"I'm just trying to figure out who the characters in the dream stand for. Pallas is the victims, Beverly, Johanna, and Phillippa. And Athena is their killer, their friend."

"And you?" my mother asks. "What about you?"

"I was there. I was watching. I could do nothing to save them."

"How do you know you were only a watcher? How do you know you weren't Athena the killer? Or Pallas the victim?"

"We went over this, Mom. I was watching." I feel as if I'm trying to talk myself out of getting in trouble with my mother for killing Athena's friend.

"But you're the author of the dream, right? You are not only in command of you, the character of the quiet observer, but you control the actions of Athena and Pallas. You are not watching someone else's dream. You are directing their actions. And in that way, you have three roles here. You are the observer, you are the killer, and you are the victim. The awake you sees yourself only as the observer, but your unconscious sees yourself in all three roles. You are each of these women."

You are the observer, you are the victim, and you are the killer.

Kate Hagen is next. The vision of the e-mail abruptly appears in my head. A shiver runs up my legs. "Maybe." It's all I can muster. There is no way I am telling her about the e-mail. She'll react drastically. We'll all end up in Colorado with aliases like Mitzi and Della.

"Go back to sleep, Mom. You have your conference tomorrow. I promise I won't wake you again."

"Are you sure you don't want me to sleep in the bed with you?"

"I'm sure." But I'm not. This is starting to get creepy.

Mom left for the conference early this morning, and I took Molly to school. Hawthorne has a security detail now. I don't recognize any of the cops, but they seem to know who I am. I feel safer there than anywhere else.

I get home. I have a couple of hours before I have to pick Molly up. I turn on the TV to see if there are any breaking-news stories.

Nada.

I pick up the phone and dial Peg's number.

"You'll be the first to know," she answers the phone.

"Pardon?"

"You called because you want to know stuff. You'll be the first to know."

I laugh. "Peg, I wasn't prying for info. I actually have some ideas here."

"Kate, I'm sure you have theories. Good theories. But there is stuff that we know that you are better off not knowing."

"Peg, if I didn't know you better, I would say that you've been taking classes in being condescending."

"It's not that, sweetheart. It's that my hands are tied."

"I get it." And I do get it. Peg knows about the Katie e-mail. And she hasn't said anything. We may be playing the same game, but we aren't on the same team. We both want to catch the bad guy, but she's the thimble and I'm the dog. I can't tell her about Liane until I have 100 percent proof that she did it. Otherwise I will just be another crackpot with time on her

278 • KAREN BERGREEN

hands who wants to use her knowledge of Greek mythology to help solve a string of murders.

I need to tell her about the Katie e-mail and about my suspicions regarding Liane. I'll have to tell her that Steve turned out to be an utter disaster, but that our fling was not in vain. For Steve is the key to this. Steve a nursery-school teacher/physicist who happens to be oversexed. He obviously picked the wrong woman to cheat on. I'll explain it all to Peg, but I'll hold on to the part about going through her computer. Friendship goes only so far.

"Kate, if I were you, I would be extremely careful until this thing has been resolved."

"Is there something you're not telling me?"

"Nothing like that."

Nothing like that. That's what Peg says when she means there's something like that.

Peg must already know about the Katie e-mail. How could she not? The whole NYPD and half of the DA's office must know about it. Obviously, if I am a target, they must have been watching me this whole time. At least, that is, until Phillippa was murdered. So the Katie e-mail is useless. The killer, Liane, used it as a red herring to throw them off the scent. She knew that the ex-husband and the friend would do everything they could to protect me so she could defeat her competition in peace.

Meanwhile, Paul and Peg and God knows who else have most likely been tracking my every move. They probably surveilled my date with Steve.

Yuck. I feel violated all over again. Suddenly I'm angry with Peg. She is supposed to be my friend. She should have told me about the e-mail. After all, they believed I was in danger. Shouldn't I have been notified? I might have had the option to flee to Canada or something.

I'm about to ask Peg about this when she says, "Just a sec." Peg attempts to put her hand over the receiver, but, as luck and her bad aim would have it, she misses and I can hear voices. I hear Jordana, her secretary, say that someone is waiting for her.

"What?" says Peg.

I'm about to scream into the phone that it's time for her to get a hearing aid because her hearing loss is now affecting her job, when I hear Jordana clearly.

"Ellen Westin is here to see you."

Ellen Westin. My Ellen—I mean Paul's Ellen Westin.

"Tell her I'll meet them at the restaurant," I hear Peg say. "Gristle's. In about twenty minutes."

Gristle's in about twenty minutes.

I can't get to Gristle's in about twenty minutes.

Shit.

"Darlin', I've gotta go. Sit tight. I love you," Peg says.

Brutus.

I hang up the phone with the intention of slamming it. I feel rage. I don't even know where to begin. But I know I have to go to Gristle's.

I run to the subway. Peg and Ellen Westin must be at Gristle's already. Meet *them* there, she had said. *Them*. Who's *them*? Paul? Is Peg's husband, Marty, coming, too? Paul has moved on and so has Peg.

My heart is pounding in my chest. No wonder Peg, a big Paul fan, has been pushing me to date. She knows that Paul and Ellen are together. She's known this whole time. Just as she knew about the Katie e-mail. Poor depressed, fragile Katie. They must have been laughing over my fling with inappropriate Steve while Paul was bringing around sophisticated Ellen.

I emerge from the subway at Chambers Street and jog past 1 Hogan Place onto Bayard Street. I have tucked my hair in my baseball cap and am wearing a hooded sweatshirt. I look like a bikeless delivery boy.

I try to calm myself down a bit.

Maybe Ellen Westin isn't a romantic interest at all. Maybe this is job-related.

But it can't be job-related. I checked out the employee roster at the police department and the DA's office. No Ellen Westin was listed.

Maybe she is going for an interview. Or she could be a reporter. She resembles Rosalind Russell in *His Girl Friday*. I could see that.

I feel a bit better as I come upon the restaurant. Should I go in?

"Yes," I say loudly before my reasonable inner voice can persuade me otherwise.

I walk in.

"Can I help you?" A hostess with a head of multi-toned brown hair shaped in a striking, but nonetheless unattractive, asymmetrical haircut asks.

I panic.

"Um. Yes. May, um, I please . . ." Do I ask for takeout? No. I need to get into the body of the restaurant. "May I please—" I am staring at her eyes, which are practically camouflaged by the thick black eyeliner and mascara.

Shoot. I am so not dressed for a table.

"May I please use your potty?" And did you by any chance apply your makeup with a Sharpie?

The hostess gives me an obnoxious look. After all, I am standing under the RESTROOMS FOR CUSTOMERS ONLY sign.

"Please," I say, imitating Molly and crossing my legs as if I'm about to piddle on their sparkly floor.

"That way." She points to the back of the room.

I skulk into the restaurant. At the center table I see them: Ellen, Peg, and Paul.

My heart sinks. As I approach them, I posit again that she is a reporter. I am standing next to the table. Paul is holding Ellen's hand, displaying it to Peg.

"Gorgeous," Peg says.

Ellen lifts her forearm from the table and admires a huge diamond ring sitting on her left hand.

I think it's okay to jump to conclusions now.

I skip the restroom and turn around, rushing by the thoroughly confused hostess.

I can't believe Paul is getting married again so soon.

Especially after we had that conversation yesterday. I can't believe I told him about the cancer. I can't believe I felt close to him, even if it was just for a moment.

Of course, it all makes sense. Paul is ready to move on to a new chapter in his life. Ellen will be in Molly's life, and he wants to make sure that I'm okay with this. For Molly's sake.

But Peg. Peg was my friend. How could she have stabbed me in the back?

Pallas.

That must have been my dream. My subconscious telling me that my friend would not literally kill me, but figuratively. An accidental stabbing. Like Paul, Peg couldn't help but fall in love with Ellen.

I would have cried the whole way home on the subway if it

hadn't gotten stuck due to a sick passenger. It takes me an hour and a half to get back. I memorize every advertisement around me. Everything is in Spanish. A college kid takes advantage of the captive audience and hands out pamphlets for a Gustave Doré exhibit at the Frick. "I'm an intern there," he boasts. No one is impressed. Bored, however, we all take the pamphlet. I glance down at the etching on the cover. It is a teeny-tiny picture of Hagar and Ishmael.

Hagar. I don't think I have thought about Hagar since I took a Bible class in high school. And suddenly she is everywhere: on St. Christopher's stained-glass window at Beverly's funeral, even Pallas's funeral in my dream, and here on this little Doré pamphlet. Maybe it's a sign. My mother thinks I look for signs where they don't exist. It's the ancient Greek in me.

Hagar. I am trying to remember the story. Hagar was the maid, really slave, of Sarah and Abraham, and when they couldn't have a baby, Abraham made a baby, Ishmael, with Hagar. And then Sarah took the baby from Hagar and raised it as her own.

So Abraham slept with the help. They didn't have more clinical insemination techniques back then. Abraham was getting a little on the side. Just like Paul. How's that for a sign? I thought it was going to be a sign about the killer because of my dream about Pallas and Athena. But, no, it's much less interesting. God is trying to tell me that men have been unfaithful since the Old Testament.

I feel warmed by solidarity with Sarah as I finally part ways with my subway car and run back to the apartment.

I give a quick hello to Alfred, who looks more sallow than usual, and I head upstairs.

My mother is at the door. "Where have you been? I thought you were supposed to stay home."

"I know, but I had to—" I'm poised to admit my ill-fated frolic so that I can tell her that I have unlocked the key to my subconscious and now know the meaning of the Pallas/Athena dream when she jumps in.

"Thank goodness you're home."

"Is Molly okay?" I chastise myself for not having picked her up from school.

"Molly's fine. It's Aimi Wentz."

"Oh my God. Don't tell me she's dead?"

"She's not dead."

"What?" I look up in horror. My heart starts racing; my mind follows. Is she the killer? I think maybe it's not Liane after all. Aimi was single and found Steve attractive. He loves kids, and it wouldn't hurt to have a man in Tess's life.

"She's in a coma," my mother says.

Okay. Back to the Liane theory. "Is she going to be okay?"

"They don't know. Paul said he would call me as soon as he knows."

"Paul?"

"Yes, Paul. He called me. I told him I thought you were with him and he sounded agitated."

Of course he sounded agitated. His engagement luncheon must have been ruined.

"He's coming over here." She pauses. There's more. I'm waiting for her to tell me that Paul's engaged. She's probably gone out with Ellen, too.

"What?" Now I'm the agitated one.

"Tess is missing."

My heart skips a beat. Tess. Little Tess is missing. "Are you sure? This isn't the killer's modus operandi. Maybe they just don't have the facts."

"I don't have the facts, but Paul made it sound that way. Kate, I'm scared."

Unfortunately, just as she says this, Molly walks in. "Why are you scared, Grandma?"

"Oh, nothing, sweetie. It's just an expression."

"Mommy, why is Grandma scared?"

I look at Grandma. I have nothing to say. Frankly I'm off-balance myself.

"Mommy, are you scared?"

"No, sweetie."

By this point, Molly has herself worked up. "Mommy, I'm scared."

This hasn't been the first time that Molly has been frightened, but it is the first time her fears are at least somewhat rooted in reality. I don't have the presence of mind to pull her into bed with me and sing "My Favorite Things," but I think of the next-best solution.

I say we can watch some TV

Molly's fears vanish. TV is a big treat in our house. I try to limit Molly's exposure to television, less for reasons of good parenting than because Molly tends to break anything with a plug or a battery. She has smashed two remote controls and jammed another.

"But, Mama, I like the buttons," Molly always defends herself. One time she had switched from *Ni Hao, Kai-Lan* to an infomercial for a bottom-shaper. "What's that?" she asked, pointing me to what looked to be a clothed rehearsal for a porn movie.

"Oh, that's a kind of show called an infomercial."

"Oh," Molly said, clearly not understanding.

"Mommy's friend Miriam is in a show like that," I said, referring to the Abbisaucer.

"Oh." Molly had lost interest.

Tonight, I hear two short knocks followed by two long ones. Paul. I'm grateful he's here.

"Daddy, Daddy, Daddy." Molly runs to the door.

But it's not Daddy. It's Miriam.

Again?

Hello, hello, hello.

Miriam is without a doubt the last person I want to see tonight. I just cannot listen to her.

"I so wanted to stop by and say hi," she says.

"Hi," I manage weakly.

"Did you love my knock?"

"Loved," I say flatly. And I double-lock the door in a passive-aggressive attempt to tell her that this wasn't acceptable.

"So funny that I completely fooled you."

"Fooled me." I wish I could put her in front of the TV along with Molly.

"So," she says.

"So, we're a little tense here so it may not be the best time."

"Tense, honey? Oh. Then it's great that I came over. Why are you tense?"

Because everyone around me is getting killed. Because my ex-husband is getting remarried. Because my best friend prefers his new betrothed to me. Because I have nothing to do but pretend I'm in my old job, which I am doing badly.

"Things," I say instead.

"Oh, honey. I totally get it. But you should use me as your ray of hope. You know how I have just had the worst luck. And you just told me to keep plugging along, and, well, any day now, Evan and I will get married and then have the kid."

I didn't know that Miriam wanted a kid. "So it's really happening?"

"Well, nothing is in stone. I just had to take care of some stuff. You know, I made so many decisions when I was single, and now that I'm with *the one,* I have to compromise."

"I think that's great. You deserve it."

"You bet I do. After all I've gone through." Miriam looks proud of herself at this moment.

"Okay then," I say, hinting for her to leave.

"Okay, then," she concludes without moving.

"Miriam, I've got to do some stuff. Molly is a little spooked and I've got my own things to worry about."

"Why is Molly so spooked?"

Why do I have to keep reminding Miriam that everyone around us is dropping dead? "Kids pick up on these things. You know, the murders and all."

"Oh, but Molly has nothing to worry about."

"Well, there's been a new development. One of the kids is missing."

Miriam doesn't ask further and says, "I'm sure Molly will be fine."

Why are you so sure? I want to ask her. Because you are getting married and it has nothing to do with you. I suddenly feel furious at Miriam. She's been waltzing in and out of my home now for three years, presenting me with the minutiae of her life, all the while blithely dismissing traumatic events that are happening around her. How does she know Molly will be fine? I'm not happy at this moment with her in my house.

"Don't you have someplace to be?"

"No. Not yet." She doesn't take the hint.

"I've got some stuff to do."

"Okay." She remains still.

I can hear my mother in the next room telling Molly that her favorite part of *Cinderella* was the pumpkin turning into a coach. "Molly, maybe you will discover a way to make fuel out of squash, too." Leave it to my mother to find the green in fairy tales.

Miriam asks if she can use the bathroom. This tends to be a huge time-eater for she tends to see any bathroom visit as an occasion to touch up her makeup and admire her appearance.

I check my e-mail. I have a message from Liane. My stomach starts to turn again as I give it a quick look.

Dear Kate:

I hope you are safe and well. I am writing to you to tell you how sorry I am for my behavior these last few days. I think we are all on edge because of the tragedies, and I have some other issues going on as well.

I don't know why I can't talk to you about this in person. Maybe it's because I am embarrassed. Maybe it's because admitting to others that something is wrong would require admitting that something to myself.

I hope that makes sense. I was never much of a wordsmith—that's why I like making jewelry and selling homes.

Here it is: I think my marriage is pretty much over. Arthur and I haven't spoken—except in front of Max, of course—for about six months now. Arthur has another apartment that he sleeps in after we put Max to bed. We have tried to go to counseling, but are on our third therapist, and things are getting dire.

Recently, I have engaged in behavior I'm not proud of. I have no excuse except that I wanted a huge distraction. And instead of cultivating what seemed to be a possible burgeoning friendship with you, I have been acting like a spoiled teenager.

I would love to call and talk to you about all this. Hopefully we will still be alive. Haha. I shouldn't joke I know, but you seem to have a sense of humor about this nightmare we are all in. So, as soon as the police have their man, I would love to take you to coffee or lunch or something with alcohol.

Stay safe,
Liane

"You didn't tell me I had bags under my eyes," Miriam interrupts my daze. "How can I be seen like this?"

"You look great." I am still wearing my hooded sweatshirt, jeans, and baseball cap. I think I need to read Liane's e-mail again.

"I need some hot water with lemon and cayenne pepper," Miriam announces.

I stare at the computer. Liane's e-mail seems so real, so genuine. Her behavior, which I had interpreted to be indicative of a serial killer, is also indicative of someone whose marriage is falling apart. I should know.

Could it be that she was onto my suspicions about her and wanted to throw me off her scent?

"Mommy! Come in here." Molly is screaming for me.

I run in. "Look, Mama: Miriam. And it's not an infomercial." She's pointing at the TV. While Miriam looks and acts like a princess much of the time, I need to tell my daughter that she isn't in *Cinderella.*

But Molly isn't watching *Cinderella.* She's watching Channel 2093, a channel I have never heard of. And there on the screen is a movie whose production values appear low. Miriam is on the screen.

She is wearing a white ski parka, tight black pants, and snowshoes.

"Don't kill me," she's screaming. *"Please don't kill me."* Her acting makes me wince.

We see that Miriam's character is about to be stabbed—not just stabbed, speared, by a huge, curved fishing spear.

"What is this?" my mother asks. "Molly should not be watching this."

"Grandma, I know this is make-believe. Miriam would never wear those silly things on her feet."

"It's *Slaughter at Snowcap*," I tell my mother. "It was one of Miriam's legit acting jobs."

"I've never heard of this."

"How did you escape that?" I whisper. "I had to watch it three times. It's awful. It's about a serial killer in the mountains who kills a bunch of women. But it's not like the killer has a signature murder method. I always thought serial killers killed everyone the same way, but this one employed a bunch of methods. One is stabbed, one is bludgeoned, one is electrocu—" I cut myself off.

I shiver at the familiarity of this. When I saw the movie, I never told Miriam how absurd it was that a serial killer would kill in so many random fashions. But she wanted to feel special. A harpoon killed her character. Could it be that the killer watched this obscure, awful movie and got the idea from that?

That is ridiculous. First of all, except for Miriam and me, no one has seen this movie.

I can hear Miriam singing the Hawthorne song. Why would Miriam be singing the Hawthorne song? First, she can't sing.

Second, she hates kids' songs, and third, why would she even know the Hawthorne song? I hardly know it.

She has been saying that she and Evan want to have a baby. Maybe she is hoping to send the baby to Hawthorne. But that wouldn't be for years. She would have to get pregnant first.

I hear Miriam's voice in my head. *We are going to have this kid.* I think back on our discussions about their romance. Evan has no children of his own, but he became attached to his ex's kid. He carried the picture around. But that kid was six years old. Too old for Hawthorne. Also, why would Evan get custody of a kid that wasn't his when the biological mother was perfectly competent?

Maybe they are adopting a kid.

And Miriam wants to send the kid to Hawthorne.

That's why she was so interested in Molly. That's why she wanted to borrow the class picture—to get herself interested in Hawthorne.

But why Hawthorne? A year ago I could understand, but I would never send my kids to a preschool with a mom murder rate.

So typical of Miriam. So out of it.

I look up at the TV screen. Miriam is dead. She looks like a little girl there—placid and vulnerable. There's no designer dress, no champagne, and her makeup is running. It brings me back to our childhoods when this was how she looked. She was so pretty, but she was less "done." And her hair was lighter. Come to think of it, I never thought of it before, but she looked a little like Tess.

Poor Tess. Missing. She could be dead or orphaned. She's such a cute kid. And Miriam liked her. Probably because she looked like Miriam and wore cute shoes. In fact, I am certain that if Aimi and Miriam were both walking on the street with Tess, everyone would assume that Miriam was her mother.

The resemblance is uncanny. Does Miriam think that as well? Does she want to adopt Tess? Is that why she was interested in her? My blood cools in my veins and I don't like where my thoughts are leading me. Liane's e-mail causes me to doubt that she is the killer, so I, what? I immediately start thinking it's Miriam?

I am officially crazy.

I bet if I look at the class picture, I will realize how wrong I am. I head into the kitchen. I realize Miriam has Molly's recent class picture and I have only last year's. I run over to my photo file to pick it up. I have only just started to sort Molly's baby pictures, but my childhood pictures are in perfect order. My mother used to take my picture every year on the first day of school and the last day of school. I look at the kindergarten pictures. There I am covering my face—shy about having my picture taken. I turn the page to see the last day of school. I have obviously overcome my bashfulness. I am staring into the camera with a big thumbs-up. And standing next to me is another girl in the same pose.

Oh my God. It's Tess. I mean it's Miriam, but the picture is the spitting image of Tess. I feel chills.

This is all about Tess.

Something falls out of my pocket. It's the Doré pamphlet. I am staring at Hagar.

Hagar—the woman who gave birth, but did not raise her baby. In Doré's picture she is in pain, not the pain of childbirth, but the pain of loss.

I turn around and see Miriam, and she has the same expression on her face.

"I think things are really turning around for me," I hear her voice behind me, and I turn around. She's holding my meat cleaver. "Evan and I will get married. Now that I have my baby, we will live happily ever after."

"You killed all of these mommies, and you killed them for Tess?" I am realizing this as the words come out of my mouth.

"Oh, no. Her name is Fiona. *Tess* doesn't work for me. I am her real mother. Aimi just borrowed her. When she didn't return her, I had to take matters into my own hands."

"You mean by killing a bunch of other moms?"

"That was your fault," Miriam says.

"My fault."

"Yes, this is all your fault. You had the wrong address for Aimi on your bulletin board. The years I have had to put up with you and your anal organization skills. And the one time I need them, you don't come through for me."

"Beverly's address!" I flash to a memory of Beverly screaming at Bree about mixing up the addresses.

Suddenly, Miriam is waving my enormous meat cleaver in the air.

"Miriam," I say gently, "what are you doing? I think you should put that down."

I am whispering in the hope that Molly and my mother will stay put.

"Kate, are you okay?" My mother comes in, screaming, with Molly in tow. It is too late.

"Hello, Virginia. Hi, Molly."

Miriam sounds casual. A little drop-in. A huge meat cleaver.

"What are you doing?" Molly is staring at the deranged woman.

"She's practicing for a play," my mother says quickly. I hope Molly cannot hear the quiver in her voice.

"Miriam has been very busy trying to get her family together," I throw in.

My mother has no idea what I am talking about, but she does her best to counsel my psychotic pal. "That can be a lot of work." Her vagueness is purposeful.

"You don't even know," Miriam says.

"She's concerned that I am going to mouth all of her private business." I clear my throat here. "To Paul and, um, Peg."

"But you hate them," my mother says.

"No, you don't," Molly whines. "Mommy loves Daddy, and she says Peg is one of the family."

I shrug.

Miriam believes Molly. "You know, Kate, I just can't do it. I always have to work around your life. Around your kid, and your ex-husband, and all of your sicknesses. Well, it's my turn, and I'm not going to let you ruin it." She waves the knife around again.

"Is this for the play?" Molly asks.

"Virginia, go into the bedroom with Molly. I want to talk to Kate first."

I know I can't talk her out of this. "Miriam, I'm really sorry you see me as self-absorbed." I am apologizing to her because I want to save my mother and my kid. I'm apologizing to her because I want my daughter to grow up with a mother. I'm apologizing because I want to live. I want to live. There is so much for me out there. I may want to work again. I may want a relationship again. I loved Paul. I even love him now, despite his betrayal and betrothal. Maybe I can find that again.

I want to stay alive.

If I didn't know of her success in killing the others, I would laugh at Miriam as she wields the meat cleaver. She looks ridiculous. But her track record speaks for itself.

I have to think fast.

"Miriam, your triceps!"

"What?"

"Have you been skipping the gym?"

"Are you kidding me?" She pulls her arm down for a second to check out her potential flab, and I grab her.

I try to wrench the cleaver from her hands, but she is holding it tight.

"Miriam, it's over."

"No, it's not. I'm fitter than you."

She pushes me to the ground and is standing on my sternum with the knife above her head. I am Pallas. She is Athena. Then I recall that Athena is the goddess of wisdom.

"Sorry, Kate, I liked you. Fiona and Molly could have been friends."

Suddenly everything goes black.

I'm not dead. I'm not unconscious.

It's dark in my house. I start to make out the figure next to me. It is Miriam. Her knife is in our table leg. She reaches toward my throat, and I am sure I'm about to die. But before I stop breathing for good, two men are on top of her.

One of them is Paul. The other is my father.

Everything gets blacker.

This time, I do pass out.

I come to I don't know how many minutes later. My mother, my father, and Molly are standing over me. I wonder for a second if I am now dead, and they are looking at my body. My mother keeps saying my name, Molly keeps saying, "Mommy," and my father, undoubtedly realizing he is only a bit player here, is looking on supportively.

I see that Paul and my father have Miriam restrained. Suddenly, Peg is here, wearing a mint-colored dress, looking a little too put together for the circumstances. She is writing in her notebook at warp speed.

Miriam is screaming, "Are you kidding me? Are you kidding me?"

"It's a pleasure to ignore you," Paul says.

I look at my family. "Are you guys okay? Molly, don't be scared."

"I'm okay, Mommy." Molly squeezes my hand. "I have a new grandpa."

I look at my mother to see if a flicker of pain is on her face. There is none.

Miriam has been in jail for two days now. Not surprisingly, Evan has abandoned her. I did not have the pleasure of meeting him, but Paul did.

"He's a decent guy. Caught up in his businesses. He met Miriam, she was pretty, she was enthusiastic, and she told him she was a single mother. Turns out he had had testicular cancer a few years ago, which left him sterile. But he really wanted children. Miriam told him that she had a daughter named Fiona. She talked about her all the time. When he wanted to meet her, she kept saying no, that it wouldn't be fair until she was in a serious, long-term relationship. That's when Evan started thinking he might want to settle down. She showed him pictures of Tess and rattled off stories about her activities—which sounded creepily similar to Molly's."

"He was going to marry her?" I ask, incredulous.

"Look, you are friends with her."

"But marriage is different."

Paul doesn't say anything. I think he is trying to find the right time to tell me about Ellen Westin, but he's worried that I might pass out.

"I think she really would have killed me," I declare out loud. "And then, my mother—and Molly—I don't want to think about it."

"I think you're right. She was desperate. And focused. For what it's worth, though, I don't think she ever wanted to kill you."

I try not to think about what would have happened. If Paul and my father hadn't come in, I'm certain Miriam would have killed the three of us.

"How did you know what was going on?" I ask Paul and my father.

Paul looks at my father. "He's the hero here. Let him tell it."

"I got worried," my father says softly, "when Virginia was talking to you about the murders after I left the other day."

"After you left?"

"Yes. I have been blessed and cursed with good hearing. I couldn't stop thinking about it. And the doorman thought I was welcome here, so I've been hanging around, you know."

"Spying on us?" I am only slightly creeped out.

"He was protecting his family," Paul interjects. "And when he heard screaming, he came up to get me."

"Did you know who he was?" I ask.

"No. He just said there was an intruder in the house. And when I got there, the door was locked. My key didn't work—"

Of course, I double-locked it to "punish" Miriam.

"And I picked it."

"It wasn't until after we had Miriam downtown that I asked this guy who he was, and then he tells me he's your father."

"I thought he would punch me," my father says.

"I thought I would, too," Paul says. "But it wasn't my place"

I'll say.

It's been exactly two weeks since Miriam tried to cleave me. Paul and Peg have been kind enough to let me help with the investigation, citing "special circumstances." We have, I think, pieced the whole story together. It wasn't too difficult, as Miriam is a big talker. She had never intended to kill Beverly. She made that clear. It's uncertain whether she had planned to kill Aimi. She just wanted Tess back.

"Fiona," she shrieked from her jail cell when she heard us talking.

She had gone to Beverly's town house, thinking it was Aimi's. As I had surmised, she rang Beverly's servants' entrance doorbell. Beverly ran downstairs to answer the door, assuming it was someone interviewing for a new staff position.

Miriam was at her door. Without any fanfare, she asked to take "Fiona." When Beverly told her that no Fiona was in the house, Miriam took a free weight out of her purse and smashed Beverly on her head.

"She was just so condescending. I don't know how you could put up with these people." Miriam was not 100 percent crazy.

"I just can't believe she carried a free weight in her purse," Peg said.

"I'm sure there was a jump rope in there somewhere," I assured her. "Someone could have gotten strangled. If it were possible, she would carry a Pilates Reformer."

When Miriam ran upstairs to get her daughter, she saw another little girl sleeping.

"It was some kid named Bitsy," she complained to Paul. "I didn't want Bitsy. I wanted Tess."

As soon as Miriam realized she had the wrong baby and had hurt the wrong mommy, she panicked and ran downstairs, out the front, more elegant, door. She didn't want to go all the way downstairs. She was afraid Beverly might still be alive.

"I didn't realize killing came so naturally to me," she said to Peg with some pride.

Miriam realized that she couldn't simply locate Aimi's house and run over to get Tess, but she remembered the plot of the movie she had been in years before. She would act as a serial killer preying on the mothers at Hawthorne school. No one would think she was the one. She had no connection to the school. She would get rid of a few moms, grab Tess, and marry Evan.

Just like that.

It was fairly easy for her to be invited into the homes of the Hawthorne moms, even after they were warned. They trusted her because she looked like them—only thinner. Johanna's doorman let her into the apartment without question when she told him she was the babysitter. The doorman helped her by telling her that the door was open, so she let herself in. She overheard the bath running and headed over to the tub. It was hard for her to focus on Johanna at first, she confided to Peg, because she had amazing bathroom furniture. But then she saw what she described as a "big-ass hair dryer" and threw it into the water.

Miriam told Paul that she picked Phillippa as a murder victim out of respect for me. She remembered some of my stories about Phillippa, and she knew she would be easy to kill. After all, the weapons were in her house: the prized sword collection.

"I really didn't want to kill anybody," she added. "I just wanted my baby girl. I'm like the grizzly bear who goes after people who steal their cubs. But I really kind of enjoyed getting rid of Phillippa. She answered the door in a stupid Chanel suit, which, I'm sorry, is so over. Coco is dead, lady. Buy de la Renta."

To gain access to the von Eck residence, Miriam used her best acting skills. She told Phillippa that the Asia Society was interested in honoring her and her husband for their contributions to all things Asian. She asked if she could look at the swords, to see which sword would be on the cover of their catalog.

"You could kill someone with a samurai sword?" I asked when we were all in the interrogation room.

"Kate," Miriam whined, "I told you to come to my gym for the Asian-warrior fitness class. I could do this stuff in my sleep."

Miriam had been slightly concerned about getting caught. That was why she wrote the *Kate Hagen is next* e-mail. She knew that Peg and Paul would waste a lot of energy protecting me, so she could be free to go after the moms and get Tess. She was exhilarated when she told us about retrieving her daughter.

"Even though you screwed everything up with the wrong address, I have to give you at least a little credit." Miriam recalled that I had mentioned that Aimi was into healthy living, so she posed as a health-food consultant. At Aimi's door, she told her she was selling detox shakes and offered to give her a free sample, which she had loaded with antifreeze just minutes before. Aimi drank it on the spot and fell unconscious. Miriam grabbed Tess and took her home, temporarily entrusting her to her hairstylist, Michael.

Paul took Miriam back in time and pressed her about Tess. Miriam did in fact give birth to her. She and I were pregnant at the same time—only she didn't know it until she was seven and a half months along. She had never wanted to have children. "I don't see the point," she would say to me during my pregnancy, and even afterward, as I rocked infant Molly in my arms. Miriam went to Los Angeles to give birth. Her friend Gigi, a makeup artist, told her about a service that helps out with adoptions. The babies all go to well-off and well-vetted families, and in return the families paid up to $500,000 for "medical expenses." The adoptions themselves were legal, but the Los Angeles district attorney is investigating the exchange of money.

Miriam was completely happy with her decision. Aside from the occasional I-wonder-what-happened-to-you-know-who moment, she had never given Tess a second thought. That is, until last year, when she ran into her at school. Immediately she was sure she knew who Tess was. Her casual curiosity intensified. She looked into the paperwork and called some of her contacts in California. At the time, she didn't want Tess. She was just nosy.

Then Evan came along. Mr. Wonderful, who was going to pull her into the marriage club. Only she had to produce a child. This was hard for her as she'd had a hysterectomy soon after giving birth to Tess. In a panic, she told Evan she had a little girl. She said that she and the baby's daddy were in the midst of a custody dispute that would soon be resolved in her favor. She told him that Fiona was at Hawthorne. She even borrowed Molly's class picture, without my noticing, to show him what her little girl looked like.

When Miriam was hauled off to central booking, about fifty uniformed officers went to Michael's house to rescue Tess. When they got there, she was sitting in front of the TV, watching *Project Runway* and eating peanut butter Tasti D-Lite. Michael's neighbor and frequent client, Eloise Langan, has been staying with her. Aimi is in the hospital and is expected to make a full recovery, but she can't go to India.

"Fuck India," she had uncharacteristically said. "I just want to hang out with my daughter."

Paul and Peg were selected to be the official cop/prosecutor leadership of the case. All in all, they were pretty good about including me in all of the questioning. Peg tried not to joke about my coming back to the office. She was worried that my predisposition to postpartum depression would also make me a good candidate for posttraumatic stress disorder—being so close to a meat cleaver and all.

Not to mention the potential murder victim of my BFF.

But my mental health has stayed on its road to recovery. Maybe it was the lifting of the burden of my father's absence. Maybe I've been ready to unload the toxicity of my friendship with Miriam. Maybe it was the fun in crime fighting.

"Maybe it's all the time with Paul," Peg suggested.

I've been spending more time at home the past few days. My mother has extended her trip. She and my father are spending a lot of time together. Their romance is clearly a thing of the past, but they have a lot of catching up to do. At least my father does. My mother's in it for the apologies and the closure. And Molly loves her new grandpa.

"He likes traffic lights," she told me.

Paul has taken a few days off work. Molly says she likes it when we are a family.

"Some of my friends have a mommy and a daddy in the same house," she told me. "How cool is that?"

Today we are at the park. Molly is on the swing.

"It's very loud," Paul comments on its squeak. "It sounds as if it is being tortured."

While the sound is awful, it no longer frightens me.

"Hey, thanks for letting me in the interrogation room," I tell Paul.

It doesn't seem as hard to be with him lately. Perhaps we're just so focused on Miriam that I'm less likely to think about all that has happened between us.

We don't talk about Ellen.

We don't talk about Steve either. Not that there is anything to say. Paul won't mention his name. When we talk about the Hawthorne staff, he refers to everyone by name, even Bree, but Steve will remain "that science guy."

I don't correct him.

He is working around the clock, helping Peg build the case against Miriam. On top of that, he keeps fretting about the jewel heists. He doesn't even seem to run out for a meal except to meet Molly.

Ellen must be out of town.

This makes it easier for me. But I have to prepare myself emotionally for seeing her every day in our building, in our lobby, in Paul's apartment, maybe even my own. I feel sick and sad at the same time, but Miriam's prosecution provides distraction.

My mother asks me how I feel about what my friend did. I think she's worried that it will send me into another depression. But it doesn't.

"We're all fragile," I tell her. "And just because Miriam is ridiculous, her pain isn't any less potent. I wish I had seen it. Instead I was just exhausted by her. In some ways, her being locked up in prison for life will make our so-called friendship easier to manage."

I thought I was making a stupid joke, but I find myself

weeping ever so slightly instead. I remember chatting with
Miriam about Miriam over a pedicure, watching her suck on
a Finn Crisp at a cocktail party, seeing her sneak in a sit-up in
my bathroom.

"She was my friend even in her cartoonishly selfish way.
It's another relationship in my life that's over. I guess I don't
like moving on."

I know my mother is thinking that I'm referring to Paul.

I think Paul enjoys that Miriam was behind all of this.
"I never liked her," he keeps repeating like a Greek chorus. "I
knew she had it in her."

"Then how come you waited until she had a cleaver next
to my heart before you did anything?" I ask.

"I wanted to lure you back into law enforcement." He
laughs. "And it worked. You were on the case the whole time.
It would have been cruel to keep you out of the fun part."

"What do you mean the whole time?" I do my best to cast
aside the now gross memory of Steve nibbling my ear on Bleecker
Street.

"Oh, come on. You don't think I knew you were snooping?"

"*Moi?*" I use all of the French I've ever learned in this three-
letter sentence.

"Kate, I'm an investigator. I know when people have been
rummaging through my computer." He looks serious.

"Why didn't you tell me?"

"I was keeping an eye on you. Peg was keeping an eye on
you. We weren't sure the threat against you was real, but we
had someone on you at all times."

"All times?" Yuck, Steve again.

"Yes." Paul does not smile at all.

"Don't be so judgmental." I tell him as I regain my hurt.
"Just because I don't have my own little Ellen Westin . . ."

"Who?"

"Your fiancée, Ellen Westin."

"I have a fiancée?" I must admit my ex-husband is a better actor than I expected.

"Paul, please don't make me pretend that I don't know. It's too exhausting."

"Pretend you don't know what?"

"About you and Ellen." I realize I am gritting my teeth. This game is unpleasant.

"Who the hell is Ellen?"

"You introduced us. You were going on a date, leaving work early."

Paul's initial look of confusion is giving way to perplexity.

"I know. Your police spy must have told you that I caught the two of you having lunch with Peg at Gristle's. Ellen was wearing quite an impressive bauble on what most would consider her engagement finger."

Paul no longer looks puzzled. He starts to laugh.

"Please don't mock me. I'm proud of the way I have been holding it together."

"Kate." He grabs my hand as kindly as he can under the circumstances. "Katie. Do you think I would be so involved with you"—he pauses, and I know he's thinking about kissing my cancer scar—"if I were newly engaged to someone?"

I pause while I take a deep breath. "Yes."

"Then you don't know me."

"Paul." My voice starts to quiver. "You were married to me and you were seeing someone else. It isn't much of a stretch for me to think you would be so, as you say, involved with me while you are engaged."

Paul stops laughing. "Kate, what are you talking about?"

Not this again. My anger returns. "Paul, please don't treat

me like an idiot. I know that you cheated on me when were married."

"Kate, I never—" He's completely somber.

"Don't lie, Paul, and don't make me revisit this. Please. I've done it a thousand times. I was lame. You cheated. You've moved on. I've moved on. I can't deal with the lying."

"But there is no lying, Katie. I've never cheated on you."

I'm tempted to leave the park, but Molly is waving to us.

"Okay. You seem to be having a memory lapse. So let me give you a summary." I put on my best examination-of-a-hostile-witness voice. "We were married. We had a baby. I was depressed and checked out. You couldn't deal. You cheated. We got divorced. Now you are marrying someone who hopefully"—I choke up a little here but am able to squeak out the words—"won't be depressed ever."

"Kate." He grabs my hand again and holds it firmly so I have no chance of yanking it away. "I was awful to you. I told you that. I didn't understand depression. To be fair, I don't think you did either. But I didn't cheat on you. Ever. I don't begin to understand where this is coming from."

I fight for control of my tears as I reprimand him. "Just before we split up, I was all set to address my depression and bring some romance back into our life. I got the number of a therapist. I even bought a new bra. It was Gel-Curve."

"Yeah." Paul looks confused. "And?"

"And I called your office to tell you to come home, and Helen Varvulis told me that you were at a seminar. A *seminar*."

"So? I was in a seminar."

"Paul. Sweetheart." The *sweetheart* is totally sarcastic. "*Seminar* was your code word for 'cheating.'" My smoking-gun moment.

"Sure, Kate. But it also means 'seminar.' That's where I was.

There is no code for my cheating because I don't cheat. If I remember correctly, the only thing that I could concentrate on during that time, aside from you and Molly, was getting Mark's Break off the ground. And I gave seminars all the time. I was invited by businesses in every corner of New York City." He looks wounded. "I would have shared this with you if you had any interest in my life."

Now I'm the confused one. "I all but confronted you with this and you didn't deny it."

"I didn't deny having an affair?"

"I didn't use those words exactly." Now I recall that I used words like *all that you have done*. These had seemed clear at the time, but they don't exactly win my case for me several years later.

"Kate, you are a lawyer. You worked for a professor of evidence. There is no evidence. *Because this didn't happen.* Listen, I was a lousy husband to you during this time. I've told you that. But I swear on my brother's grave that I never cheated on you. Ever. For the record, I still haven't been with anyone else."

Now I know he's lying. "Oh, so did you and Ellen Westin enter into an abstinence pact? How sweet."

"Kate, there is no such person as Ellen Westin." He's getting angry.

"Can't you keep track of your lies? Paul, you introduced me to her."

"There is no such person as Ellen Westin. That was Tanya Cirilla. She's a cop. We were doing an undercover operation involving a bunch of jewelry-store heists. And just so you know, she is in a very happy relationship with her life partner, Wendy."

"How was I supposed to know that?" My voice is still hard, but I feel the germination of relief.

"You weren't. It was undercover. And it never occurred to me that you might have thought Tanya and I were a couple." He starts laughing.

"Oh" is all I can manage.

We are silent.

"So you don't have a girlfriend at all?"

"Nope."

"And you didn't have a girlfriend at all?"

"Let me put it this way, Kate. The last girlfriend, and I use that in every sense of the word, I ever had was you."

I feel myself crying again, remembering the pain I had felt at his betrayal. "I thought—" I'm in full-force sob by now.

Paul pulls me into him. "You thought wrong, Kate. I never cheated on you. It didn't occur to me to cheat on you. I loved you. I ended the marriage only because that's what you wanted. You couldn't look at me. I felt as if I had no choice. Honestly, do you think I would move into the apartment above you if I were sleeping around?"

Come to think of it, that does make little sense.

"I moved in there because I wanted to be near Molly." As if on cue, Molly waves at us again, and we wave back. "But I also wanted to be near you. I care about you. I wanted to make sure you guys were okay. There's no fiancée. There's no dating."

Wow. I'm not sure how to respond. "I just can't believe you were in a real seminar."

"I was."

"And I can't believe Ellen Westin is a lesbian."

"No, Ellen is straight." Paul laughs. "Tanya is definitely into the ladies, though."

"And you didn't cheat?"

"I didn't cheat."

"All this time?" I say this slowly. "All this time and you aren't the man I thought you were."

"No, it turns out I'm better."

This makes me cry even harder. "But I . . . I . . . I—" I'm blubbering so hard that the words can't come out.

"You jumped to conclusions." Paul keeps me in his embrace but puts his arm on my shoulder. I'm ready for a *There, there* but instead I get "You are great with the law, Katie, but you should leave the police work to me."

I am silent as I watch Molly playing. Paul is quiet, too.

"What's going on in your head?" he asks.

"I'm in a surreal state of half joy and half sadness. Sadness for the wasted time. I've spent years resenting you, hating you even. And for what? All that we went through, we might have been able to avoid. And joy because . . . because . . . I don't know how to say it."

"Because there are still opportunities here. We are still alive. We have a beautiful daughter. We're young."

"Ish," I say.

"Youngish and healthy. You are totally hot and I am not a bad specimen myself."

"There are still opportunities here."

"Do you want to go out sometime? I'd like to break my abstinence pact."

I laugh as tears are streaming down my face. "Okay."

"That's wonderful. And could you wear the Gel-Curve bra?"

Again, we both wave at our daughter.